GHOST CANYON

ANTHONY M. STRONG

ALSO BY ANTHONY M. STRONG

JOHN DECKER THRILLER SERIES

What Vengeance Comes

Cold Sanctuary

Crimson Deep

Grendel's Labyrinth

Whitechapel Rising

Black Tide

Ghost Canyon

Cryptid Quest

JOHN DECKER SERIES PREQUEL

Soul Catcher

COLUM O'SHEA THRILLER SERIES

Deadly Truth

THE REMNANTS SERIES

The Remnants of Yesterday

The Silence of Tomorrow

STANDALONE BOOKS

The Haunting of Willow House

Crow Song

West Street Publishing

Cover art and interior design by Bad Dog Media, LLC.

ISBN: 978-1-942207-18-4

For Izzie and Hayden (who was the inspiration for Tieg).

CLASSIFIED UNIVERSAL SPECIAL PROJECTS

VERUM CONQUISITOR

GHOST CANYON

PROLOGUE

AUGUST 1874—SOUTHERN NEVADA

The two men and the mule moved through the darkness; their way illuminated only by the glow of the full moon that hung low in a cloudless sky. Karuk went first, leading his companion along the mountain trail with confidence despite the younger man's unease.

"Are you sure you know where you're going," Travis Biggs asked, peering nervously towards the rocky landscape that spread out on each side of them, rising steeply as they went higher. They had left the mining town far behind and could no longer hear the faint tinkle of the piano or the raucous laughter coming from the bordello that sat on the dusty main street. "Why couldn't we have come out here in daylight?"

"You know why. We can't be seen." Karuk glanced back, the moonlight illuminating his finely sculpted features. A subtle blend of Native American and Old World that highlighted his position as an outcast in both cultures thanks to the union between a white man and his Ojibwe mother. "Do you want to do this, or not?"

"It's that or share the gold, and there's not enough in that vein for everyone."

"Then shut up and stop complaining. We're almost there," Karuk said, then lapsed into silence.

They continued on for another fifteen minutes until the trail ended at a rocky plateau dotted with creosote bushes, sagebrush, and Joshua trees. Beyond this the terrain rose even further but was completely impassable.

Karuk led them to a spot marked only by a pile of gathered rocks. He removed them one by one, casting them aside while Travis watched, one hand holding the mule's reins.

"Hand me the shovel," Karuk said once he had exposed the ground underneath the rock pile.

Travis led the mule to a bush and tied the reins around a sturdy branch, then removed a shovel from the packsaddle and handed it to his companion.

Karuk took it and began to dig, removing the top layer of sand and dirt. He hadn't dug far when the white dome of a skull revealed itself, wiry tufts of hair still attached in places.

"Is that what we're looking for?" Travis asked, suppressing a shiver of revulsion.

"Not the skull," Karuk said, moving more dirt aside with the shovel's blade.

There were more bones now. Vertebrae and a rib cage. Arm bones, including the humerus and radius. Moving lower, Karuk uncovered the pelvis and leg bones. He gently lifted a femur and held it out to Travis.

"Here, take this," he said.

Travis accepted the bone and slipped it into a leather bag hanging from the mule's pack.

Karuk removed several more bones, passing them to Travis before taking the shovel and pushing dirt back over the now desecrated remains. He piled the rocks back in place, and then stepped aside. "We should leave. The spirits will be angry."

Travis nodded. He didn't like it up here. "You won't get any argument from me."

He unhitched the mule and together they retraced their steps down the trail, picking their way slowly through the treacherous landscape. When they reached the end of the trail, the pair veered off instead of following the path back into town.

"You're sure you want to do this?" Karuk asked as they approached the entrance to the Ghost Canyon Mine.

"You're not going to get cold feet now after we already did the hard part, are you?" Travis responded. He'd been concerned about partnering with the half-breed. The man was a loose-lipped alcoholic and spent most of his time hanging around the bordello even when he wasn't working there sweeping the floors and picking up after the miners and their women. But Karuk knew the legends. He also knew where the disgraced Paiute warrior, Shilah, rested far from the traditional burial grounds.

"I'll go through with it." A troubled expression passed across Karuk's face. "I don't like playing with dark forces, that's all. It's bad luck."

"It'll be bad luck for Scratchy Bill and his boys when they come down into this mine tomorrow. That much I know." Travis chuckled. He sure would like to see the faces of the other miners when they found out what would be waiting for them in the darkness. But he wouldn't be there. Travis would be far from here in the bordello, enjoying a glass or two of rye whiskey and toasting his own newfound good luck. "Let's get on with it. I want to get back to town."

"Hand me the bag with the bones," Karuk instructed. "Quickly, now."

Travis unhitched the leather satchel from the mule's pack, gave it to Karuk. He eyed the mine opening. "How far in do we need to place the bones?"

"Near the seam. We want to make sure that no one comes out alive."

"We have to go that far into the mine at this time of night?" Travis felt his gut clench.

"You don't need to come. I can take care of it if you want. Someone should stay and watch the mule, anyway."

"Sounds fair to me." Travis unclipped a lamp from the pack and held it out to Karuk. "You'll need this."

"Thank you." Karuk took the oil lamp and lit it, then slung the leather satchel over one shoulder. "I'll be as quick as I can. Wait for me here. Don't go anywhere."

"I'll be right here when you get back," Travis replied.

"Make sure that you are." Karuk headed off toward the mine entrance.

Travis watched him enter. For a while he could see the glow from the miner's lamp as Karuk moved deeper into the tunnel, but soon even that faded, and Travis was left with only the mule for company.

He glanced back down the trail, wishing he could return to town and partake of a couple of Mule Skinners, rye whiskey cut with blackberry liquor. His throat was dry and dusty from the trek up into the mountains. But he'd promised Karuk that he wouldn't leave, and he would be as good as his word. His plan wasn't fully executed yet. There was one thing he still needed to do once Karuk returned. Then there would be no one else to lay claim to the seam. As far as anyone knew, the mine was tapped out, which was why most of the miners had already departed the town looking for new opportunities. Some had gone to California. Others headed north toward Carson City. He briefly considered following them, but then Travis and his crew had found a fresh source of gold in the Ghost Canyon Mine. And since they'd sworn each other to secrecy, no one else knew about it.

From somewhere out in the desert a coyote howled, the

sound lonesome and chilling. It sent a shiver down Travis' spine. He looked toward the mine entrance and willed Karuk to return. How long could it take to scatter some old bones?

He'd barely finished thinking the question when he saw a yellow glow light the entrance. Moments later, Karuk emerged with the satchel still slung across one shoulder.

"You get it done?" Travis asked as Karuk drew close.

"It's taken care of." Karuk extinguished the lamp and hooked it back onto the mule pack along with the satchel. He pulled his duster tight around his thin frame and walked past Travis toward the path leading back to town. As he did, he spoke over his shoulder. "Bring the mule and let's get out of here. I'm thirsty."

"Right behind you," Travis said. But instead of following along, he reached down to the six-shooter holstered at his hip. He pulled the gun free and took aim at the retreating man, cocking the hammer at the same time.

Karuk registered the slight noise and started to turn, alarmed, just as Travis pulled the trigger.

The bullet slammed into Karuk between his shoulder blades and sent him to the ground in a spinning tumble.

The mule whinnied, frightened by the sudden noise.

Travis pulled the hammer back again and kept the revolver trained on the prone man as he approached him. But Karuk was in no shape to fight back. He lay in a swiftly widening pool of his own blood and looked up at Travis with pleading eyes.

"Help me," he said in a wheezing voice. "It hurts."

Travis said nothing. He merely released the hammer and slipped the revolver back into its holster. There was no need to make more noise than necessary and shooting Karuk again would only waste a good bullet. He bent down and took Karuk's arms, then dragged him to the side of the path.

"What are you doing?" The older man's eyes widened in terror. He coughed up a mix of phlegm and blood.

Travis ignored the question. He paused a moment to catch his breath, noting how Karuk's face was already becoming slack as his spirit took flight. Then he gripped his dying companion with both hands and pushed him off the path.

Karuk half slid, half rolled down a steep incline and disappeared from sight into the dense brush at the bottom.

The unpleasant task completed, Travis kicked dirt over the blood until it was no longer visible and then returned to the mule. Tomorrow the other miners would come up here and walk into the trap that he and Karuk had laid for them. Then, once they were as dead as the half-breed, he would enter the mine, collect the bones, and reinter them now that he knew where the old warrior was buried.

Then the gold would be his, and his alone.

CHAPTER ONE

TODAY—HALEY GHOST TOWN, NEVADA

Robyn Miller stood on the front porch of the Last Chance Saloon and Hotel and looked at her watch. It was already gone eleven in the morning and the group of geologists she was waiting to meet were late. Standing at her heel was Tieg, the blond mop of a mutt she'd rescued from the animal shelter three years before. He looked up at her and let out a low woof, as if he agreed that the men Robyn was waiting for were unacceptably tardy.

She sighed and went back inside, the dog tagging along at her side.

The sound of hammers and various power tools echoed through the building thanks to the workers renovating the rooms on the second floor. The hotel's restoration was behind schedule, with the third floor not even touched yet. She had resigned herself to the fact that it wouldn't be open before the spring.

"Are you still waiting on those guys from Vegas?" Carlton Miller, her great uncle, appeared from the direction of the recently completed saloon bar. He stood on the other side of the lobby, arms folded, and observed her with a stare that barely concealed his animosity.

"I'm sure they'll be here soon," Robyn replied. Carlton reminded her of an old crow, with a gaunt face and beady black eyes that hid an intelligent yet sardonic personality. She wished, not for the first time, that he wasn't a one-third owner in the old ghost town that had been in their family for generations. He was a thorn in her side. A constant prickle that refused to go away. That she owned the other two-thirds of the property was a bone of contention that would never resolve itself until the old man was in his grave. Not that she wished him dead. She merely wanted the curmudgeonly senior to share her vision for what could become a profitable business and restore the family fortunes.

Tieg, who liked Carlton about as much as Robyn did, slipped off to the back of the building, pausing once to look back at his owner, then disappearing into the small office behind the stairs where his bed was located.

Carlton shook his head in disdain. "I bet they're not coming. They probably found something better to do."

"They're coming. Why wouldn't they? I made the arrangements weeks ago." But even as she said the words, Robyn felt a pang of anxiety. What if they had forgotten the appointment? If she couldn't get the mine inspected to make sure it was safe, she wouldn't be able to take people down there. That would remove a much-needed income stream, especially since she'd already shelled out the money to have the entrance blasted open again.

"I don't know why you want to play around with that dirty old mine, anyway." Carlton let out a derisive snort. "It's a foolhardy venture, if you ask me."

"No one's asking you." Robyn turned away and glanced back

through the open door. The long and dusty canyon road into town was still empty.

"Like you didn't ask me about doing up this place," Carlton said, sweeping his arms around the old hotel's lobby. "Who the hell's going to want to stay in a rickety old bordello, anyway?"

"Lots of people." Robyn had gone through this with her great-uncle before and had no desire to relitigate old arguments. "We're less than an hour's drive from Las Vegas. You should know. You've been living up here and selling unofficial tours for years."

"There's a big difference between letting folks who drive out from the Strip wander around for ten bucks a pop and pretend they're cowboys for a few hours and trying to get people to give up their glamorous hotels and fancy restaurants to stay in a falling down old wooden box that saw its heyday in the 1870s."

"Well, I disagree." Robyn was getting antsy. If the geologists would hurry and arrive, she could end this conversation. "Unusual wedding venues are big business these days, and we need somewhere for the guests to stay if we want to turn this into a true destination."

"That's another thing. You're ruining the integrity of the town with that ridiculous wedding chapel you want to build. Not to mention the camping area. That's all we need, a bunch of hulking RVs driven by yahoos cruising in and tearing it up."

"How in blazes am I ruining the integrity of the town? I'm burning with curiosity. Please, tell me?" Robyn felt the familiar surge of frustration that bubbled up whenever she dealt with Carlton. "Before I got here, this place was practically falling into the ground. You weren't doing any maintenance on the buildings and you didn't even have liability insurance. All it would've taken was one person to slip and fall or cut themselves on one of the rusty relics of cars and machinery you have lying around here, and we'd have lost the place to a lawsuit."

"That wouldn't happen. People aren't stupid."

"You don't know that. One careless mishap and we'd lose everything."

"Good riddance. If it were up to me, I'd have sold the town when that developer was buying up all the land hereabouts for their fancy-ass planned community."

"Which never got built because we're too far out. It wouldn't be profitable."

"Just like this old place will never be profitable, no matter how many fancy ads you take out in wedding magazines and tourist guides. We can't compete with Vegas."

"We don't need to. We're unique. That counts for something. Besides, it isn't up to you. I'm the majority owner of this town and the land it sits on. I'm not selling out to some developer for a fraction of what it's worth so they can capitalize on it and make all the money. No thanks." Robyn shook her head. "And even if they made us a fair offer—which they never would—I still wouldn't sell. Those people are nothing but opportunist snakes."

"Snakes or not, they had cash, and we don't."

"I have money. How you think I'm doing all this stuff?"

"By cashing out your retirement account, selling your home in Chicago, and getting into a mountain of debt with the bank, that's how."

"That's my choice. I haven't asked you to chip in even though you'll be taking a third of the profits."

"And I'm not going to chip in. If I had a dime, I'd be out of here tomorrow. I've had enough of this dust bowl."

"Then why don't you go? Just sell me your share of the town and make yourself a life somewhere else. It's that simple." But Robyn knew he wouldn't sell his interest, at least not to her. If he couldn't convince her to hand the place over to some developer for pennies on the dollar, then he would stay. And not because he thought the wedding venue was going to be a roaring success he could participate in, but because the decades-old feud with his brothers, which would never end since one of them was already dead, had left him so bitter that he'd rather stay and sabotage his own family than be reasonable and sell her his share. It didn't help that Carlton's brother, who had died the previous spring, had bequeathed his share to her. The fact that her own grandfather had gifted her his third of the town, thus making her majority owner, only poured fuel on Carlton's anger. He was, in short, a bitter old man with nothing better to do than make her life miserable.

"Bah. You're going to be the ruin of me." Carlton waved a dismissive hand and turned his back, then disappeared into the barroom, no doubt to find himself a glass of whiskey.

Robyn rubbed her temples, behind which a tension headache was throbbing, and walked back out onto the veranda. This time when she looked down the road, she spotted a white quad cab truck, leaving in its wake a billowing trail of dust. The geologists had finally arrived.

CHAPTER TWO

William Fenton, who more often than not just went by the simpler name of Bill, brought the quad cab to a halt in front of a ramshackle looking three-story building that was by far the largest structure in the old ghost town known as Haley. Sitting next to him in the passenger seat was Corey McDaniel. Carlos Philippe, the third member of the team, occupied the quad cab's rear bench. He had been playing with his phone since they left Las Vegas, but now looked up and peered through the side window.

"What a crap hole," he said, letting his eyes wander across the row of dilapidated buildings that would have long ago disintegrated into piles of rotten lumber if it weren't for the sporadic upkeep of the landowners. As it was, several of them looked like they were about to give up the ghost. All except the one in front of them. Its state of restoration stood in stark contrast to its surroundings. His gaze fell upon a slim, attractive woman in her early thirties who was standing hands on hips upon the wraparound porch staring at them. She did not look happy. "Why would anyone want to come and stay out here in this godforsaken wilderness?"

"You'd be surprised." Fenton turned the engine off and opened his door. "City folk will pay big money to feel like they're roughing it. Living the pioneer life for a few days."

"Yeah. Just so long as they've still got comfortable beds, hot running water, and Wi-Fi," Corey chuckled, opening his own door and hopping down to the ground.

"Nothing wrong with a comfortable bed," Fenton replied. He slammed the truck's door and mounted the steps to the veranda. When he drew close to the woman, he smiled and held out a hand. "Bill Fenton with Geology Partners, Inc."

"Robyn Miller. You're late."

When she didn't immediately take the proffered hand, Fenton hesitated. He was about to drop his arm when she finally reciprocated. He put on his best customer service voice, which wasn't particularly good because he was a geologist. "Yeah, sorry about that. We would've been here already, but we were all the way over on the north side near Nellis Air Force Base earlier today, so we had to drive clear across town. Traffic was pretty heavy on the interstate. It didn't ease until we got past Boulder City."

"Nice place you have here," Carlos said, barely bothering to keep the sarcasm from his voice. He leaned against the truck and wiped sweat from his brow with the back of his hand. It was early November, a month in which it wasn't uncommon to see daily temperatures ranging from the mid-fifties to eighty-five degrees or more. Today was on the high end, topping out at almost ninety.

Fenton ignored his colleague. "We're ready to start when you are. We just need to grab our gear from the back of the truck and then you can show us the mine."

Robyn nodded. "Of course. It's not far, only about half a mile, but we'll have to walk. We're going to widen the trail and pave it to allow easy vehicle access, but we haven't gotten that far yet. Right now, it's pretty narrow and overgrown."

"Not a problem. We're used to walking." Fenton descended the steps again and went to the truck. He dropped the tailgate and removed hardhats with dome-mounted halogen lights, coils of rope, handheld flashlights, and fluorescent jackets. He distributed the gear between his men, then went to the truck's cab and retrieved a digital SLR camera and a large yellow toolbox. When he turned around, Robyn was standing behind him.

"What's that for?" She asked, nodding toward the toolbox.

"It contains our equipment. We'll need to measure the air quality in the mine and take temperature readings. That sort of thing."

"Air quality?" Robyn looked concerned. "Do you think there will be a problem?"

"Probably not. If I understand it right, you won't be going much further than a quarter of a mile in and sticking to one level. We're just looking at walking tours, correct?"

"Yes." Robyn nodded in agreement.

"You should be fine, then. We'll need to check though, just to be on the safe side. These old mines are littered with dangers. There might be subsurface water that contains heavy metals. We could find cyanide or mercury compounds up there, not to mention high concentrations of methane, carbon monoxide, or hydrogen sulfide. It's less likely here, but not unheard of. The mines of the Comstock Lode were notorious for gas buildup. Another hazard we need to watch for is blackdamp."

"What's that?"

"Its air with low oxygen levels. It leaves only a mix of unbreathable gases like nitrogen and carbon dioxide. It mostly occurs deeper underground than we're going, but it can be deadly. I wouldn't worry too much about it. It's unlikely that there will be any problems with oxygen levels or gas buildup so close to the entrance. Plus, you'll be keeping close to the adit. That's the entrance tunnel."

"That's the plan. We don't want to lose anyone in there." Robyn led the three men away from the cluster of buildings toward a winding path that led up a slope toward the mountains overlooking the ghost town.

Halfway up, they passed a rusty truck sitting on the side of the trail amid the bushes. It probably hadn't moved since the fifties and now sat on bare axles. The glass enclosing the cab was long since gone, as were the boards that once made up the bed of the truck. Its metal skin was red and oxidized without a trace of paint left.

"Will you look at that," Corey McDaniel said, speaking for the first time since exiting their own, much newer truck. "I'll bet this was a beauty before she ended up here rotting away."

"There are relics like that all around the town." Robyn moved them past the old truck without pause. "There's even the wreckage of a light aircraft further up the canyon. It crashed in the seventies after developing engine trouble and trying to make an emergency landing. Miraculously, the pilot walked away unscathed."

"That's one lucky guy," Fenton commented. "I would not want to bring a plane down on this terrain."

"That's probably why he crashed," Carlos said.

The mine entrance was in view now. Robyn led them the last few yards and stopped. She glanced toward the jagged hole in the mountain's side, now blocked by a pair of sturdy metal gates she had installed to keep trespassers out after blasting the rubble from the entrance. "Did you want me to wait for you here?"

"No need," Fenton said. He donned his hardhat. "It'll probably take us an hour or two to do our job. We'll go further in than you'll be taking tourists, just to be on the safe side. We can find our way back down on our own once we're done."

"Perfect. I have a lot to do," Robyn said. "I'll be in town, then."

"Sounds like a plan." Fenton placed the toolbox on the floor and put on his fluorescent jacket. He opened the toolbox and removed three small yellow boxes with LED screens. He clipped one to his jacket and handed the others to his companions.

"What are those for?" Robyn asked.

"Multi-gas detectors," Fenton replied. "They will alert us instantly if methane or other harmful gasses are present in the mine." He smiled. "I wouldn't worry too much, though. It's just a precaution. Like I said, we're unlikely to encounter much this close to the surface. The air flow should be pretty good, and gasses mostly accumulate deeper underground."

He closed the toolbox and waited for the others to activate their detectors, and then made his way to the mine entrance.

Robyn produced a key and removed the chain and padlock holding the gates closed. She swung them open.

Fenton turned on his helmet light and checked his equipment. Then he crossed the threshold into the abandoned mine with his colleagues a step behind.

CHAPTER THREE

The darkness beyond the Ghost Canyon Mine's entrance would have been absolute if it were not for the flashlights and lamps attached to the hardhats of the three geologists who now pushed their way deep within the mountain.

They were probably the first individuals to set foot this far inside the mine for almost a century and a half. Knowing this, they proceeded with caution, picking their way along and playing their flashlights to the left and right, looking for any sign of instability in the tunnels.

About fifty feet in, old mining carts blocked the passage. These had once been used to transport ore from the deeper sections of the mine back to the surface for processing. The three men edged their way past the decaying equipment and continued on, soon losing sight of the opening through which they'd gained access.

"This looks like a suitable spot to take some readings," Fenton said, not long after they passed the ore carts. He stopped and placed the toolbox on the ground and opened it, removing a handheld anemometer. Used to check air temperature and flow, it looked like a chunky TV remote control with a fan on top.

Even though the hard rock mine was underground, there was a cool breeze moving through the passageways, a sign that air was entering the mine through passages and ventilation shafts that remained unblocked.

"How far in do you want to go?" Carlos asked.

"Half a mile should do it," Fenton replied, returning the anemometer to the toolbox before starting off along the passage again. "Maybe a bit further if we see anything of concern."

"I'm not seeing much so far," McDaniel said, glancing up at the wooden support beams and timber braces that lined the tunnel walls and ceiling. "It all looks pretty tight for a mine that's been closed this long."

"I agree." Fenton nodded. He paused, lifted the DSLR camera and took a shot of the tunnel. The automatic flash lit up the rocks in stark relief. He took a few more from different angles before continuing onward. "They'll have to install permanent monitoring equipment and string lights down here, but it shouldn't be that big a deal to run tours. It's all nice and clean."

"I don't get why folk want to pay good money to wander around old mines." Carlos shook his head. "I can think of better things to do with my cash."

"What, like feed it to the slot machines on Fremont Street?" McDaniel chuckled.

"Everyone needs a hobby." Carlos adjusted the lamp on his helmet as they continued deeper into the mine. "If you must know, I've made a tidy pile of cash playing those slots."

"No, you haven't. You're always complaining about how much you lost."

"Not saying I win all the time, but I have a system. I come out on top in the long run." Carlos glanced sideways toward his colleague. "Besides, I don't see you raking in the winnings."

"That's because I'm not stupid enough to waste my money in casinos," McDaniel retorted. "It's a mug's game."

"Yeah, well, you do what you want, and I'll do the same."

"I wasn't getting at you." McDaniel shook his head. "I don't care what you do with your money. I was just pointing out that you aren't some freaking slot genius."

"Knock it off, you two," Fenton growled, glancing back toward his companions. Up ahead, the passageway widened into a small, excavated room with new passages running off at forty-five degrees from each other.

The three men came to a halt.

"Which way, boss?" Carlos asked, absentmindedly scratching his chin.

"Let's take the right-hand passage first and see what we have, then we can come back and explore the other one."

"What if the passages keep branching?" Carlos asked. "You know what these old mines are like. There could be a hundred miles of tunnels and shafts down here. Surely, we've gone far enough. They aren't going to bring tourists further in than this and I'd like to get back to town."

"What have you got going on that's so damned important?" McDaniel asked.

"Never you mind," Carlos said, as Fenton and McDaniel started off into the right-hand passage. He cursed under his breath and glanced down the passage to his left. He was about to turn and follow the others, when he noticed an object laying half-buried in the loose gravel floor. It glinted white under his flashlight's beam. His eyes widened with surprise. "Hey, guys, hold up. You might want to see this."

"What now?" Fenton returned with a scowl on his face.

"There's something in that passageway." Carlos nodded toward the narrow tunnel that ran off to the left. "Looks like a bone. You see it?"

"I don't see anything," Fenton snapped, shining his flashlight across the ground ahead of him. But then he saw it. A sliver of white against the dark brown gravel that lined the passage floor. He took a step closer, his eyes narrowing. "What is that?"

"I'm telling you, it's a bone," Carlos said.

"If it is, then it probably belongs to a hapless mule, or maybe some poor wild animal that got stuck in here and died," Fenton replied as they drew close to the object. He kicked at it with his foot, nudging it free.

"That's not from a mule," McDaniel said, wide-eyed.

"No, it's not." A shudder ran through Fenton as he looked down at the uncovered bone, which comprised a long shaft with bulbous ends.

"That looks like someone's leg." There was a tremor in McDaniel's voice.

"I think it's human," Carlos said in a low voice. "Why would that be here?"

"We don't know that it's human," Fenton replied, but deep down he suspected Carlos was right. Sensing that they had stumbled upon something important, he fired off a couple of quick photos, zooming in close for the last one. "This complicates things. We'll need to get the sheriff up here. Those tours might not be happening anytime soon."

"Even if it is human, it's probably been down here for a century or more."

"Or it could belong to a murder victim." Fenton trained his flashlight further down the tunnel, noting that it curved out of sight some thirty feet distant. "It wouldn't be the first time someone hid a body inside an abandoned mine."

"I don't see how." McDaniel shook his head. "They only blasted the entrance a few weeks ago."

"Doesn't mean there isn't another way in." Fenton started off down the passageway toward the curve. "Come on, let's see if there's anything else."

"I'd sooner leave that to the sheriff," Carlos replied, but he tagged along behind, anyway.

"Aren't you curious?" Fenton said as they approached the bend.

"Not really." Carlos glanced back at the exposed bone and made the sign of the cross, even though he hadn't attended church in twenty years.

"Don't be such a baby," McDaniel said, but when they rounded the bend, he came to a halt and now it was his turn to feel afraid.

The tunnel ended not far beyond where they were standing. Pickaxes and other tools leaned against the walls. Others lay scattered across the floor, as if the miners excavating here had simply abandoned them. To their left a wide seam of quartz ran through the rock, within which they could see glittering ribbons of gold. But this wasn't what frightened them so. It was the three corpses that sat with their backs to the roughly hewn rock, still wearing the tattered remains of the clothes that were on their backs when they walked into the mine. Their skin was brown like tanned leather and so shriveled that the miner's skeletons were easily discernible. They stared back at the newcomers from dead eyes that hadn't witnessed a living person since Ulysses S. Grant occupied the White House.

"¡Dios mío!, what are they doing here?" Carlos backed up, shocked. His gaze fell to a symbol scratched into the floor in front of the miners. A circle with two arrows facing inward toward a central dot. "And what's that?"

"Looks like they were drawing in the dirt," Fenton said.

"I don't care if they were playing banjos and having a hoedown," McDaniel said, stumbling backwards. "I'm getting out of here."

"Wait," Fenton replied. He raised the camera, waited for it to focus, and took several photographs in rapid succession. Then he backed up. "Good enough. Let's get topside and call the authorities. This is definitely not my area of expertise."

"No arguments there," Carlos said, hurrying along behind his boss.

They arrived back at the chamber where the paths forked.

Fenton turned right and took the tunnel leading back to the surface. He hadn't gone far when he heard McDaniel speak.

"I hear something." McDaniel had stopped with Carlos next to him. He was staring down the other tunnel, his face creased with fright. "We're not alone down here."

"Don't be ridiculous," Fenton said. But now he heard it too. A creaking, like groaning timbers, only higher pitched. This was followed by a shuffling noise, getting louder.

"There's a figure in the tunnel," Carlos said. "I can see them coming toward us."

"That's crazy. There's no one else down here. It's impossible." Fenton took a step back toward his colleagues. "Would you hurry it up?"

But neither man replied. They stood transfixed, staring into the blackness, wide-eyed.

"Guys?" A shudder of fear worked its way down Fenton's spine. He was about to go back and get his friends, snap them out of their fugue, but something made him hesitate. Instead, he backed up, his gaze still rooted upon the two transfixed men.

Then, out of the corner of his eye, there was a movement. His gaze drifted toward it, and what he saw made him turn and flee in terror, even as his colleague's dying screams rang in his ears.

CHAPTER FOUR

When Robyn Miller returned from the mine, there was no sign of Carlton, much to her relief. She entered the hotel and crossed the lobby, then climbed to the second floor where the workers still labored. Most of the rooms on this level were already completed. Soon they would shift their attention to the top floor, which still waited in a sad state of dilapidation.

She stepped inside the closest room, which looked like something right out of an old Western movie. Sage green patterned wallpaper covered the walls. Silk curtains held with tiebacks adorned the window. A lighter inner curtain of lace covered the windowpane. An ornate mirror with a teak frame hung on the wall. The only items that didn't look authentic were the modern electric lighting, the flatscreen TV sitting on the bureau opposite the bed, and the en suite created by sacrificing the room next door and cutting it in half to create a pair of bathrooms for the adjacent bedrooms.

It was an added expense that had pushed the cost of renovation much higher than she would have liked, but nobody wanted to stay in a hotel that forced them to share the facilities.

This was especially true of wedding parties who might book

a stay to feel like they had stepped back in time but didn't want the experience to be too real. With Las Vegas and its swanky hotels right down the road, she had a lot of competition, as Carlton had gleefully pointed out.

Robyn returned to the corridor and made her way to the far rooms where work was still going on. When the construction crew's supervisor saw her, he stepped into the hallway, rubbing his hands on his shins. He was a big man named Hank, with a shock of ginger hair and a pale complexion that Robyn thought was unusual given the area of the country in which he lived. She wondered if he owned shares in a sun block manufacturer, or just had a naturally pale complexion.

"Come to make sure we're working hard, have you, Miss Miller?" Hank asked with a grin.

"I just wanted to see how far along we are," Robyn replied. "I love how the place is coming together. It's exactly what I wanted."

"Pleased that you like our work." Hank hesitated, his expression becoming serious. "I know you want to get this done as quick as you can, but I got some bad news, I'm afraid."

"What now?" Robyn's heart sank. "You're not going to tell me there's another delay, are you?"

"That I am." Hank dropped his gaze. "The plumber's working a job at a new condo complex on the north end of the Strip. He should have been finished next week, but they're behind schedule so he's not going to make it back here anytime soon to run the piping for the bathrooms on the third floor."

"Just great." Robyn grimaced. "How long a delay are we looking at?"

"Three weeks. Maybe a month if they run into more issues."

"What issues could they possibly have? Its new construction."

"They've been having an argument with the building

inspector. As expected, he won. They have to redo a bunch of the plumbing."

"It can't be helped, I guess." Robyn felt a flicker of disappointment. Not that it mattered. She would not be open before the spring, anyway. "We can't use another plumber?"

"With the amount of construction in these parts? Are you kidding me?" Hank let out a snort. "We're lucky to have a plumber at all, given that we don't have the deep pockets of the gaming industry. You know what it's like. They're building new casino hotels almost as quick as they can tear the old ones down. Labor's at a premium."

"I get it. Doesn't mean I have to like it," Robyn said. "Just get him here as quickly as you can, okay?"

"Sure." Hank glanced back into the half-finished bedroom, where the sound of construction had come to a halt. "What the hell?"

The three workers, who until now had been replacing the rotten plaster with modern drywall, were standing at the window, staring out.

Hank crossed the room to see what they were looking at, then turned to Robyn, brow furrowed. "I think you have a problem."

Robyn hurried to join him. One of the workers stepped aside to let her through. A figure was stumbling down the trail from the old mine, waving his arms and screaming at the top of his voice. As he drew closer, she realized it was the lead geologist, Bill Fenton.

A chill ran through her. Had there been an accident? She turned and ran from the room, taking the stairs two at a time before hurrying across the hotel lobby and out onto the dusty street. She barely noticed Tieg, who had come bounding out from his bed at the sound of her footfalls, and now stood looking up at her with expectant eyes, his tongue lolling out excitedly.

But Robyn didn't pay the dog any heed, because Fenton was drawing closer now and she could see the terror in his eyes. The man looked positively beside himself.

"What's wrong? Did something happen?" Robyn asked, afraid of what he might say. If there had been an accident inside the mine, like the roof had caved in on the geologists, or one of them had fallen into an open shaft, she would never get this place open for business.

"You've got to help me," Fenton screeched as he reached her. He gripped Robyn's shoulders with powerful hands and looked into her eyes. "They're still up there. It got them."

"Your men are still in the mine?" Robyn's world crashed down around her. "What got them? Tell me."

"The creature with the red eyes. It came out of the darkness and ripped them apart." Fenton was hysterical, close to tears now. He looked over his shoulder toward the trail, then back to Robyn. "We have to get away from here. It will come for us next."

CHAPTER FIVE

Two thousand eight hundred miles away across the other side of the country, John Decker stood on a wide balcony at CUSP's facility on a rocky island off the coast of Maine, his coat pulled tight against the November chill. Behind him, the main building rose three floors. Below him, dropping away from the railing that Decker now leaned on, was a rocky cliff that ended eighty feet below in a horseshoe-shaped pebble beach upon which angry waves now crashed.

It was a remote spot, far from civilization. The only close habitation was a small town on the neighboring island, accessible only at low tide by a narrow causeway. It was this remoteness, no doubt, that had inspired CUSP to build here, adding on to a nineteenth-century mansion constructed on the island by an eccentric railroad magnate. It was the mansion's original owner that built the causeway, intending to run a rail line directly from a small train station a mile from the house, all the way across to the mainland. The idea was to use the specks of land in between in much the same way that Henry Flagler's Overseas Railroad linked Key West to the Florida mainland with bridges running between the intermediate islands.

The railroad magnate abandoned the project when he determined that the frequent inclement weather off the Maine coast posed too much of a challenge. A prescient decision, given that a hurricane destroyed Henry Flagler's railroad in a location far less prone to severe weather, less than twenty-five years after he built it.

The only part of the Maine railroad ever constructed was the causeway, originally intended as a platform upon which to run the rail bridge. Now it served as a road allowing CUSP personnel to escape the facility for a few hours.

"Decker, you made it." Adam Hunt strode out onto the balcony. Walking next to him was a familiar figure.

"Now there's a sight for sore eyes," said Colum O'Shea, a broad smile upon his face. "I haven't seen you since London."

"That feels like a long time ago." After he and Colum faced a resurrected Jack the Ripper in London, they had sent Decker south to French Guiana, where he barely escaped with his life during a harrowing mission on the ocean floor. That assignment had ended with a roller coaster ride up from the seabed in a preserved German U-boat. A submarine that was now moored out of sight in a sheltered inlet on the north side of the island. After that had come a well-deserved break, spending six weeks with Nancy at their rented house on the Gulf Coast. "What are you doing in these parts?"

"Same thing as you. Checking in with the boss and getting up to speed with the latest intelligence. I won't be around long though. Flying back out first thing in the morning."

"That's a shame. It would be nice to catch up," Decker said.

"There's always tonight." Colum looked at his watch. "But right now, I have to be at a briefing on the third floor. I'll catch up with you guys later, okay?"

"Sure thing," Hunt said. He watched Colum depart, then joined Decker at the railing. "What do you think of our little island fortress?"

"This isn't the first time I've been here, you know," Decker replied.

"The last visit was so brief," Hunt said. "You barely had time to see anything other than the U-boat."

"Speaking of which, how are the surviving crew getting along?"

"You know I can't answer that." Hunt stared out over the ocean.

"You don't need to give me specifics, but I would like to know how they're holding up. It must be quite a shock to set sail in the Second World War and not step back on dry land until almost three quarters of a century later."

"They're acclimatizing, slowly. I can tell you that much," Hunt said. "It's our hope that we can eventually provide them with new identities and set them up with a quiet life somewhere."

"Under your constant supervision, of course."

"That goes without saying. Our observation will be unobtrusive, naturally."

"So, they'll never be completely free."

"Is anyone?" Hunt glanced sideways toward Decker and raised an eyebrow. "Freedom is a shared delusion made possible by a collective unspoken agreement not to scratch too far below the surface."

"That's dark."

"It's the truth." Hunt's gaze drifted back out over the water. "Have you finished your assignments for the day?"

"Yup. I've been up since six. Spent two hours at the range playing with all sorts of lethal toys, then they gave me a physical which was completely unnecessary."

"I wouldn't go that far. You've had more than your share of scrapes recently. Abraham Turner sliced up your shoulder pretty good in London. On your last mission, you were attacked, shot at, and hit over the head."

Decker shrugged. "Goes with the territory."

"Does Nancy share that sentiment?"

Decker remained silent.

"I thought so." Hunt slapped Decker on the back, then turned and made his way toward the building. "Come with me."

"Where are we going?" Decker followed behind.

"I think it's time you got the full tour." Hunt stepped inside and held the door open for Decker. "Now that your probationary period is over."

"My probation is over?" Decker furrowed his brow. "That was quick."

"You think so?" Hunt replied as he led Decker through a central atrium filled with light thanks to a glass ceiling three floors above them. To their left rose the walls of the original mansion, the once exterior stone old and weathered. This was the accommodation block and more resembled a luxury hotel than staff quarters. There was even a hotel style lobby which housed a bar and buffet restaurant that served as the facility's canteen. "You've completed three missions now, the last of which you handled solo."

"That surprised me," Decker said. "I was expecting you to send a more senior agent along with me."

"You handled yourself fine." Hunt led Decker toward a set of elevators near the atrium's far wall.

"I almost got everyone killed. I should have recognized Thomas Barringer for what he was much earlier."

"Don't be so modest. It was your idea to reach the surface using the sub." Hunt pressed the elevator's call button and waited. "Without that, Barringer's plan would have worked."

"True," Decker admitted.

"CUSP has a certain expectation of its field operatives," Hunt said. "We recruit based on prior experience and don't like to waste time on unnecessary training. We bring you on board, verify that our initial opinion was correct, and then throw you in the deep end. You either sink, or you swim."

"What happens to those recruits who sink?"

"They get permanently silenced." There was an ominous tone in Hunt's voice.

Decker glanced toward his superior, alarmed. "You kill them?"

Hunt shrugged. "We have to maintain anonymity."

Decker pushed his hands into his pockets and looked away, stunned.

Hunt milked the uncomfortable silence for a few moments longer, then a broad smile cracked his normally stoic face. "That was too easy."

"You were winding me up." Decker felt a rush of relief.

"Despite what people think, I do have a sense of humor."

"Apparently," Decker said dryly, as the elevator arrived.

When the doors opened, Hunt stepped inside and motioned for Decker to follow. "The ability to remain jovial is a necessity in this line of work. Without it you may end up in a very dark place, as our next destination will highlight."

"Exactly where would that be?" Decker asked.

"Somewhere we take every operative once their probationary period is over." Hunt leaned toward an optical scanner and waited while the elevator verified his identity, then turned his attention to a panel with five buttons, labeled D1 through D5. He pressed the button marked D1 before turning to Decker. "We're going to The Zoo."

CHAPTER SIX

The black and white Ford Explorer with a nudge bar over the front grill and Las Vegas Metropolitan Police written along each side tore along the canyon road toward the ramshackle town of Haley with its light bar blazing.

Behind the wheel was Officer Charlie Walters. Next to him, Officer Glenn Barrow, on the job for less than a year and still learning the ropes, was busy telling dispatch they were only a minute away. After he finished, Barrow turned to his partner.

"Must be unusual to get a call this far out," he said. "Isn't this place nothing but a ghost town? Can't be more than a handful of people living out here."

"Try two," Walters replied. "Carlton Miller, and his nephew's kid, Robyn. She's only been around for six months, but the old man has lived here for decades, letting people poke around for ten bucks a pop for years even though he didn't have a business license. He's called us out a few times to get rid of tourists he claimed were taking souvenirs from the ghost town."

"Really?" Glenn peered through the windshield as they approached a ragtag cluster of buildings. He shook his head. "Why would anyone want to steal from a crap hole like this?"

"They wouldn't. But Carlton's a mean old buzzard. He's spent so long living out in the desert that the sun's fried his brain." Charlie brought the police interceptor to a stop next to a dusty quad cab truck. "The woman is nice, though. She's the majority landowner, despite Carlton calling us up here to have her escorted off the property for trespassing earlier this year. I was the responding officer. Once I found out who she really was, I almost charged him with wasting police time."

"Why didn't you?" Glenn asked. "Sounds like he's a piece of work."

"You want to do all that paperwork over something so trivial?"

"Good point."

"I gave him a verbal warning and left it at that." Charlie saw the young woman, Robyn, exit the newly renovated hotel and wave to them. He pulled on his door release. "I really hope this isn't another of Carlton's hijinks."

"It doesn't sound like it." Glenn exited the car and followed the senior officer toward the building. "Dispatch said there were two men dead in the mine, some kind of accident."

"We'll see," Charlie said, mounting the steps to the veranda. He introduced himself and followed Robyn into the building.

She led them through a lobby that smelled of sawed wood and fresh paint, and past a set of double doors with inset etched glass panels into a saloon that looked like something from a Western movie set. A bar spanned one end of the room, standing in front of a mirrored wall decked out in dark wood shelves. The walls were lined with old photos of the mining town's heyday, housed in gold frames. There was no liquor on the shelves yet, but Charlie spied a solitary bottle of whiskey on the bar top next to a shot glass.

Carlton sat perched on a stool within arms-reach of the whiskey, a look of displeasure pasted across his face. The room's other occupant was a younger man sitting at a round table. He was in his late forties with a shadow of graying stubble darkening his chin. He wore a yellow florescent jacket and tan hiking boots. A hard hat with a light attached sat on the table in front of him.

"This is the guy that reported the deaths in the mine?" Charlie asked, glancing toward Robyn.

"Yes." Robyn nodded. "He's one of three geologists that went up there. We hired them to inspect the stability of the mine entrance and passageways so that we can run walking tours in the mine."

"And that's what they were doing when the incident occurred?"

"Yes. They went into the mine together, but he's the only one that came out. I tried talking to him but didn't get far." Robyn glanced toward the geologist. "Most of what he's said so far sounds like gibberish to me. He keeps talking about monsters with glowing red eyes."

"I told you nothing good would come of opening that mine," Carlton said. "Now look at the mess we're in."

"Don't you have something better to do?" Robyn asked, glaring at the old man.

"Not really." Carlton reached for the whiskey and poured some into the shot glass. He pounded it back and smacked his lips. "I'm comfortable right here."

"If you must stay, keep your opinions to yourself."

"Hey," Charlie said, stepping into Robyn's line of sight. "Deep breath. He's just trying to rile you up."

"He's doing a good job of it, too."

"We won't achieve anything with the pair of you snapping at each other." Charlie motioned to Glenn. "Why don't you take Miss Miller out into the lobby and take her statement."

Glenn nodded. He placed a gentle hand on Robyn's elbow and steered her out of the room.

Charlie watched them go and then turned his attention back

to the man at the table who hadn't yet spoken a word. He approached and pulled a chair out.

"Mind if I sit down?" Charlie asked.

"Free country," the man replied. He looked up, then quickly dropped his gaze again.

"Thanks." Charlie took a seat and observed the man for a few moments, noting the distant look in his eyes, as if he were barely aware of his surroundings, and the way he rubbed his hands back and forth on his thighs. "What's your name?"

"William Fenton. Bill."

"Hello Bill," Charlie said. "I'm Officer Walters. Going to ask you a few questions. Is that okay?"

Fenton nodded.

"Good." Charlie leaned forward with his elbows on the table. "First things first, we need to find out what happened to your friends. Get them out of that mine."

"You can't go in there." When Fenton looked up, his face was a mask of terror. "It's not safe. Besides, you won't find them alive."

"That's something we'll have to confirm for ourselves." The geologist's answers and demeanor confirmed what Charlie already suspected. The man was suffering from psychological shock. "How far in were you when the accident happened?"

"It wasn't an accident. Something attacked us."

"That's not possible." Charlie shook his head. "The mine's been closed for years."

"I'm telling you, there's something in there. It had the devil's eyes, and it tore my friends apart like they were confetti." Fenton looked at the police officer with wild eyes. His bottom lip trembled.

"Okay. Calm down." Charlie was aware of Carlton, still watching from the bar. He wished the man would leave. "This is important, Bill. Where were you when this happened?"

"I don't know. About half a mile in, maybe more."

"How do I find that location?" Charlie knew that the gold and silver mines dotted throughout the surrounding hills were akin to underground mazes. He'd accompanied rescue teams a few times over the years, pulling out lost hikers. Sometimes alive, but more often, not. "Can you take us back there?"

"There's no way I'm going back into that mine, and you can't make me."

"Then you're going to have to tell me how to find your friends."

"Just follow the adit until you come to a fork where the drifts go off in different directions. That's where it happened."

"Drifts?"

"The horizontal passages in the mine. The adit is the entrance, the rest of the tunnels are drifts. There are probably some vertical shafts in there too, but we never came across any. Didn't go deep enough."

"Ah. Got it," Charlie said. He sensed movement to his rear and glanced around.

Glenn was standing in the doorway. "Paramedics are here. Search and rescue too. They're antsy to get up there. You find out where we need to go?"

"I think so." Charlie stood up. He tapped his fingers on the table and looked at Fenton. "I'm going to pull your friends out of that mine now. I want you to stay here, understand? I may have more questions when I return."

"Sure." Fenton met Charlie's gaze. "If you make it out alive, that is."

CHAPTER SEVEN

Hunt fell silent for the swift journey down into the bowels of CUSPS's island facility. Decker stood anxiously next to him, unsure if he wanted to see where his employer kept those it deemed too dangerous to remain free in the world. It wasn't exactly a prison. There were other facilities serving that purpose. The residents at this location were of a more unusual persuasion. It was here they transported Grendel after the confrontation in Ireland, spirited away along with his mother by an elite squad known as the Ghost Team. The Zoo, Decker surmised, was an apt name.

When the elevator arrived at level D1, the doors slid open. Hunt and Decker stepped out into a large room with a concrete floor and walls. The only furniture was a metal table and a chair, upon which sat a man wearing a uniform that Decker recognized from his encounters with the Ghost Team. On the wall facing the desk, a row of monitors flicked between different views of The Zoo. When the guard saw Adam Hunt, he swiftly stood and snapped to attention.

"Sir," he said. "I wasn't expecting any activity today."

"As you were," Hunt said. "This is an informal visit. I'm giving our latest recruit the grand tour."

"Very good." The guard retook his seat and watched as Hunt approached a second optical scanner, this one mounted next to a steel door directly opposite the elevator.

"We took a retina scan during your physical this morning," Hunt said to Decker. "It will allow you to move through the restricted areas of the facility based upon your security clearance."

"I wondered what they were doing," Decker said, remembering the laborious eye test they had given him. He now realized that it was more than that. "How will I know which areas I can enter?"

"Every secured door is color-coded," Hunt said, pointing to an orange decal affixed to the wall next to the optical scanner. "There are five access levels with light blue being lowest security and red being the highest."

"Where does this door fall on that scale?" Decker asked, nodding toward the orange decal.

"One below red. Security zone four. Your clearance allows you to access zones one through three, which are represented by light blue, dark blue, and yellow color codes. We've given you onetime temporary access to enter The Zoo. It's good for one retina scan only, after which it will expire." Hunt nodded toward the scanner. "We allow only one person at a time through. I'll go first. Wait for the door to close behind me and then follow my example."

"Understood."

"If you have any issues, speak to the guard," Hunt said. Then he leaned in and let the scanner do its work.

A brief alarm sounded, and the door opened. Hunt stepped through before it swung closed again.

Decker heard the clunk of hidden locks re-engaging.

He glanced toward the guard, who was paying no attention,

his unwavering gaze still fixed upon the monitors. Decker stepped up to the scanner and leaned close, looking directly at the optical reader. After a moment, a red light on the scanner turned green, and he heard the locks draw back again. Seconds later he was standing with Hunt on the other side of the door.

The corridor was featureless, with blank white walls, a white floor, and a ceiling that exuded light with no visible fixtures. It ran thirty feet to a second door identical to the one Decker had passed through moments ago. The only visible items were two small security cameras, one mounted above each door. Decker felt strangely claustrophobic and hurried after Hunt to the second door.

"This corridor acts as a safety valve between The Zoo and the outside world," Hunt said. "The system only allows one door to open at a time. The guard in the antechamber we just left can also override the optical scanners and instigate a lockdown to prevent either door from opening if the situation warrants it."

Decker didn't ask exactly what circumstances it would require for a lockdown. He wasn't sure he wanted to know. Instead, he remained silent while they repeated the process with the scanners, and then he stepped out of the corridor and into a place unlike any he had ever seen.

"Welcome to The Zoo," Hunt said, clearly amused by the look of surprise on his companion's face.

"This is nothing like I expected." Decker had visited many prisons, and The Zoo resembled none of them. He stood on a high gantry that ran through the middle of a vast space that fell away beneath them. Other gantries ran off at right angles leading to metal doors set into the cavernous chamber's exterior walls. On the levels below, he could see more doors. Like the corridor they had just left, the ceiling was one large, illuminated block with no visible fixtures. It flooded the chamber with clean white light.

Hunt gave Decker a few moments to take in the spectacle before he spoke. "Each level has room for one hundred and twenty containment pods, which we call suites. There are sixty bays on each side, accessed only by these suspended walkways."

"Containment pods? Suites? Those sound like fancy words for a jail cell."

"An accurate assessment. We try to avoid associating this facility with a regular prison. We use the containment pods to transport those we bring to The Zoo from the location of their capture. Once the pod arrives at this facility, we move it to an empty bay where it becomes part of the structure."

"The transportation doubles as the inmate's permanent cell."

"Again, we don't like to use terms like inmate or cell," Hunt replied. "But yes, at least partly. The pod becomes part of a larger suite designed for the occupant's specific needs."

"Got it," Decker said. "How many levels are there?"

"Five, all of them independently accessed via the elevator we just rode down here."

"There's no movement between levels from this chamber?" Decker asked.

"No." Hunt shook his head. "Each level has its own access point and security. That way we can control entry to different parts of The Zoo. For example, your own temporary security clearance will only allow entry to this level. Travel down to D3 and you won't get in. Likewise, we can set security clearances suite by suite. If you have business with a particular guest, as we call the occupants of The Zoo, you won't be able to gain admittance to any of the other suites unless your basic clearance level allows it." Hunt started along the gantry. "Follow me."

"This place is incredible," Decker said, glancing around as they traversed the high walkway. He looked over the railing to the levels below, noting how the bottom floor contained rows of tables and chairs much like the rec area in a conventional prison. The occupants of that level, it appeared, enjoyed greater freedom than those on the floors above.

"You haven't seen anything yet," Hunt replied. He turned left and led Decker along one of the branching gantries. They stopped in front of the metal door and once again repeated the ritual with the scanner in order to gain access.

The door opened.

Decker stepped over the threshold into a dimly lit room with an opaque wall made of a shiny material that resembled glass.

Hunt crossed to a narrow podium that held a touchscreen. He played with the controls for a moment and then, much to Decker's surprise, the wall's opacity faded and became transparent to reveal the room beyond.

Decker took a step forward, his eyes wide. A dim cavern sat behind the glass, with rugged stone walls and a gravel floor interspersed with small boulders. Beyond this, at the edge of darkness, Decker could see animal bones strewn in the dirt. He looked sideways at Hunt. "What are you keeping in here?"

"You'll see." There was a smile on Hunt's face. As if reading Decker's mind, Hunt motioned toward the bones. "Before you ask, we're feeding it sides of beef and pork ribs. We are not sacrificing goats to it or anything."

"Feeding what?" Decker moved closer to the glass and peered into the gloom. From the darkness, a pair of yellow eyes glowed. Then a familiar figure stepped out of the shadows and returned his stare.

Hunt joined Decker and stood, arms folded, mesmerized by the creature beyond the glass. "Not so scary now, is he?"

"I wouldn't go that far." Decker felt a shiver creep up his spine. He approached the glass and Grendel did the same. Their eyes locked briefly, and Decker suppressed a shudder of revulsion. "He's just as frightening as I remember."

CHAPTER EIGHT

They made their way up the canyon path toward the mine opening. Charlie went first, followed by two paramedics and the three-person search and rescue team. Glenn, Charlie's rookie partner, was last.

When they arrived at the Ghost Canyon Mine, the search team commander, a man named Ryan Colbeck whom Charlie had worked with a few times before, took charge. He made sure everyone was wearing their protective headgear and handed each member of the group a flashlight. His colleague, a young woman named Sasha Martin, gave out two-way radios. Before entering, she warned the group to stick close to each other. It was easy to get disoriented underground, and she didn't want to lose anyone. Then the group stepped out of the sunlight and into the mine's cold, dark world.

They proceeded slowly, with the search and rescue team taking the lead. Glenn looked around anxiously, his flashlight beam bobbing off the walls and ceiling.

"First time in a mine?" Charlie asked, glancing sideways toward his partner.

"Yeah." Glenn nodded. He looked uneasy. "How far in do we have to go, anyway?"

"About half a mile according to our witness back in town." Charlie kept his own flashlight pointed straight ahead. He knew from experience the dangers that lurked in old mine tunnels. "You okay with that? You look a little green there."

"It's narrow in here, that's all."

"You can go back and wait for us at the entrance if you want," Charlie said.

"Not a chance."

"Just putting it out there."

"Yeah, and how would that look if something happened to you down here, with me waiting back up top like a sissy. We're partners. Where you go, I go."

"I thought you'd say that."

Charlie returned his attention to the mine tunnel. There was an obstruction up ahead. At first he wasn't sure what it was but quickly realized it was old ore carts abandoned when the mine closed. He wondered just how much junk was actually down here, rotting away in the darkness. Judging by the amount of crap littering the ghost town they had just come from, probably quite a lot. It amazed him how people left so much stuff behind when they moved on, especially out in the desert where there were entire communities abandoned once the flow of precious metals that sustained them dried up. He guessed it was just too much trouble to move everything. When he was a kid, his parents had taken a drive out to Death Valley. They'd stopped at a settlement full of nothing but tumbleweeds and dust. At one time it had been a booming frontier settlement that made its money pulling a mineral called rhyolite out of the surrounding hills. All that now remained were a few crumbling stone buildings that had long ago lost their roofs. But the thing he remembered most was the train station. It was the only structure that had survived intact. It sat empty and dark, the rail line that brought prospectors and bankers and women of ill repute to that desolate town long gone. It was hard to tell where the tracks had even been. It was a sad and lonely place. A moldering temple to the lust for money that drove men into a harsh and hostile wilderness. It was somewhere he would never forget.

"Watch your step," Colbeck shouted back as they edged their way around the ore carts. "There are some sharp edges here. Don't want anyone to cut themselves."

The sudden voice snapped Charlie back to the present.

"You see anything yet?" He shouted forward to the front of the group.

"Not so far," came the reply. This was a man Charlie hadn't met before, but who Colbeck had introduced at the mine entrance as Enrique.

They carried on walking and met no more obstacles. After a while Glenn spoke again. "You believe what that guy back in town said?"

"About what?" Charlie asked.

"That something is down here, and it killed his colleagues."

"Not really." In Charlie's experience, there wasn't much that hung out in old mines. There might be rattlesnakes around the entrance, or even a bobcat or two looking for a cool place to lay awhile. But this far into the tunnel there should be nothing bigger than a bat, and maybe a few spiders.

"Then what do you think happened?"

Charlie was about to answer when a shout went up at the front of the group.

"The tunnel splits here. I see something. This might be the place."

"I guess we're about to find out." Charlie pushed his way past the paramedics and joined the search and rescue crew, who had come to a halt twenty feet ahead at a spot where the adit branched, and two new tunnels ran in opposite directions to each other.

"This matches the place described by your witness," Colbeck said.

"What do we have?" asked Charlie. He glanced around but didn't see much, and certainly not a pair of mutilated corpses. "Doesn't look like there's anything here."

"There's something, alright." Sasha trained her flashlight onto the tunnel floor. The beam picked out a dark viscous stain sitting atop the loose rock and dirt.

"That looks like blood," Colbeck said. "A lot of it."

"There's more here," Enrique said, playing his flashlight across the rock walls. "Spatter. Something nasty went down here, that's for sure."

"Then where are the bodies?" Charlie asked. He sensed someone behind him and turned to find Glenn off his right shoulder. Lingering a few paces behind were the two paramedics, who looked lost without a victim to work on.

"Maybe they're wounded and wandered deeper into the mine." Glenn said.

"Not with this much blood." Colbeck shook his head.

"And not without these." Sasha bent down and plucked an object from the floor near the tunnel wall. She held it up and Charlie saw it was a bloody flashlight with a smashed lens. She nodded further down the drift. "There's another one over there."

"Put that back where you found it and don't touch anything else," Charlie said, a chill enveloping him. He motioned the paramedics and rescue team to move back, away from the blood. "This might be a crime scene. We don't want to contaminate it."

"What? You can't just abandon them down here." Sasha aimed her flashlight further down the empty tunnel. "We don't know for sure that they're dead. We have to confirm it."

"And we will," Colbeck said. "But we're going to need a bigger team to conduct a thorough search. We need the proper gear too. There must be miles of tunnels down here. As it is, we could wander for days and never find them, and just end up getting lost ourselves."

"I have a question," Glenn said. "Since we all agree there was a struggle, and that with this amount of blood it's unlikely the victims survived, is anyone else curious where the bodies went? I mean, we know there's no wildlife in the mine to drag them off, so if those men died here, they should still be here."

"Unless our witness back in town is the real killer, and he's covering his ass by claiming a creature attacked them." Charlie played his flashlight beam over the bloodied ground once more. "He could've murdered them, dragged the bodies deeper into the mine, and dropped them down a shaft before running back to town and claiming a monster got them."

"That doesn't sound like a very believable story if you want to get away with murder."

"You would be surprised," Charlie said. "I've heard perps come up with some real crazy shit to stay out of jail. But yes, I agree. As explanations go, it's not very sound."

"Especially when he could just say that they fell down the mine shaft. He doesn't need to invent an unknown assailant," Glenn replied. "And why attack them so violently? There must be a hundred ways to kill someone down here without leaving all that blood behind."

"When we locate the bodies, we'll have our answer." Charlie said. "But right now, we should return to the surface and regroup. It's not safe to go further under the circumstances."

"Maybe the old guy, Carlton, will have a map of the mine."

"It's possible."

"Let's go, then." Colbeck said. "We'll return better prepared and make a full search." He turned to head back the way they'd come.

They had only gone a few feet when Sasha stopped and held up an arm. She turned back toward the dark tunnel. "Wait. I hear something."

Charlie stopped and listened. "I don't hear anything."

"I do," Glenn said. "It's like a low moan."

Then Charlie heard it too. A whispering moan that echoed from the direction of the unexplored tunnel. A shiver ran up his spine. "What on earth is that?"

"Maybe it's one of the lost geologists," Sasha said. She pointed her light down the tunnel, but there was nothing there.

"It was probably a breeze," Charlie replied, but even as he spoke the words, he knew it wasn't stirring air.

"Hush," Sasha waved them quiet.

Then Charlie heard a new noise. A shuffling, dragging sound, and this was definitely no breeze.

"It must be the geologists. They aren't dead," Sasha said, her eyes wide. She took a step toward the sounds. "We need to help them."

"No." Colbeck reached out to stop her. "It isn't safe."

"We can't just abandon them." Sasha shrugged his hand away and kept going.

"Wait," Charlie said. He had a bad feeling about this situation. "We don't even know that it's them."

"Who else could it be?" Sasha glanced back, briefly meeting Charlie's gaze. "If the rest of you don't want to help, I'll find them myself." Then she turned and took off down the tunnel at a sprint.

"Sasha," Colbeck shouted after her.

But it was too late. She was already gone.

CHAPTER NINE

It was early evening in Maine. Decker sat at the bar in CUSP's strangely hotel-like accommodation block, nursing a whiskey sour. He leaned on the bar and stared down into the untouched drink, watching the ice melt. His tour of The Zoo had left Decker with a deep sense of unease. Knowing that such a place existed, and seeing firsthand, were two different things. It drove home the reality that his work had consequences long after the end of a mission. Despite Adam Hunt's assurances that the German sailors released from their purgatory on the U-boat were being well taken care of, Decker couldn't help but wonder if CUSP had created a prison for them just as restrictive as the one Grendel now occupied.

That Hunt referred to the prison cells in the subterranean facility sitting beneath the island as *suites* only heightened Decker's sense of disconnect. He understood that creatures such as Grendel, and his mother, Astrid, were dangerous. He knew they could not be allowed to roam free, killing at will. But he also possessed a strong sense of justice, or more accurately, due process. In his previous life there was a line that separated men like him, who apprehended bad guys, and the judiciary who weighed their fate with impartiality. In his new job, Decker had become judge, jury, and executioner. It was this shift in the dynamic of his life that left Decker uncomfortable.

"That whiskey has probably aged about as much as it's ever going to," a familiar voice said to his right. "If you're not going to drink it, you should probably pass it over here. I'll put the blighter out of its misery."

"You wouldn't like this," Decker said, dragging his gaze from the glass and glancing toward Colum. "It's bourbon."

"So?" Colum raised an eyebrow.

"I thought you Irish lads were of the opinion that anything made outside of the Emerald Isle wasn't a true whiskey."

"Don't sweat yourself." Colum climbed onto a stool next to Decker. "I'll drink it now and go to confession later."

"That easy, huh?"

"Perks of being raised Catholic."

"And how does that Catholic God feel about your current profession? Do you think he'd be happy that we round up his creations and lock them away?"

"Oh, hell." Colum shook his head. "Adam Hunt gave you a tour of The Zoo, didn't he?"

"Yeah. Something like that."

"It's a lot to take in." Colum caught the bartender's eye and ordered a drink. "I remember the day he took me on a tour of that place. Just about scared the bejeebers out of me. I didn't sleep for a week."

"I find that hard to believe." Decker lifted his drink, finally, and took a sip.

"It's true. I saw some bad things when I was in the service. Not to mention the Troubles when I was growing up. What people will do to each other, it's terrible. But what I saw down there was different. It's a shock when you discover the creatures that prowl your nightmares are real."

"I've been there," Decker said, remembering his encounter

with The Cult of Anubis in New York, and Annie Doucet's transformation into a Cajun werewolf. "Even when you know that monsters are real, The Zoo is a lot to take."

"You're lucky in that respect. You already knew that creatures like Grendel were out there even before you went to Ireland. I was completely unprepared the first time I walked into The Zoo." Colum let out a mirthless chuckle. "Adam Hunt, man. I think he just enjoys scaring people. I don't envy you chasing monsters for a living. Thank heaven most of my assignments are more mundane. Speaking of which, have you spoken to Mina recently?"

Decker nodded. "We keep in touch. I kind of feel responsible for what happened."

"That's all on Abraham Turner. He's the one who stabbed her and tried to steal her life force."

"I'm the one that got her involved in the first place."

"She got herself involved. She practically blackmailed us to let her help." Colum's drink arrived. He lifted the pint and gulped a quarter of it before continuing. "I'm just glad it worked out okay in the end."

"Yeah." Decker wasn't sure how well it had worked out for Mina. She was still struggling with the aftereffects of her encounter with Abraham Turner. It had changed her, and what those changes meant in the long term, they had yet to find out. He said none of this to Colum, though. Even Adam Hunt didn't know the full extent of Mina's transformation, and Decker wanted to keep it that way for now. He wasn't sure they could trust CUSP to stay away, and he didn't want her to end up somewhere like The Zoo. She had, after all, absorbed much of Abraham Turner's power. Deciding they were heading into dangerous territory with further conversation regarding Mina, Decker changed the subject. "I assume Hunt has you off on another mission tomorrow?"

Colum nodded. "I have a briefing first thing in the morning

and then I'll be gone. I have no idea where, yet. You know what Adam's like. That man likes secrets more than anyone I've ever met. I swear, he wouldn't even tell us his own name if he thought he could get away with it."

"We don't actually know that he *has* told us his name," Decker pointed out. "Adam Hunt could be an alias."

"Good point," Colum said, polishing off the rest of his pint and motioning for a refill. "I bet his real name isn't anywhere near as cool. It's probably something lame like Reggie Braithwaite or Barry Smith."

"That sounds like a pair of truck drivers," Decker said, laughing.

"Or plumbers," Colum added.

"Gentlemen," a voice said from behind the pair.

Decker turned to see Hunt there with his arms folded. "How long have you been standing behind us?" He asked.

"Long enough," Hunt said. "And for the record, my name is neither Reggie, nor Barry."

"But is it really Adam?" Colum asked, grinning.

In response, Hunt merely flashed an enigmatic smile and motioned to an empty barstool. "My work is done for the day. Would you mind if I join you?"

"Knock yourself out," Colum said. He glanced down the bar, looking for his second pint, which had not yet arrived. "And since you have some sway around here, maybe you can get that bartender to pour me a drink."

CHAPTER TEN

In the moments after Sasha bolted down the tunnel, the group stood in stunned silence. Then, regaining his wits, Colbeck unclipped the two-way radio from his belt and activated it.

"Sasha. Do you copy?" He released the talk button and waited, but empty static was his only reward. He tried again, toggling the talk button, and barking into the radio to no avail. If Sasha could hear him, she was not responding.

"We have to follow her," Glenn said, taking a step forward.

"No. Not you." Charlie shook his head. His own first instinct was also to give chase, but he was responsible for the remaining personnel and didn't want to lead an inexperienced group deeper into the mine. He turned to Glenn and spoke quickly; aware they didn't have much time. "Take the paramedics back to the surface and wait for us at the entrance."

"What? Why?" Glenn looked shocked. "We should stick together."

Charlie shook his head. "We don't know how stable this mine is, and I don't want to be responsible for more folk than necessary. I'm taking the search and rescue team and we're going after Sasha. If we come across anyone that needs medical help, and they can't walk out under their own steam, we'll come back and get you. But right now, it's too dangerous for everyone to be down here."

"But—"

"No buts. That's an order." Charlie wasn't budging. He pointed back toward the entrance. "Go."

"Fine, but just for the record, I'm not comfortable with this."

"Understood, but I'm the senior officer here."

"Yeah. I know." Glenn let out an annoyed snort. He hesitated a moment, perhaps debating if he should argue further, then turned and stomped back toward the mine entrance with the paramedics in tow.

Charlie watched him leave, then turned his attention to the pair of remaining rescuers.

Colbeck was still busy trying to raise Sasha on the radio. Receiving no response, he lowered the radio. "Dammit. Why isn't she answering?"

"I don't know," Charlie replied. "Maybe there's too much rock between us and her."

"Maybe."

"Forget the two-way. We're wasting time," Charlie glanced backwards to make sure that his partner was still returning to the surface. He could see flashlights bobbing in the darkness, getting further away. Satisfied, he turned back to Colbeck. "Let's go find her before she gets herself in trouble."

"No argument there," Colbeck replied through gritted teeth. He touched Enrique's shoulder and set off down the tunnel. "Come on."

Charlie cast another quick glance back toward the mine entrance, then followed along.

The three men passed by the pool of blood, taking wide steps over it to avoid contaminating the scene more than necessary, and pressed deeper into the mine. They moved at a fast clip, aware that Sasha might pull ahead of them. If they reached another fork before they located the missing woman, they would have to pick a passage and hope they'd made the right choice or split up. Charlie didn't like either option. He prayed they would catch up with her before encountering that scenario, or that she would come to her senses and double back.

Charlie kept his ears open, listening for the strange noises that had lured the overzealous search and rescue team member away from the group in the first place. He heard nothing and wondered if it really was just a momentary breeze blowing through the tunnel.

Until he heard the scream, high pitched and full of terror.

It echoed down the tunnel before being abruptly cut off.

"Holy crap, what was that?" Enrique came to a stumbling halt. He stared into the darkness; his face flushed with fear.

"My guess would be Sasha," Charlie said, pushing past the alarmed man and taking off at a faster pace than he should, given the unfamiliar terrain. He sped along the tunnel, playing his flashlight across the ground ahead to make sure he wasn't going to run headlong into a mineshaft and fall to his death. Colbeck followed close behind, his pounding footfalls and labored breathing loud in the confined space.

They reached a spot where the tunnel curved to the left, the walls rough and pitted with chisel marks where the miners had followed the seam of gold. Further back came more footfalls as Enrique hurried behind.

"She can't be that far ahead," Colbeck said, drawing level with Charlie.

"That scream didn't sound good." Charlie hoped Sasha hadn't stumbled into a vertical shaft and plummeted to her death or impaled herself on some piece of rusty equipment in her haste to find the missing geologists.

"Sasha, can you hear me?" Colbeck called out as they rounded the bend.

The only answer they received was a low moan.

Charlie felt a prickle of fear. Instead of pulling two injured or dead people out of the mine, they might have now made it three, adding Sasha to the casualties.

A hundred feet distant, the tunnel turned again, switching back upon itself like an undulating snake. Charlie swept his flashlight beam across the ground ahead and covered the distance at a jog. When he took the corner, his feet almost slid out from under him on the loose grit covering the floor. He caught himself just in time. Even so, Charlie stumbled, the flashlight beam dancing wildly until he regained his feet. Then, when he saw what lay ahead, his first instinct was to turn and flee back in the other direction.

Sasha was further down the tunnel, sitting propped against a pile of rocks. Her head was bent low, her chin almost upon her chest. But it was the figure crouched over her that filled Charlie with dread. It looked like a collection of bones wrapped in desiccated flesh. It straddled the stricken woman, pinning her to the wall with bony arms that ended in taloned fingers. It hunched low, bald head buried somewhere between her breasts and navel, where it appeared to be slurping noisily at a viscous dark fluid that Charlie realized, with horror, was the woman's own blood.

Colbeck rounded the bend with Enrique a step behind and came to a skidding halt. His eyes flew wide, and he opened his mouth to speak, but Charlie put a hand up and silenced him. The creature, whatever it was, hadn't noticed them yet. It was too busy chewing on their colleague.

But then, as if sensing the three sets of eyes gazing upon it in mute horror, the creature lifted its head and turned toward them.

Charlie's hand flew to his gun. He pulled it from its holster and raised the weapon.

The creature hauled itself upright on wasted legs and stood blocking the passage ahead of them. Charlie aimed his service weapon but didn't fire. He had no idea how fragile the tunnel was and didn't want to bring it down on top of them. Besides, the creature wasn't advancing. It was just standing there. Charlie had the strange sensation that it wasn't afraid. In fact, just the opposite. It was confident they would become its next victims.

Charlie's eyes flicked from the impossibly animated skeletal figure down to Sasha. She was obviously dead. Her arms hung limp at her sides, and she didn't appear to be breathing. But that wasn't how Charlie knew Sasha was gone. The creature had flayed her stomach open and tore the skin back like so much thin fabric, before discarding her innards next to the body in a bloody heap. Charlie had attended many homicides. He'd seen gunshots and stab victims. He'd witnessed strangulation and drowning. But he had never seen a body wrecked this violently. It was almost too much to bear.

He lifted his eyes from the shattered corpse just in time to see Colbeck shamble past him toward the monstrous creature. And tagging along behind, like a dutiful pet, was Enrique.

"What are you doing," Charlie hissed.

Neither man answered. They were looking straight ahead, their eyes locked upon the withered husk that had so violently dispatched their co-worker.

"For the love of God…" Charlie reached out and gripped the man's arm, but Colbeck shrugged the restraining hand off and kept going.

And then Charlie noticed the creature's face, and the blood-red eyes set into sunken dark sockets. Eyes that glowed with an inner luminescence that held him in a hypnotic fog and filled his mind with suggestive whispers to come closer. With some effort, Charlie shook off the strange sensation. But it took all his willpower. He wondered what would happen if the creature diverted its attention and actually met his gaze. Would he still be able to escape its pull?

He didn't want to find out.

Deciding that a tunnel collapse was a risk he was willing to take, Charlie lifted the gun, took aim, and fired four shots in rapid succession.

CHAPTER ELEVEN

All four of Charlie's bullets slammed into the skeletal creature, knocking it backwards into the darkness. He couldn't tell if he'd inflicted a mortal wound, or even if the hellish animated corpse could die, but his rapid-fire shots achieved one thing. They broke whatever hypnotic connection the creature held upon the two rescue team members. The men stopped their forward march, looking momentarily dazed, then hurried back toward Charlie.

"We have to leave, right now." Charlie kept the gun aimed forward. He swept his flashlight across the tunnel ahead, but the passageway was empty. Their attacker had retreated further into the tunnels, at least for now.

"Not without Sasha," Enrique said. He ran to her and kneeled down, checking her vitals, even though she was obviously deceased.

"Leave her," Colbeck instructed. "There's nothing we can do."

"He's right." Charlie didn't know where the creature had gone, or how long it would stay away. He knew one thing. They might not be lucky enough to fend it off a second time. "She's dead."

"I'm not leaving Sasha down here with that thing." Enrique slipped his arms under her body and lifted. "I'll carry her out. She deserves nothing less."

"Do whatever you need to," Colbeck said, glancing nervously down the tunnel. "But if she slows us down—"

"She won't." Enrique grunted under Sasha's weight as he stood up. He cradled her in his arms, ignoring the blood that stained his jacket. With noticeable effort, he started down the tunnel back toward the mine entrance.

They retraced their steps, following the serpentine route back to the site of the original attack, then turned and followed the adit toward the mine entrance. The ground rose gently as they walked, carrying them closer to the exit, and safety.

No one spoke, either too shocked to talk, or afraid that any sound might draw their attacker back toward them. Charlie brought up the rear, ready to use his gun again if the creature appeared a second time. He couldn't explain how he knew it, but he was certain there would be only a momentary window within which to fire before he succumbed to its hypnotic gaze. But they weren't being followed, and soon, much to his relief, Charlie saw a rectangular patch of daylight up ahead.

They pressed on with renewed determination, even though Enrique was sagging visibly under his dead friend's weight. A few minutes later, they emerged from the mine and into the bright, warming Nevada sunshine.

Enrique stumbled forward and dropped to his knees ten feet from the mine entrance. He deposited Sasha on the hard ground, then scooted out of the way for the paramedics, who scrambled into action at his approach.

"What happened in there?" Glenn had been sitting on a large rock near the entrance, fanning himself with his hard hat, and jumped up as they exited the mine. Now he approached Charlie, a look of shock on his face. "Did she fall?"

"We were attacked." Charlie turned to face the mine with his gun raised. If there was even a hint of movement in the darkness beyond the entrance, he would be ready. "Probably the same creature that killed those two geologists."

"Creature?" Glenn looked at the dead woman, then glanced back toward the mine. "Seriously? That guy back in town was telling the truth?"

Charlie glanced over his shoulder. The paramedics were working on Sasha, even though they surely realized their efforts were futile. "I think we can safely rule him out as a suspect. I don't know exactly what attacked us, but I shot it four times at close range and barely phased it."

"That's not possible. You put four bullets in a man, he doesn't walk away."

"I never said it was a man." An image of the emaciated corpse flashed through Charlie's mind. The way it walked, lurching forward on impossibly thin limbs. The way its eyes burned with unholy fire. Worst of all was the creaking, shuffling sound it made, like joints popping and shifting with each step. He shuddered and pushed the dire memory away. "It might have once been a man, but right now, that thing is about as far from human as you can get."

"You're not making sense. You sure you didn't stumble into a pocket of stale air and inhale too many fumes?"

Charlie pointed to Sasha. "Does that woman look like she was killed by fumes?"

"Hey. I'm just saying—"

"What we saw in that mine was no man." Charlie felt a flash of anger. "I was there. You weren't."

"Okay. Take it easy. I believe you." From the tone of Glenn's voice, he still wasn't convinced. "Creature or not, we still have two missing people in there. How do you want to proceed?"

"I don't know. I've never encountered a situation like this before," Charlie replied. There was no way he was walking back into the mine anytime soon, that much he knew. He watched the paramedics unfold a rescue stretcher and lift Sasha's body onto it. A few steps away, Ryan Colbeck and Enrique lingered in shocked silence. He guessed their colleague's death was sinking in now the adrenaline had worn off. He looked back toward the mine entrance. "Either way, we have to call it in. Maybe we can get someone up here who knows more about this kind of thing."

"Who would that be?" Glenn looked incredulous.

"Beats me," Charlie admitted. "We'll make our report and pass it up the chain."

The paramedics had finished strapping Sasha's body to the stretcher. They hoisted it between them and started off back down the path toward the old ghost town.

Charlie waited for the two remaining members of the search and rescue team to tag along behind, then followed up the rear with his partner, casting nervous glances back toward the mine. When they were far enough away that he could no longer see the yawning black hole in the mountainside, Charlie slipped the gun back into its holster, but even so he kept a hand on it, ready to draw should the need arise.

"You going to tell dispatch what you told me?" Glenn asked as they made their way down the narrow trail.

"Not much choice. It's the truth."

"Good luck getting them to take you seriously." Glenn wiped a sheen of the sweat from his forehead with the back of his hand. "I'm your partner. I know you wouldn't invent a crazy story like this, and I'm still not sure I believe it."

"I know," Charlie said. He didn't need to be told how crazy his story sounded. He tapped the body cam affixed to his torso. "But I have proof. My camera was rolling the whole time."

"I don't know, it's pretty dark in those tunnels. What if it didn't record anything but blackness."

Charlie nodded toward Colbeck and Enrique. "Then I have two witnesses to back me up."

"Let's hope that's enough."

"It will have to be." Charlie was feeling better the further they walked down the trail. Soon this would be someone else's mess, and he could try and forget what he'd seen in the Ghost Canyon Mine. The problem was, he didn't think he would.

CHAPTER TWELVE

Robyn Miller observed the commotion on her property with growing dread. A third person had lost their life inside the mine. A member of the search team. And by all accounts it was violent. There really was something up there, although the cops had been tightlipped about exactly what.

Robyn felt bad about the death. It was dreadful, of course. Yet she couldn't help wondering how this would affect the future of the business she was trying to build here. Who in their right mind would want to take a tour in a mine linked to such a recent and horrific tragedy? It was hardly a fun day out when all anyone could think about were the number of deaths that had occurred there. Not that anyone would be going anywhere near that mine in the immediate future. After the cops returned from the mine, a whole bunch of people showed up in a variety of vehicles. There was even a SWAT team who actually drove their armored truck up the trail. No mean feat, since the path wasn't wide enough for a regular car, let alone a hulking tactical assault vehicle.

She was confined to the hotel's saloon bar for most of the evening, along with the surviving geologist, Carlton, and Tieg.

The dog sat at her feet looking bewildered as a parade of officials came and went, asking questions, taking the opportunity to confer under air conditioning, and occasionally helping themselves to tall glasses of iced tea from jugs she'd put out on the bar top. It was during one of these frequent refreshment visits that she overheard a couple of senior police officials discussing their next move. The SWAT team were going to enter the mine, even though it was getting dark. The buzz of activity increased in anticipation of this event. There was even a helicopter circling overhead. At first she thought it was a police chopper monitoring the action on the ground, but then she spotted the logo emblazoned on the side as it made a low pass over the town. The local news station. Her heart fell. This would be plastered all over Channel 10 by midnight.

Then, in no time at all, the mood changed.

Two men in khaki pants and matching white polos showed up like a pair of escapees from some golf tournament. They arrived in an unmarked sedan so dull that it screamed government. This pissed off the cluster of LVMPD captains and lieutenants, at least judging by the heated exchange that started in the hotel lobby and then spilled into the saloon. Maybe they felt their toes were being stepped on, or maybe they just didn't like the newcomers, who were obviously Feds. Either way, the dynamics of the situation shifted. Within thirty minutes the SWAT vehicle was back, recalled before the heavily armed team even entered the mine.

A couple of uniformed officers erected A-frame barricades across the entrance to the trail and stuck a sign in the dirt which read, AREA CLOSED, and in smaller lettering underneath, BY ORDER OF LVMPD.

After that, the police activity subsided. Cruisers and unmarked vehicles pulled U-turns in the street and headed back toward the city. It felt like an exodus, which was weird because they still had not found the two missing geologists, and if anyone knew what was attacking people in the mine, they weren't saying.

Pretty soon there were only a couple of vehicles left. A lone police cruiser was parked near the barricades with a bored officer staring out across the dusty landscape at the mostly dark ramshackle buildings. He was obviously on guard duty even though there was no-one around except her and Carlton to even attempt a trip up to the mine. And the two Feds, of course.

They parked their car out front in the spot previously occupied by the geologist's quad cab, which the police department had towed away a couple of hours earlier after bundling the traumatized geologist into the back of an ambulance.

The Feds themselves were standing on the wide veranda out front. One of them leaned on the railing and stared toward the trail leading to the Ghost Canyon Mine, while the other paced back and forth talking on his phone. Afterward, he slipped the phone into his pants pocket and made his way inside with his partner a few steps behind.

When they approached Robyn, Tieg jumped up and ran to greet them, tail wagging. The dog was, Robyn thought, a better ambassador for the ghost town than Carlton, and certainly more friendly.

One of the Feds, the younger of the two, kneeled and petted the dog, rubbing his head and scratching behind his ears. Tieg grinned and his tongue lolled out.

The other agent only gave the dog a cursory glance and then spoke to Robyn. "I'm Special Agent Elton Fowler with the FBI's Las Vegas field office. My partner over there, the one practicing his interrogation techniques on your dog, is Special Agent Jackson Barnes."

"Hello, Special Agent Fowler," Robyn said. She was sitting at a table near the bar and motioned to an empty seat. "Won't you sit down?"

"No, thank you." Fowler shook his head. "I prefer to stand."

"Okay." Robyn resisted the urge to stand up, even though she was uncomfortable with the agent standing over her in such close proximity. She wondered if he really wanted to remain standing, or if it was a way to assert his authority. She'd once read an article about the CEO of a large corporation wanting an office chair that raised higher than the other chairs in the room so that it would force his employees to look up to him, which would instill in them a feeling of subservience. Was Agent Fowler doing the same thing, possibly subconsciously, or did he just dislike being comfortable? "Is there something I can help you with, Agent Fowler?"

"Yes, indeed." The FBI agent reached up and straightened his collar, even though it wasn't out of place. "As I understand it, you have rooms available."

"I do have rooms, yes, but we're not open yet. We probably won't be accepting reservations until the spring."

The other agent had finished playing with the dog. He stood and approached them. Fowler waited for his partner before speaking again. "But you do have renovated rooms that will be suitable for habitation."

Habitation? Robyn thought. It was an odd turn of phrase. Even so, she nodded. "We've finished the renovations on most of the second floor. Why?"

"Excellent. Agent Barnes and I would like to procure two such rooms for our use while we investigate. Unless you object, of course, in which case we shall make alternate arrangements."

"No, it's fine." Robyn wasn't sure what to think, but she had to admit, having a couple of armed FBI agents on the property after what had occurred today would not be the worst thing in the world. "I can put fresh sheets on the beds. I have to warn you though, it still smells of paint up there."

"That won't be a problem," Fowler said. "And of course, the FBI will reimburse you for the nights we're here."

"Also, as I'm sure you can see, the bar and restaurant are not yet open, but we have plenty of food and I'm more than happy to whip up meals should you require them. It will give us a chance to practice before we open to the public. Kind of like a dry run."

"In that case we will take you up on that offer," Fowler replied.

Robyn nodded. She stood up and called to Tieg. "I'll take care of those sheets right now. There's a bottle of whiskey on the bar if you'd like a drink."

"Thank you, but not while we're on duty." Fowler paused, then spoke again. "And if it's not too much trouble, maybe you could make up a third room, too."

"Another FBI agent?" Robyn asked over her shoulder as she headed toward the door with the dog at her heels.

"Not quite," Fowler said. "The situation here is rather unique, so my superiors called in a favor. We have a specialist on the way. Someone who's dealt with this kind of thing before."

CHAPTER THIRTEEN

Decker's accommodation was a well-appointed room on the third floor of the mansion overlooking the bay. This space, unlike the one Grendel was being kept in many levels below, could legitimately be called a suite. Decker didn't know how many people worked at the facility, but he estimated there were at least fifty rooms if you counted both the mansion and a newer wing on the east side of the property.

After a light supper in the canteen, he retreated upstairs and called Nancy. It was late, almost 11 o'clock, but they talked for an hour. Taylor was not far down the coast, attending college in Boston, and Nancy had toyed with the idea of traveling up with Decker and visiting her daughter while he continued on to Maine. But the plan had not come to fruition. Taylor hadn't been in school long, and they decided to give her some space since Christmas was less than two months away and she would be returning home for the holidays. Even so, Decker sensed a tinge of sadness in her voice, and he wondered if she regretted not making the arrangements. Nancy had been struggling to readjust ever since the events in Wolf Haven, and Decker felt helpless to resolve the situation.

When she hung up, he climbed in bed and lay there for a long while, thinking.

He awoke next morning and made his way to the cafeteria. Colum was already there, sitting alone and digging into a hearty plate of bacon and eggs. A travel bag sat on the floor next to him.

Decker went to the buffet and helped himself to a ham steak, hash browns, fried eggs, and chunks of honeydew melon, which he figured offset the dubious choices he'd made with the rest of his breakfast. He placed the plate on the tray and then poured a coffee before making his way back through the cafeteria toward his colleague.

"Mind if I join you?" Decker asked as he drew close to the table.

"I'm almost done here," Colum replied, looking up briefly from his food. "But I'll take the company."

"What time's your flight?" Decker placed the tray on the table and pulled out a chair.

"Eleven o'clock. I'm booked on a commercial flight out of Portland International. There's a helicopter standing by to take me there just as soon as I finish breakfast."

"Going anywhere nice?" Decker asked, then held up a hand to stop the almost certain protest. "Yeah, I know you can't tell me the specifics, but at least tell me that Hunt has you going somewhere pleasant."

"You're right, I can't tell you specifics." Colum had just about finished his breakfast. He popped the last piece of bacon in his mouth and chewed before talking again. "But I'll give you a clue since you asked, I'm off to Eastern Europe. I'd love to tell you which country…"

"But then you'd have to kill me?"

"See, now you're getting it. We'll turn you into a shady government spook yet."

"And thus, my childhood dream will finally be realized,"

Decker said, chuckling. He cut into his ham steak and started to eat. He had only taken a couple of bites, however, when Colum nodded toward the cafeteria entrance.

"U-oh. Here comes the boss, and he's looking at you."

Decker twisted to see Adam Hunt striding across the room. And Colum was right. He was heading directly for them, gaze fixed firmly upon Decker.

He didn't look happy.

"What did you do?" Colum asked, mopping up bacon grease from his plate with a slice of bread.

"Nothing." Decker shook his head. "I haven't been here long enough to get into any trouble."

"Well, something has pissed him off. I'm sure glad he's not looking at me."

Decker would have replied, but at that moment Hunt reached the table.

"Good, you've had breakfast already," he said to Decker. "That will save some time."

Decker glanced down at his plate of food, barely touched. "Actually, I've only just—"

Hunt cut him off with a wave of one hand. "I got a call this morning requesting our assistance for an unusual situation out west. To be precise, I didn't actually get the call. That honor went to someone higher up the chain, and they bumped it on down to me."

"A call from who?" Colum asked, his interest piqued. "I thought we operate autonomously."

"We do." Hunt looked like he'd been sucking on a lemon. "But the nature of our business requires that we form relationships with other agencies, both domestic and foreign. It's the only way to obtain much of the information we rely upon. Most of the time that works in our favor…"

"But sometimes they want to collect on the favor, instead?" Colum said.

"Exactly."

"So, who came knocking?" Decker asked.

"The FBI, after someone came knocking on *their* door. The Las Vegas Metropolitan Police Department, to be precise."

"Sweet," Colum said, grinning at Decker. "Looks like you snagged an all-expenses-paid trip to Sin City." He settled back in his chair and looked up at Hunt. "Any chance he needs a sidekick? I'd be up for a trip to the bright lights."

"Not going to happen," Hunt replied. "You have your own mission in Europe."

"Yeah. Eastern Europe."

"Still counts."

"Barely." Colum looked disappointed.

"What's the problem out in Vegas?" Decker asked.

"I don't want to discuss that here." Hunt glanced around the room. "I'll brief you in private once you've packed your bags. For now, all I'll say is they have a need for a monster hunter."

"On second thought," Colum said. "Eastern Europe sounds fine. I've had enough of monsters for a while."

"Indeed." Hunt glanced at his watch, then turned his attention to Decker. "I'll see you in my office in forty-five minutes. Don't be late. You'll be sharing the helicopter ride with Colum and we can't afford any delays. We have a private jet waiting for you at Portsmouth International."

"Lucky you. Riding in style," Colum said. "All I get is a coach class ticket and no legroom. Still, on the bright side, the only monsters I'll be chasing are human."

"Which doesn't make them any less deadly," Hunt replied. He tapped his fingers on the table and focused on Decker. "I've had the concierge transfer everything you'll need to your room."

"What might I need?" Decker asked.

"A sturdy pair of boots for a start. You'll be out in the desert. We don't want you getting your ankle bitten by a rattlesnake."

"Concierge," Colum said with a snort. "When I was in the army, we called them quartermasters."

"You're not in the army now," Hunt replied. He nodded toward Decker. "Eat up. Time's wasting."

Then he turned and strode back in the direction from which he'd come.

CHAPTER FOURTEEN

Harlan Biggs, Jr., who liked to think of himself as one of Las Vegas's great hoteliers, rose early, as was his custom, and headed down from his penthouse suite atop the Prospectors Paradise Hotel and Casino, to the small gymnasium on the second floor. The penthouse was in reality no such thing, except in Harlan's own head. It was really just two hotel rooms knocked into one on the sixth floor at the back of the aging building, overlooking an alleyway stuffed with dumpsters and trash cans. On a good day there was only the faintest whiff of garbage seeping in through the gaps around the window mounted air conditioner unit. On a bad day, in the height of summer when it was a hundred and ten degrees in the shade, he could smell the collective trash of the surrounding buildings slowly roasting inside the plastic refuse containers.

He rode the elevator, noting how it clanged and creaked its way to the second floor. That would soon be addressed. The hotel was in the middle of a much-needed renovation, its last facelift having occurred when Sinatra was still living it up at The Golden Nugget over on Fremont.

Harlan's own hotel and casino, the gambling equivalent of an off-off-Broadway show, sat nowhere near either Downtown or the Strip. Instead, it was located over a mile east and was more of a hangout for locals than tourists. After its three-million-dollar spruce up, he hoped that would change. This figure was still frugal compared to the amount spent on most such endeavors, especially in a place like Sin City, but it was all Harlan could lay his hands on, and even that had not been easy.

He stepped out of the elevator, a towel slung over one shoulder, and headed toward the gym. He encountered no one in the hallway. The hotel was currently closed and would remain that way for at least the next two months. He had toyed with the idea of getting rid of the gymnasium, an amenity added in the 90s at the expense of one of the guest rooms. But the economics that drove his old man—who still ran the hotel back then—to provide the seldom used facility was still valid. Tour operators and hotel booking sites handed out star ratings by the number of creature comforts afforded the guest. Having a gymnasium might make the difference between being a two-star property or getting three stars. There was no standard across booking sites, and you could never tell what would or wouldn't move you into a higher category, but if an empty gymnasium meant he could charge a couple of dollars more for a room, and get five percent more bookings, so be it.

Harlan stepped into the gymnasium and dropped his towel on the elliptical. He hated exercise, but he also loved good food and better scotch, two habits he'd picked up from the senior Harlan Biggs. If thirty minutes of exercise each day kept him from following his father to an early grave, Harlan figured it was time well spent. At least he didn't smoke cigars one after the other like his old man. That was one vice that never interested him. In fact, the smell of those big fat stogies had made him want to wretch. Even now he hated the odor of cigar smoke, which was a problem when you ran a Vegas casino.

Harlan eyed the treadmill, willing himself to step onto it and get his morning torture session over with. Below him, on the partially gutted ground floor, he could hear the workers starting their day. The lobby was an empty shell ripped back to the studs. The casino and its adjacent restaurants, which occupied most of the remaining floor space, were further along, and the results were better than he'd expected. After his workout, he would change into more suitable attire, and head down to oversee the work. Or more accurately, check in with his general manager, Wagner Mitchell, whom Harlan had entrusted with the day-to-day supervision of the various contractors.

Except that he didn't need to check in with Wagner. His GM came barging through the door, red-faced and panting.

"Harlan, you might want to make yourself scarce." He bent over, hands on his knees, and sucked air. "Oscar Rossi just pulled up out front with two of his goons. He doesn't look happy."

"Shit." Harlan felt his stomach clench. "Go down to the casino and see what he wants. Tell him I'm not here."

"He's not going to fall for that," Wagner said. "I'm sure he wants what he always wants. Money."

"He'll buy it if you sound convincing enough. Tell him I went over to Henderson to pick out the new slots for the casino."

"What if he checks and discovers we lied to him? He'll just come back in an even worse mood."

"It's not a lie. I do have to go there today. All we're doing is fudging the time."

Wagner shrugged. "It's your kneecaps." He turned to leave, but he hadn't even made two steps when a figure appeared in the doorway.

Oscar Rossi, who looked a good decade younger than his sixty-eight years, was dark-skinned even for a man of Italian heritage who lived in a place with over three hundred days of sunshine each year. Harlan had often wondered if he was just naturally swarthy or if he achieved his well-done complexion via a sunbed in one of the dozen massage parlors he operated around the city, mainly to launder dirty money.

"Harlan," Oscar said in a sing-song tone that still managed to sound menacing. "I hope I'm not interrupting your morning exercise routine."

"Not at all. Always a pleasure to see you, Oscar," replied Harlan. It was not, in fact, a pleasure to see Oscar Rossi. Ever. "Is there something I can help you with?"

"Don't play coy, Harlan. You know why I'm here." Oscar glanced at Wagner and hitched his thumb toward the door. "Don't you have somewhere else to be?"

Wagner hesitated, casting a furtive glance toward Harlan. Then, deciding he was better off out of it, the GM scurried toward the door.

Oscar stepped aside to let him through, and Harlan glimpsed two burly men loitering in the hallway outside. The closer of the pair, a musclebound slab of flesh with tattoos covering both arms, leaned in and pulled the door closed, blocking Harlan's view, and leaving him alone with Oscar.

"Shall we get down to business?" Oscar asked.

"Doesn't look like I have much choice," Harlan replied. He wished he'd brought the gun he kept in his nightstand drawer down with him. A Glock 48. He felt vulnerable, alone and unarmed in a room with Oscar Rossi, who surely had at least one weapon stashed about his person. Although even as he harbored the thought, Harlan realized that being armed would be of little use. If Rossi wanted him dead, the goons would be in here, not the boss. And they wouldn't engage in polite conversation or give him time to draw his own gun. Upon reflection, a chatty Oscar Rossi was better than a couple of tight-lipped enforcers.

"Now then, how about you tell me why I'm here." Oscar said, pushing his hands into his trouser pockets, which pulled his jacket open just enough for Harlan to confirm what he already suspected. Oscar was wearing a shoulder holster. "I want to hear it from *you.*"

Harlan's throat was dry. He swallowed, hoping the meager amount of spittle would provide enough lubrication to prevent his voice cracking. "Your interest payment."

"That's right. It should have been on my desk three days ago." Oscar nodded. He glanced toward the closed door, then looked back at Harlan. The implied threat was obvious. "Here's how this is going to work. You give me your excuse for not paying, and I'll decide if I like it enough to cut you some slack."

"Okay." Harlan nodded, his mind racing.

"And make it good." Rossi smiled and glanced toward the weights machine, which made what he said next even more disturbing. "I'd hate for you to have an accident while you're working out. That truly would be a shame…"

CHAPTER FIFTEEN

Robyn Miller slept fitfully, her dreams haunted by images of torn bodies and dying screams. She woke at 8 AM and rose, thankful the night was over, then dressed and headed from her bedroom on the ground floor at the back of the building behind the saloon bar. The room had once been a lean-to storage area, but she had rebuilt it, blocking off the outside door, and opening a new entry from a corridor running adjacent to the bar. It was small, but functional, and best of all it didn't deplete her stock of guest rooms on the floors above.

She made her way to the brand-new commercial kitchen and put on a pot of coffee. While it brewed, she fed Tieg, and then strolled through the saloon bar and into the lobby.

There was no sign of Carlton. He lived in a dilapidated cabin at the other end of town, which was not actually far away considering that the entire town was comprised of fourteen structures in various states of repair, and a dusty, unpaved street. This was in stark contrast to how the settlement would have looked during the town's heyday. Back then there were many more buildings, including a bank and an assay office. At its height, the town boasted a population of two thousand. Most were prospectors lured by the promise of riches buried deep in the surrounding hills. There were at least six different mines operating. They were mostly small, abandoned when the miners realized that the promise did not live up to the reality. There was not as much gold hereabouts as it first appeared. The only operation that produced any large quantity was the Ghost Canyon Mine, which was also the closest to town, and even that had dried up after a few years. Without the lure of precious metals to keep them there, the town's fortunes dwindled along with its population until there was nothing left but a bunch of dusty old buildings baking in the sun.

Robyn stepped onto the veranda. Tieg followed her out, still licking his chops. The dog flopped down with a grunt, head on his paws.

When Robyn looked back up, she noticed the police car was no longer stationed at the foot of the trail. The A-frame barricades were still there, but they were now unguarded. Then she noticed movement further up the canyon. It was the two FBI special agents. They were picking their way back down from the direction of the mine. They still wore khaki pants and polo shirts, but at least they'd had the good sense to swap their sneakers for hiking boots.

When they drew close, the younger of the two, Agent Barnes, waved a greeting. She waved back and waited until they reached the hotel and mounted the steps onto the veranda.

"Out for an early morning walk?" She asked.

"We felt it would be prudent to check the mine and see if there was any activity," Agent Fowler replied.

"And was there?" Robyn asked hopefully. They had closed the metal gates at the mine's entrance the previous evening, but had not padlocked them, hoping the two missing geologists were still alive and would find their way out.

"There was not, I'm sorry to say." Agent Fowler shook his

head. "And given the circumstances of their disappearance, I must conclude both men are dead."

"I concur." Agent Barnes stepped past Robyn and kneeled to pet Tieg again. He scratched behind the dog's ears, which elicited a satisfied snort from the animal.

"But you're still going to look for them, aren't you?" Robyn asked.

"Not at this time," Barnes said, glancing up. "Those tunnels aren't safe. It would be foolhardy to send more searchers in when it could very well lead to more deaths."

"Safety has to be our number one priority," Fowler agreed. "Given the extremely slim odds of finding them alive, we cannot risk more casualties. We did, however, leave the gates unlocked, should either of them have survived."

Robyn nodded. She understood their concern but wished something more could be done. Then she remembered Agent Fowler's request that she prepare a third room for a specialist. Someone who could resolve the situation. For the first time since the lone geologist stumbled back down the trail, wild-eyed and terrified, she felt a glimmer of hope.

CHAPTER SIXTEEN

Decker sat in the Gulfstream jet's spacious seat and watched the ground slip away beneath them as the sleek aircraft took to the sky.

He reflected on the briefing that had occurred two hours previously. Adam Hunt kept it short, telling him only that three people had died under mysterious circumstances in an abandoned gold mine outside Las Vegas and the local FBI field office had requested CUSP's help. It was a quid pro quo situation. CUSP operated as an international organization free of oversight by any single government. Yet they needed access to the resources of other law enforcement and military organizations, both clandestine and otherwise, in order to do their job. If they needed satellite images of a certain region, they could access NSA spy satellites, for example. CUSP had operational agreements with organizations as diverse as England's MI5, the CIA, the French intelligence service known as DGSE, and of course, The FBI.

It didn't take a genius to figure out Hunt was not pleased about sending one of his operatives on a goodwill mission, but he knew future cooperation between their agencies rested upon

CUSP fulfilling their part of the bargain when called to do so. He also admitted that the situation in Nevada matched Decker's unique set of skills. The killer was a skeletal being with glowing red eyes. It was rare that law enforcement agencies took such claims seriously. If that were the case, Decker would do nothing but fly all over the country at the request of every sheriff's office and police department whenever anyone thought they'd seen a UFO or arrested a perp who claimed *voices told them to do it.*

But in this case, there was corroborating evidence, not the least of which were eyewitness accounts by members of a trained search and rescue team and an experienced Las Vegas police officer who was wearing a body cam. Since the attacks took place in a mine, the resulting footage was blurry and dark. There was one brief sequence, however, which captured the killer on film. Once the Special Agent-in-Charge of the Las Vegas field office realized what they were dealing with, he contacted his superiors in DC, who called in a favor with Decker's employer.

So here he was, jetting out to Sin City.

Even better, he had the entire jet to himself, except for the two pilots and a company flight attendant who wasted no time in approaching him as soon as they were at cruising altitude. He requested a bottle of water and then settled in for the five-hour flight.

He spent the first couple of hours going over the eyewitness statements the FBI had forwarded to Hunt. He also watched the police officer's body cam footage several times.

One piece of information that intrigued him was the statement given by a man named William Fenton. He was one of three geologists who entered the mine to conduct a survey. He was also the only one who made it out alive. His two companions were still missing. But this wasn't what caught Decker's attention. It was a section of his statement that mentioned three mummified bodies huddled at the end of the tunnel next to a seam of gold, as if they had just sat down to die.

The three long-dead prospectors and the current attacks were related. Decker was sure of it. Especially since there was a strange symbol drawn in the gravel in front of them, although Decker had no clue what it was. Fenton had possessed the good sense to take photos, and Decker studied these with interest. The killings in the present had their origins in the heady days of Nevada's Gold Rush.

Finally, having studied the information to the best of his ability, Decker closed his laptop and settled back for the duration of the flight. He felt a tingle of anticipation, mixed with a large dose of unease. Something had gone horribly wrong in the small ghost town south of Las Vegas. Three people were dead, and a creature of possibly supernatural origin was to blame. His thoughts drifted back to the frigid town of Shackleton, Alaska. He had traveled there to solve a series of gruesome killings by an unknown creature, much like his current assignment. It was also the first time anyone called him a monster hunter. He smiled at this, remembering his first encounter with Mina. Then the smile faded when he remembered she might be a monster of sorts now herself, thanks to him. With this thought weighing heavily on his mind, Decker reclined his seat and closed his eyes, hoping to get some shuteye and arrive refreshed and ready to go. But instead, he found the monsters of his past creeping from the corners of his mind and consuming his thoughts, just like they so often did. Frustrated, he returned his chair to the upright position and opened the laptop again.

CHAPTER SEVENTEEN

Oscar Rossi waited for Harlan's reply, as if it might change the outcome of his visit to the Prospectors Paradise that morning.

It would not, and Harlan knew this. He should never have borrowed money from Rossi in the first place, but he was desperate. Now he would, most likely, pay the price. "The hotel renovation is costing more than I planned. I've had to put extra money in from my pocket. It's left me short."

"And why is that my problem?" Rossi asked.

"It's not. I understand that." Harlan was starting to sweat. "I just need another week, maybe two, that's all."

"A week?" Rossi drew in a long breath and shook his head. "You're already three days late. I think I've been more than generous. Wouldn't you agree?"

"You have, yes. Goes without saying." Harlan was being backed into a corner and he knew it. He would need to tread carefully, or Rossi might bring the goons in, and then he wouldn't be able to tread at all. "I'm transferring money from an offshore account. It's enough to cover the next two interest payments. By then the hotel should be open again."

"We had a deal, you and I." Rossi raised an eyebrow. "Did we not?"

"Yes."

"And what did you agree would happen if you didn't abide by the terms of that deal?"

"I'd forfeit the hotel." Harlan licked his lips. They felt dry. "Look, Oscar, we go way back, our families. You know that. Surely we can work something out."

"It is true that your father provided me with many years of faithful service. He was always there when I needed him." Rossi glanced around. "If only these walls could talk... But it was a different time, and your father's gone now, God rest his soul."

"And he was faithful to the last," Harlan said, pressing his advantage. "He could have rolled when the DA came calling, gave you up. But he didn't. He kept his mouth shut even when they tried to take away his casino license. He let you funnel money through here for years at no small risk to himself."

"All of which is correct." Rossi nodded thoughtfully.

"He knew things that could have sent you down for a long time, but he kept them to himself. Just like I have."

"Are you trying to threaten me?" Rossi asked, a flash of anger glinting in his eyes.

"No. That's not what I'm doing." Harlan realized he might've overplayed his hand. "I was just pointing out that my family has always been loyal to you, is all."

"Good. That's what I thought. But just in case the idea enters your head to use the small amount of knowledge you possess as leverage, don't. If you so much as whisper one word in the wrong direction, I will hear about it, and then interest payments will be the least of your problems. Do I make myself clear?"

"Like spring water."

"Excellent. I liked your father. I like you. It would be a shame for our relationship to end on a sour note."

"On this, I think we can agree."

"Wonderful." Rossi removed his hands from his pockets and clapped them together. "I'll tell you what. Take the extra time. I'll give you two full weeks. Your father's dedication and years of service have earned you some leeway. But don't mistake my generosity for weakness. I shall expect your payment two weeks from today."

"Thank you." Harlan felt a rush of relief. He didn't know what would happen in two weeks, but at least Rossi's enforcers waiting in the corridor wouldn't get to have any fun today.

"For a ten percent late fee, naturally."

"What? Ten percent on top? You can't be serious. That's another sixteen thousand."

"If you don't like my terms, we can keep negotiating." Rossi shrugged. He glanced toward the closed door, then back to Harlan.

"No need for that," Harlan said quickly. He'd witnessed Rossi's negotiating style before, and it involved a lot more screaming than it did talking. "Those terms are fine."

"That's what I thought." Rossi took a step toward the door, then glanced back over his shoulder. "And since you offered, you might as well include next month's payment too. Then you'll be ahead of the game."

This last demand left Harlan temporarily speechless. By the time he mustered up the courage to reply, it was too late. Rossi was already out the door and halfway down the corridor with his burly sidekicks in tow.

Harlan stood and watched him leave, then he turned and sat on a bench. He cursed his own stupidity. Why had he told Rossi he was transferring two months' worth of payments? He was transferring squat. There was no offshore account. It was a spur-of-the-moment lie to buy more time. And it worked, to a degree. He had another fourteen days. But at that point he would need to pony up two full payments plus ten percent on top. It made him want to cry. He cursed ever going to Oscar

Rossi for a loan. But there was no one else. He had tried the banks and credit unions and approached a slew of legitimate investors. With the way the casino's profits had declined over the last few years, and his family's reputation, no one would touch him. Which left Rossi, who jumped on the opportunity like fleas on a dog.

It was a terrible deal. A three-million-dollar loan at an eye-popping rate of interest. Sixty-five percent. Which was surely illegal, assuming any financial regulators ever got to inspect the paperwork, which they would not. But Harlan knew he had no choice. Either he renovated, or his business would keep sinking until he lost the hotel. With no recourse, Harlan agreed to the terms, figuring he would only need the loan for a few months, and then he could repay it in full once the hotel was operating again. With fully booked rooms, and a bustling casino, he could recoup the money in no time. Except Rossi neglected to include the early settlement clause, and instead strong-armed him into a loan for thirty years, which meant paying nothing but interest for two-thirds of that time. He had, in effect, unwittingly gone into business with Oscar Rossi. But worst of all, if he didn't pay, Rossi's enforcers would get to dance on his skull, just enough so he wouldn't care about the hotel anymore. Then Rossi would swoop in and steal it out from under him. Between the two alternatives, Harlan would rather keep his hotel and avoid getting beaten to within an inch of his life, which meant coming up with the monthly payments. The only problem was, he didn't have them. This was, Harlan thought, shaping up to be one crappy day, and he hadn't even eaten breakfast yet.

CHAPTER EIGHTEEN

Robyn spent the morning working in the saloon bar and listening to the hammering of the workers as they finished up the last rooms on the second floor.

She unpacked glasses of various sizes from boxes and stacked them on the shelves under the bar and then turned her attention to the newly restored bar back. It was ornate with shelves to hold liquor bottles and a mirrored glass backing etched with intricate designs. Original to the building, it had deteriorated badly over the decades. At first, Robyn thought it would need to be torn out, but then she changed her mind and decided to keep it, despite the high cost of restoration. In the end it had taken a team of three carpenters almost four weeks. It was worth it, though. She wanted to save this magnificent piece of history, not only because it added authenticity to the hotel but also because of its history. On a normal day, she would've looked at this rescued piece of the Old West and marveled at the things it had witnessed. Bar fights settled by lead, drunkenness and debauchery, and decades of prospectors quenching their thirst.

But not today.

Robyn tried her best not to think about what had happened in the mine, but the three deaths weighed heavily upon her and so by early afternoon she packed it in for the day. She went to the kitchen and made lunch. While she was there, the two FBI special agents wandered in, so she made them a meal too. Ham and cheese sandwiches with plenty of mustard. The three of them ate at the kitchen table with Tieg watching hopefully, his brown eyes flitting from person to person, beseeching one of them to offer him a morsel.

"Will your specialist be arriving today?" Robyn asked between bites.

Agent Fowler nodded. "He's on the way as we speak. He'll be here by dinnertime."

"And then we can get to work," Agent Barnes added. "I don't like all this sitting around. It's a waste of time."

"We had no choice." Fowler bit into his sandwich and glanced toward his partner. "You heard the eyewitnesses. You saw the body cam footage. We have protocols for this kind of situation."

"What footage?" Robyn asked. "If there's video of whatever is in my gold mine, I want to see it."

"Classified, I'm afraid," Barnes said. He had finished his own sandwich in record time and was now sucking remnants of mustard from his fingers. He picked up a napkin and wiped his hands.

"Maybe she should see it," Agent Fowler said. He looked at Robyn. "You've been living out here for a while, correct?"

"About six months, but Carlton has lived here for decades."

"Yeah. We spoke to him a little while ago." Fowler grimaced. "He wasn't terribly helpful. Told us we should buzz off and leave him in peace."

"That isn't exactly how he put it," Barnes said. "It was a mite more colorful."

"It was, indeed," Fowler agreed. "But since there's a lady present, we don't need to repeat his exact choice of words."

"I wouldn't worry about it," Robyn said. "I've heard just about every cuss word there is come out of that man's mouth. If swearing were an Olympic sport, he'd have a pile of gold medals."

"Regardless, he wasn't terribly helpful, and I don't expect him to become any more so."

"He doesn't appear to like authority figures," Barnes observed.

"That's putting it mildly," Robyn replied. "Now, what about this video?"

"I'll fetch my iPad." Fowler stood up. He took his plate and placed it in the sink on the way out the door.

Robyn heard heavy footsteps on the stairs leading to the second floor. She looked to Agent Barnes, but he had removed his cell phone, and appeared to be checking his mail. Tieg, who was growing impatient, took the luling conversation as an opportunity to make his case for tidbits. He nudged Robyn's leg then sat looking up at her. Robyn couldn't help grinning, and pulled a piece of ham from her sandwich, which she had yet to finish. The dog wolfed it down and then chuffed with pleasure. At that moment, Agent Fowler returned with the iPad in his hand.

"The video is pretty blurry and dark," he said, retaking his seat. He placed the iPad on the table and pushed it over to her. "I've forwarded to the relevant section. There's some pretty gruesome stuff there, when they first come across the missing search team member. I skipped past most of it, but even so, you should be prepared."

"You don't need to watch if you don't want to," Barnes said.

"It's fine." Robyn looked down at the iPad, and the frozen video image displayed on the screen. Now that she thought about it, she wasn't sure she actually wanted to view the footage. She hadn't slept well last night as it was. Seeing the events in the mine firsthand would not make sleeping tonight any easier. She hesitated, her finger hovering over the play button, and then, deciding she had to know what was roaming her property, she clicked play.

Agent Fowler was right. The video was grainy and at first, she couldn't make out what she was looking at. Then the video came into focus and she saw a flashlight beam bobbing off craggy tunnel walls. It swung left, then right in wild arcs, and Robyn wondered if there was anything on the video worth seeing, but soon it picked out a figure standing astride a body that Robyn realized was Sasha, the search team member who had lost her life. But it was the strangely wraith-like figure that made her gasp. It was like nothing she could ever have imagined. A walking corpse with skin stretched tight over its bones. It resembled a monster from a Hollywood movie, something conjured up to scare teenagers at sleepovers. But she knew it wasn't. This was very real. And those awful eyes...

"Well?" Agent Fowler studied her with a deadpan stare. "Have you ever seen anything like this before?"

"Are you kidding me?" Robyn paused the video and pushed the iPad back toward the FBI agent. "If I saw something like that coming toward me, I wouldn't stop running until I reached Canada. Why would you think I could be of any help identifying whatever the hell is on that video?"

"Because you live here. You're the one who opened up the mine. I was hoping there might be a local legend to shed light on this creature. There's a buttload of folklore in these parts. It wasn't unreasonable to think you might know some of it."

"I moved here from Chicago. Besides, since when does the FBI rely on folklore to solve murders?"

"When we encounter a situation that conventional science can't explain. This isn't the first time we've come across a scenario like this."

"You've seen one of these creatures before?" Robyn asked, incredulous.

"No." Fowler shook his head. "Not this. But the agency has encountered other unexplainable situations, and we've learned the hard way to take them seriously. There are certain individuals in every field office around the country tasked with identifying and handling such things."

"Unexplainable?" Robyn wasn't sure whether to laugh or cry. The surreal nature of the situation was not lost upon her. She was sitting at a table with a pair of government agents discussing what could only be described as a monster. "The FBI really has agents who deal with spooky shit, just like in that TV show?"

"We're nothing like the TV show." Fowler sounded offended. He'd obviously heard this before. "But yes, there are specially trained agents around the country."

"And when we feel the situation requires it, we call in help," said Barnes.

"Which reminds me," Fowler said, glancing at his watch. He picked up the iPad and closed the cover. "We must leave for a couple of hours. The specialist's flight will be landing soon, and we should be there to meet him."

CHAPTER NINETEEN

Darwin Andoe finished loading the camping gear into the back of his Jeep Cherokee and leaned against it, waiting for his girlfriend, Tiffany Kent, to make an appearance. He was looking forward to the three-night camping expedition into the wilderness south of Las Vegas. He'd been planning it for a month, despite Tiffany's objections. If it were up to her, they would head out to Boulder City or even Reno and spend their time gambling, downing free drinks, eating too much shrimp at the buffet, and enjoying a high-priced hotel room. But this trip was a delayed birthday present for Darwin, who turned twenty-six a couple of weeks previously, and he wanted to sleep under the stars and watch the Milky Way spiral above them. As far as Darwin was concerned, there was nothing better than a dose of solitude and a roaring campfire.

"Hurry it up in there," he yelled in the general direction of the two-bedroom block house they'd rented after moving out to Nevada from Colorado two years before so Tiffany could complete her graduate studies at the University of Nevada. "I want to leave before it gets too late."

"All right, already." Tiffany emerged from the house and

pulled the front door closed. "What's the big hurry. We're driving out to the desert. Check-in time is, like, whenever we get there."

"You won't be so blasé if we have to pitch our tent in the dark," Darwin retorted. Tiffany was struggling toward the car carrying a pair of large duffel bags. He took and heaved them into the Jeep, grunting at their unexpected weight. "What the hell did you pack in these, your entire closet?"

"Just the necessities," Tiffany replied. "I can't wear the same clothes for three days."

"I don't see why not," Darwin said. "It's not like we have dinner reservations. We'll be the only ones out there. You can sit around the campfire in your undies for all I care."

"You'd like that, wouldn't you?" Tiffany grinned despite herself.

"Maybe." Darwin went to close the trunk, then remembered something. "Wait there, I'll be right back."

He sprinted toward the open garage door, ducked inside, and returned with a shovel.

"Almost forgot this," he said, throwing it atop Tiffany's ridiculously over-packed duffels.

"Dare I ask why we need a shovel?"

"So that we can dig a hole to poop in."

"You can't be serious." Tiffany looked aghast.

"How else do you think we're going to handle bathroom breaks?" Darwin asked. "You want to drive back to Vegas every time nature calls?"

"But it's so... gross. Plus, you'll be able to see me." Tiffany folded her arms, pouting. "I can't do it. Why don't we just go to a hotel instead?"

"This is supposed to be my birthday trip. I get to choose. When it's your birthday, we can go to some swanky spa and let them put mud on our faces."

"Oh, that's happening, have no fear."

"Not until you come camping with me, it isn't." Darwin flipped up the box on the garage door keypad and punched the number in to close the door. When it started trundling down, he walked back to the Jeep, slammed the trunk, and climbed in. "Are you coming, or not?"

"Guess I don't have much choice," Tiffany grumbled, climbing into the passenger seat next to him. "Just so we're clear though, the first scorpion I see, we are out of there."

"Have no fear, I'll protect you from whatever nasty creatures we encounter," Darwin laughed.

"Ooh, my hero." Tiffany glanced toward him and batted her eyelids. "Which is why I had to get rid of that spider in the bathtub last week."

"Hey, I was going to take care of it."

"When? After you stopped screeching like a baby?"

"It caught me by surprise, is all."

"Whatever you say." Tiffany smirked. "Did you pack the coolers containing the food?"

"You think I'd forget something like that?"

"I wouldn't put it past you," Tiffany replied. "You probably want to catch our food."

"Now, there's a good idea. Maybe I should take the coolers back inside the house."

"Don't you dare!" Tiffany shot Darwin a withering look. "Unless you want me to go back inside along with them."

"I guess we'll just have to eat store-bought provisions then," Darwin replied. "Even though it won't be as authentic."

"Plus, we won't starve. Don't get me wrong, but I don't put much stock in your foraging abilities."

"Hey, I've been going camping since I was a kid. My dad used to take us all the time."

"Okay, Mister Wilderness. I stand corrected." Tiffany settled back into the seat and fiddled with the AC until it was blowing a steady stream of frigid air upon her. "Are we just going to sit in this car all day, or are you actually thinking about going somewhere?"

"Now who's suddenly keen to get out into the wilds?" Darwin put the Jeep in gear and pulled away. "Nature, here we come."

"Yay. I can hardly wait." Tiffany sighed and rooted in her purse, taking out a lipstick and applying it. She flipped the visor down and checked her makeup in the vanity mirror. "Three days with no phone or internet."

"I know, right?" Darwin grinned. "It's going to be great."

"For you, maybe." Tiffany pushed the visor back in place and returned the lipstick to her purse. "But some of us actually have a life."

"Stop complaining. You can live without constantly texting your girlfriends for a few days."

"And apparently I can also take a crap out in the open, but it doesn't mean I want to," Tiffany said with the barest hint of sarcasm. "How long will it take us to reach the camping site, anyway?"

"Forty-five minutes. Maybe more if there's traffic on the interstate."

"Awesome." Tiffany removed her phone from her purse along with a pair of Bluetooth earbuds. She pushed them into her ears and closed her eyes. "Let me know when we get there. I'm going to enjoy the benefits of civilization while I still can."

CHAPTER TWENTY

The plane carrying John Decker landed a little after 4 PM local time in Las Vegas. It taxied to a private hanger where two men were waiting next to a government issue plain black Ford Crown Victoria when he deplaned.

"You John Decker?" The taller of the two asked as Decker stepped out of the aircraft. He was leaning against the car and now pushed himself up. He slipped a hand into his pocket to retrieve a slim leather case, which he flipped open to reveal his credentials, with the initials FBI written in large blue lettering across the uppermost card. He closed the wallet and returned it to his pocket. When he did so, Decker saw the silver FBI badge attached to his belt.

"That's me." Decker nodded and stepped from the Gulfstream's built in airstairs. In one hand was an overnight bag that contained a few changes of clothing, a pair of hiking boots, and a toiletries bag. Over his other shoulder was a laptop case. When he reached the car, he set them both on the ground. "And you are?"

"Special Agent Fowler." He nodded toward the other man. "This here is my partner, Special Agent Barnes."

The shorter man raised a hand in greeting but said nothing.

"You ready to go?" Fowler asked. "You waiting on luggage?"

"What you see is what you get," Decker replied. "I travel light."

"Great. Let's get on the road." Fowler popped the trunk so that Decker could stash his bag and laptop case. Barnes climbed into the back seat so that Decker could sit up front, and soon they were on their way.

Fowler steered the car out of the hanger and onto a service road that ran to the airport's perimeter. At the gate he flashed his badge to a security guard and a few minutes later they were on the Strip.

The sun was setting. It slipped below the distant mountains, painting the horizon a dazzling orange. To the left and right of them, casino resort hotels jostled for attention with bright lights and outlandish themes. Traffic was moderate, but despite this, the going was slow as they moved along the main thoroughfare in fits and starts, stopping at intersections clogged with tourists. Decker had only visited Las Vegas once before, many years ago, and he peered out of the passenger side window, fascinated by the garish facades of the larger hotels and casinos.

Agent Barnes, in the backseat, watched the passing scenery with disinterest. "You a gambling man, Mister Decker?" he asked, eventually.

"Depends how you define gambling. I've taken a risk or two over the years as a law enforcement officer. If you're wondering if I have a desire to spend hours throwing money away in one of these casinos, the answer is most definitely no."

"That's a good thing," Fowler said. "Because where we're going, you'll be lucky to find a strong drink, let alone a craps table."

"I read the briefing file during my flight," Decker said. "It's a ghost town, right?"

"Is it ever." Barnes didn't sound happy. "There's only one habitable building in the entire place. The rest of it is falling into the ground. I swear, we get the worst assignments."

"It's not that bad," Fowler said. "The landowner renovated the hotel, and it's actually pretty comfortable. There is a saloon bar but is not officially open yet. As for the rest of the place, there's an old man that lives in a dilapidated cabin, and there are a few other buildings, mostly crumbling shells."

"What about the gold mine?" Decker asked. They had left the city behind now. The bustle of the Las Vegas Strip had given way to smaller businesses and new housing developments scattered around the outskirts of the gambling mecca, and then to open desert with little sign of habitation. "What condition is it in?"

"It's stable enough. At least according to the surviving geologist. The trusses and beams holding back the rock are still in good condition considering how old they are, and the tunnels are mostly free of obstructions. We should be able to enter with no trouble."

"Except for whatever is lurking inside," Barnes added. "If we run into that, we could be in a whole heap of trouble. The last two groups that went in there didn't fare so well."

"I've been briefed," Decker said. "I assume you still haven't found the two missing geologists?"

"Correct." It was dark now, and they were driving up into the mountains. Fowler flicked on his high beams. "They were almost certainly killed, and since the rescue team that went in to look for them almost met a similar fate, we decided it was best to retreat until we could bring in expert help."

"That would be you," Barnes said.

"One person on that rescue team did meet a similar fate," Decker observed. "From the witness statements I read on the flight, it was lucky that any of them made it out alive."

"I assume you watched the footage retrieved from the responding Vegas PD officer's body cam."

"Yup," Decker responded.

"First impressions?" Fowler asked.

"Whatever that creature is, it's been there a long time," Decker said. "If I had to guess, I'd say it dates all the back to the Wild West."

"What makes you say that?" Barnes asked.

"Because I also saw the photos taken by the geologist. Those three mummified prospectors didn't just decide to sit down and end their days in that mine on a whim. Something scared them so much that they didn't dare walk out."

"Unless they got lost down there and couldn't find their way back to the surface," Fowler suggested.

"They didn't. For one thing, they weren't that far from the entrance. If the surviving geologist is correct, they're only about half a mile in and close to the adit leading out of the mine. They also carved a symbol into the dirt. I suspect this was for protection, but I'll know more once I do some research."

"Sounds plausible. Is that all you've got?"

"No. The current owner of the ghost town only recently reopened the mine entrance. No one had stepped foot inside for generations until those three geologists entered. I suspect that renewed human activity awakened whatever is in there, with tragic results."

"Now for the million-dollar question," Fowler said as they crested a rise and drove toward a cluster of lights that Decker assumed was their destination. "Do you know how to deal with it?"

"Not yet," Decker admitted. He watched the lights grow brighter and soon he could make out the shapes of ramshackle buildings sitting at the base of a mountain pass. One structure stood out, in better condition than the rest. This, he assumed, was the hotel where he would bed down for the foreseeable future. He lifted his gaze to the mountains beyond the town, now nothing more than dark silhouettes against the night sky, and wondered what horrors awaited him in that long-abandoned mine.

CHAPTER TWENTY-ONE

The confrontation with Oscar Rossi left Harlan Biggs shaken. He'd known on an intellectual level that this day was coming, especially after he failed to make the latest loan payment, but until Rossi walked through his door, Harlan had convinced himself that it would all work itself out in the end. It was now clear that it would not.

In an effort to instill some kind of normality to his day, and possibly to kid himself the world was not collapsing around him, Harlan hurried from the hotel shortly after Rossi departed, and drove out to Henderson where the vendor supplying his new slot machines was located. He spent the next three hours going over the casino floor plan with his account manager, selecting machines. Since Prospectors Paradise wasn't a top-tier casino, he wouldn't be receiving the newest slots. Many of the machines, while an upgrade to his old ones, would still be a year or two old. Worse, only a small percentage of the machines would be owned by the casino. He simply didn't have the money to purchase all the slots he needed outright. His gaming floor was small compared to many of the big boys. A strip casino might have fifteen-hundred slots or more, but Harlan was only looking at a paltry three hundred. Even so, that would add up fast at a minimum of ten grand for each machine. Even with the amount he'd made selling off the old machines, his budget only allowed him to purchase a third of them outright. He would have to lease the rest for a cut of the proceeds. The thought of giving a third of his slot profits to the gaming supplier made him feel physically sick, especially after his conversation with Rossi, but it was that or have a half empty casino floor.

By the time he returned to the Prospectors Paradise his mood was even darker than before. He parked his black metallic Porsche Cayman on the employee level of the parking garage and made his way back into the casino. He couldn't really afford the flashy sports car, which was also leased, any more than he could afford the gold Rolex on his wrist, but he needed to project the right image to be taken seriously in a town where money was king.

When he entered the hotel on the mezzanine overlooking the lobby, he ran straight into Wagner Mitchell, his GM, who was standing at the railing watching the new lobby floor being installed.

"How did it go?" Wagner asked, turning toward his boss.

"Fine, I guess," Harlan grumbled in reply. "A month from now we'll have three hundred slightly used slot machines in our casino, and the supplier will be skimming thirty percent on two-thirds of them."

"No, not that." Wagner shook his head. "Rossi. How did it go with Oscar Rossi?"

"How do you think it went? He's given me two weeks and if I can't make the interest payment, I'll have the dubious pleasure of having my legs broken by his enforcers."

"Hey, sorry I asked." Wagner turned his attention back to the work going on below. "The new floor is looking good. We should be able to put the check-in desk back in by the end of the month. That should cheer you up, huh?"

"Yeah. Great." Harlan sighed. "I'm sure Rossi will enjoy his new lobby."

"Don't be like that, boss. You'll think of something."

"You'd better pray that I do," Harlan replied. "Or Oscar Rossi will be cutting your paychecks, and I'm pretty sure he's not as much fun to work for as I am. He'll probably have you dumping bodies out in the desert within a month."

"Not going to happen. We've weathered hard times before."

"Not like this, my friend." Harlan turned toward the elevators and pressed the call button. A door slid open immediately. "I fear I may have overplayed my hand this time."

"I hope you're wrong."

"Me too." Harlan stepped into the elevator and pressed the button for the sixth floor. He saw Wagner throw his arms up in the air and shout something at the installers on the floor below. Then the doors slid closed, cutting off his view of the mezzanine.

When he reached his destination, Harlan stepped out and made his way to the penthouse. He stepped inside and closed the door, then proceeded to the living room. He turned on the TV and went to the bar that occupied one entire wall of the space. He poured himself a drink, making sure that it was substantially larger than anything he would ever allow one of his bartenders to serve in the casino. He looked down into the amber liquid, lost in thought, at least until the television drew his attention.

He turned around. The TV was tuned to a local news station. Something big was going down. They were playing footage shot from a helicopter hovering over the desert. There were police cars, an ambulance, and even a SWAT team. The news ticker, a band of scrolling text at the bottom of the screen, identified the location as the Ghost Canyon Mine.

Harlan stood there a moment, frozen by surprise, then he scooped up the TV remote and pushed the volume up further.

He listened to the newscaster recapping the previous afternoon's events. There had been an accident and people had died. The LVMPF press liaison was authorized only to say that it was an animal attack. Another source, speaking on condition of anonymity, added that the offending creature appeared to live in the mine, and that the survivors all mentioned glowing red eyes.

Harlan stood staring at the screen, transfixed.

Because the news story ignited a memory. Something he hadn't thought about for many years. An old family legend.

He put his drink down on the counter and took out his cell phone. He needed more information, and quickly.

Luckily, Rossi was not the only one with friends in high places. Harlan might not have the DA or a district judge on his payroll, but there were people in town who owed him—like that stupid cop who got in over his head on the craps tables a few years back. He was a sergeant now. The five grand Harlan had written off back then, on the hunch that a grateful Vegas police officer was worth more than turning a quick profit, might just pay off. Harlan smiled. Then he muted the TV, searched his phone's contacts, and placed a call.

CHAPTER TWENTY-TWO

The campsite was even worse than Tiffany had feared. It was nothing but a moderately flat patch of brown earth surrounded by sagebrush, nestled on a plateau beneath towering rock formations of limestone and dolomite. The ride up had been smooth enough until Darwin left the highway behind and took to the wilderness back trails to a spot he'd camped at the year before with friends. And judging by the remains of several fire pits, he wasn't the only one who decided this spot was a great place to bed down.

They pitched the tent, which Darwin assured her was big enough for two people but looked like a tight squeeze to Tiffany. After that, hot and sweating, they sat in the Jeep for a while with the air running and ate a light meal of turkey sandwiches from one of the twin coolers containing their provisions. They washed it down with bottles of water and then got back to work. It would be sundown soon, and Darwin wanted to light a fire.

He dug a shallow hole and gathered stones into a circle around it, then retrieved a fire log from the back of the Jeep.

He'd learned from a previous trip that this was easier than trying to gather firewood, especially in the arid desert.

Tiffany sat on a rock a few feet away and watched him work. The temperature was dropping already from a high of seventy degrees. The forecast predicted it would drop as low as fifty-five overnight, and Tiffany was glad that she had packed several sweaters, not to mention her thickest flannel PJs, which might disappoint Darwin but would keep her toasty.

After a few minutes, he got a roaring fire going and warmed his hands over the flames. That done, he got a blanket from the Jeep, which he spread over the ground.

"Want to join me?" He asked, flopping down.

"Sure." Tiffany pushed herself up from the rock and joined him on the blanket, huddling close against the mounting breeze, which made the temperature feel a good five degrees colder than it actually was.

"We should have brought marshmallows," Tiffany said, enjoying the fire's warmth and watching the flames leap and dance. "We could've made s'mores."

"Your wish is my command," Darwin said, jumping up. He returned to the Jeep and fumbled around in one of the coolers, then came back with a Hershey's family sized bar, a box of graham crackers, and a bag of white fluffy marshmallows. He held a pair of metal skewers in his other hand, one of which he offered to her. "Wouldn't be a camping trip without s'mores."

Tiffany grinned. "Did you pack a guitar too, so that we can have a sing-along?"

"Dang it," Darwin said, laughing. "I knew I was forgetting something."

"That's it, then. Might as well pack up and head home." Tiffany tore open the marshmallows and pushed one on to her skewer. "I only came out here for the campfire songs."

"Trust me, if I brought a guitar out here and tried to play it, you would beg to go back. I took lessons in high school. It was not pretty. Talk about all thumbs."

"Sounds like my singing." Tiffany held the marshmallow near the fire and watched it brown. "I actually got kicked out of choir in tenth grade. It was so embarrassing."

"Really?" Darwin chuckled. "Wish I was there to see that."

"How about I serenade you right now, then?" Tiffany grinned. "That will guarantee you don't bring me camping again."

"I'm sure you sing like an angel," Darwin replied.

"Good answer." Tiffany nodded. "Continue like that and I might keep you warm in the tent tonight."

"Looking forward to it already." Darwin plucked a graham cracker from the box and broke it in half, piling it with chocolate and toasted marshmallow. He popped the creation into his mouth and chewed, then took a second marshmallow and skewered it.

Tiffany ate her own s'mores and watched the sun drop below the mountains, the sky turning a fiery shade of red before fading to deep blue and finally black as night crept across the landscape. A million stars looked down upon them, bright points of light splashed across the heavens, a twinkling river in a never-ending cosmos. She looked up in awe, surprised by the intensity of the night sky.

Darwin, sensing her wonder, took her hand in his. "Everything is so much more vibrant out here at night," he said. "There's no light pollution from the city to get in the way."

"It's incredible," Tiffany whispered. "I've never really paid much attention to it before. I can see why you like to camp out here."

"If you look long enough, you'll see a shooting star." Darwin was craning his neck upward. He pointed to the fast streak that arched over their heads before fading away. "There's one now."

"That was pretty neat."

"Now you glad we came out?"

"Absolutely." Tiffany inched closer to Darwin and put her arm around him. She looked into his eyes and when they kissed it tasted like chocolate and marshmallow.

She let out a contented sigh and rested her head on his shoulder. The air was crisp and clean. The fire cast an orange glow that made her feel sleepy. It crackled and popped while further away the breeze whistled through the rocks. And then, rising over it all, a shrill resonant howl that rose and ebbed as it bounced off the canyon walls.

Tiffany let out a small cry and tensed. She looked around, wild-eyed, into the darkness beyond the campfire. "What was that?"

"Don't worry. Probably just a coyote." Darwin hugged her tight. "It's nowhere near us. We're perfectly safe."

"Okay." Tiffany took deep breaths to steady her jangled nerves, but it was no use. Instead, she pressed close to Darwin, and peered out into the darkness, praying that she wouldn't see a pair of eyes looking back from the gloom.

CHAPTER TWENTY-THREE

The Last Chance Saloon and Hotel was an oasis of comfort surrounded by a sea of dilapidation. Decker stood in the grand lobby and studied the ornate staircase winding up through the building to the second and third floors, and the carved double doors with inset etched glass leading into the saloon bar.

"Quite a place, huh?" Special Agent Fowler said, noting the look of surprise on Decker's face.

"It's nicer than I expected," Decker replied. "Hard to believe it's in such a run-down location."

"It needs to be nice," a female voice said to Decker's left. "Otherwise, it won't be much of a wedding venue. The rest of the town might not be much to look at now but come back next year and you might be surprised."

Decker turned to find an attractive woman with dark brown eyes and even darker hair standing at the base of the stairs. She wore a white tee tucked into a pair of tight jeans.

"I'm sorry, I didn't mean to offend," Decker said. "You're the owner of this place, I assume."

"Part-owner. Sixty-six and a bit percent. The other thirty-three percent is probably polishing off a bottle of my good liquor in his cabin on the other end of the property. I'm sure you'll have the displeasure of meeting him in due course, and for that I must apologize in advance." The woman feigned a rueful look. "My name's Robyn Miller."

"John Decker."

"Ah. The specialist."

"That's a better description than I usually get," Decker said with a smile. "Who exactly is the other owner?"

Agent Barnes cleared his throat. "Carlton Miller. He's a gem. I'd like to say something nice about him but haven't found a suitable example yet."

"Although we haven't been here very long," Special Agent Fowler interjected quickly, no doubt worried about offending Robyn. "I'm sure we just caught him on a bad day."

Robyn smirked. "No, you didn't. You might find this hard to believe, but he's actually on his best behavior right now."

"He's not well-liked, then?" Decker asked.

"That's an understatement," Robyn replied. "Take a step outside, look around at the falling down buildings and old junk lying around. Pay particular attention to the *no trespassing* signs and rather dubious threats that he will *shoot first and ask questions later* posted wherever he doesn't want people nosing around, and that should give you a clue about the old sot's temperament."

"I see," Decker said.

"Carlton's been living up here for decades and the isolation must've stripped away whatever social skills he once possessed. He wasn't too happy when I showed up after inheriting majority ownership of the town," Robyn said. "I haven't been here long enough to do much except renovate the hotel so far, but this place will be unrecognizable by the time I'm finished. Not that Carlton's going to like it." She folded her arms defiantly. "But that's just too bad. Of course, recent events might put a crimp in those plans, which I'm sure the old bastard will appreciate. We were all over the local news last night, and they've been milking it all day. It's a disaster."

"I'm sorry to hear that," Decker said.

"Meh. What are you going to do?" Robyn shrugged. "But enough about my troubles. I'm sure you want to settle in after your long trip. You flew in from Maine, correct?"

"Yes." Decker nodded. "My employer is there, although right now I'm living in Mississippi."

"I've never visited either place, although I'd love to visit New England in the fall. I've heard it's spectacular."

"It is," Decker agreed. "Cold though, especially when you're used to southern climates."

"I'm a Chicago girl, myself, so the exact opposite. I'm always sweating. The heat here in high summer is intolerable." Robyn motioned toward the stairs. "But enough talk of the weather. If you'd like to come with me, I'll walk you to your room."

"That would be nice." Decker realized he was still holding his bags. His arms were aching.

Robyn motioned for him to follow and started up the stairs. At the top she turned left and stopped outside of a door halfway along a narrow corridor lit by wall fixtures that must once have been gas but were now converted to electricity. They looked original. Decker found it refreshing that Robyn had retained the building's character rather than rip everything out and start anew.

She removed a key from her pocket and unlocked the door, then stepped aside for him to enter. The bedroom was restored with as much love as the rest of the building. The furniture had been selected to mimic the Old West, and the attention to detail was exquisite. Decker felt like he had stepped back in time. The only item that looked out of place was the flatscreen TV mounted above the dresser, but even this had been artfully disguised, with an ornate gold frame placed around it to blend more fully into the surroundings. A mild odor of fresh paint and sawn wood hung in the air. The sheets on the bed looked crisp and new.

Decker set his bags on the floor and turned back to Robyn. "This is better than I expected."

"I'm pleased to hear that," Robyn replied. She offered Decker the room key. "Once you've freshened up, you can head down to the kitchen and I'll make you something to eat, if you'd like."

"That would be fantastic," Decker said. He'd eaten on the plane, but that was hours ago. He was getting hungry again. "I'll be right down."

"Whenever you're ready." Robyn retreated to the doorway. "I'm a night owl, so I'll be up late."

"Understood."

Robyn nodded toward a closed door to her left. "The en-suite is through there. Originally these rooms would've had chamber pots, but we thought we'd go a little more civilized."

"I'm glad to hear that," Decker said.

"Back in pioneer days, if you wanted an actual toilet, you would need to venture beyond the hotel to the outhouse."

"Well, I'm glad you didn't get *too* authentic," Decker replied. "That doesn't sound like much fun."

"Especially when you consider your toilet paper would be corn husks. Not the kind of feature a modern bride wants for her wedding." Robyn smiled. "Anyway, I'll see you downstairs soon."

Decker nodded and watched her leave. He closed the door and took another glance around the room before picking up his travel bag and putting it on the bed. As he unzipped it, a sound drifted from the darkness beyond the bedroom window. A lonely warbling howl. Probably a coyote. He went to the window and peered out but saw no sign of the animal. He could hear it yipping though, most likely up in the mountains. Something had agitated the beast. Decker wondered if it was responding to a mundane threat, like another alpha-male in its territory, or if it could sense the creature lurking in the dark mine tunnels beneath its feet, hungry for a new victim.

CHAPTER TWENTY-FOUR

Harlan Biggs paced back and forth while he waited for the phone to connect. When it finally did, a gruff voice came on the line.

"What do *you* want?"

"Sergeant Lawson, it's Harlan Biggs."

"I know who the hell it is. I have you listed in my contacts as *never again*."

"Cute. If you'd kept your gambling habit under control in the first place, I wouldn't be in your contacts at all."

"Yeah, well, it's a little late for that now. Still doesn't mean I want to talk to you."

"Trust me, the feeling is mutual."

"If you're calling for a favor, forget it. I made that speeding ticket go away back in February, and I smoothed it over when your pit boss got a little handsy with one of the customers."

"That guy was counting cards. My floormen had every right to ask him to leave. Wasn't our fault he got belligerent."

"Harlan, your boy was heavy-handed, and you know it. Besides, there was no proof the guy was cheating outside of the fact that he'd won a butt load of money and you didn't like it. You're lucky he didn't sue your ass."

"Hasn't happened since, has it?" Harlan was growing impatient. "Can we get down to business?"

"I've already told you, there is no business. I'm done doing favors for you. Go find someone else to bother."

"Okay. I can do that," Harlan said. "Just a quick question, though, are Internal Affairs still on the same number?"

"Dammit, Harlan. You don't want to do that. It will only draw attention to you."

"Never said I was going to give them my name. What is their stance on cops being indebted to casinos, anyway? I can't imagine they look favorably upon it."

"All right, you win." There was an audible sigh on the other end of the line. "Tell me what this is about so I can get rid of you."

"That's more like it." Harlan stopped pacing and went to the window. The air conditioner unit was chugging away loudly. The noise was distracting, but he liked to stand close to the unit anyway when he was doing shady business. It was unlikely that he was under surveillance, but you could never tell, and the sound would make it harder for bugs to record him. At least, that was what he hoped. "I need some information from you about an incident up at the Ghost Canyon Mine yesterday."

"Yeah, I heard about it. Caused quite a stir."

"Tell me," Harlan said. "I'm listening."

"Well, I'm not part of the investigation and I haven't seen the report, but apparently three people went and got themselves killed inside the mine. We had two of our own up there, and one of them witnessed the third death. The rest of the search team barely escaped with their lives. Then a couple of Feds showed up and closed us down."

"FBI?"

"Yeah. Pair of stiffs from the Vegas field office. Took charge and sent everyone away. Didn't care that they were stepping on toes."

"Tell me more." Harlan felt a tingle of anticipation. "How did the victims die?"

"Some kind of animal attack by all accounts. Beyond that, everyone's keeping it pretty close to the vest."

· "Dammit," Harlan cursed. "You haven't told me much more than I got from the local news."

"That's all I know. I wasn't at the scene. Sorry."

"Not good enough."

"It'll have to be. Like I said, I haven't seen the report."

"Okay. Fine, I believe you." Harlan let out a frustrated sigh. "Can you find out more?"

"Maybe. But if I do, we're even. Deal?"

"I'll decide when we're even. But if you get me that report, it will go a long way toward it."

"I've heard that before."

"And you might hear it again," Harlan replied. "Or you might not, if you help me out on this."

"I'll do what I can." Lawson didn't sound happy.

"Perfect." Harlan stared out the window. He looked down toward the neighboring building, a burger restaurant. He could smell the meat grilling and it made him hungry. "Can you get it to me by morning?"

"Mercy, Harlan. You don't want much, do you? I'm not even working right now. My shift ended two hours ago."

"Like I care about that," Harlan said. "I'm sure you'll figure something out."

"Fine." Lawson sounded like he wanted to reach through the phone and throttle Harlan. "Give me until ten AM. My shift starts then, but I'll go in early."

"Doesn't sound like I have much choice." Harlan stepped away from the window. "Email it to me. You know where."

"Yeah, I know where," Lawson said. "Is that it? We done?"

"For now."

"Great. I'd love to say it was a pleasure talking to you, Harlan, but I don't like to lie."

"Just get the damn report." Harlan jabbed a finger at the screen and cut the call off without waiting for Lawson to reply.

He returned to the counter, and his untouched scotch. He downed it, then went to pour himself another, but thought better of it. Instead, he made his way to the small office adjacent to his bedroom. He went to a bookshelf behind the desk and pulled down an old leather-bound volume. This had belonged to his great-great-grandfather, a man named Travis Biggs. It was his journal. He'd been a prospector in the late 1800s, at least until he went and got himself lost in the Ghost Canyon Mine. He was probably still down there somewhere, his bones lying in the darkness.

Harlan sat at his desk, opened the journal, and flipped through the pages until he found the entry he was looking for. He'd read this journal often as a boy, sneaking into his father's study when the old man was preoccupied by the casino. He was fascinated by it. Later, as a teenager, he decided it was nothing more than the fevered writings of a crazy old miner. Now he wasn't so sure. And if the long-dead prospector's rambling tale was true, Harlan might yet be able to save his casino from Oscar Rossi. With a glimmer of hope, Harlan started to read.

CHAPTER TWENTY-FIVE

The creature that had lived in darkness for the last hundred and thirty-five years, made its way slowly through the pitch-black tunnels and up the adit toward the outside world. Centuries ago, when the land overflowed with bison, elk, and mountain sheep, and decades before the white man showed up, the collection of taut dry skin and creaking bones that now shambled through the mine had been the mighty warrior, Shilah.

Now it was something entirely different.

To the Ojibwe people who inhabited the Great Lakes region, it was the Baykok, or Bakaak, which meant bones draped in skin. The algonquin called it the Pakak. To the men who collected the disgraced warrior's bones, and summoned the creature to guard their gold, it was a means to an end. But to all who encountered it, the creature was death.

Now, having tasted flesh for the first time in over a century, it wanted more. Which was why the creature ventured closer to the surface than it ever had, exploring the periphery of its domain, and looking for a way out.

It reached the gates set into the mine's entrance and left

unlocked so the two missing geologists, if they somehow survived, could find their way out. But instead, something much worse stepped out into the darkness and looked up toward the night sky, full of glittering bright stars. It was a sight that would have been familiar to Shilah, had the creature he became still possessed the ability to comprehend such things.

It stood there a while, unsure of this unfamiliar world. Then, realizing it was confined no more, the creature lifted its arms and unfurled flaps of leathery translucent skin, much like the wings of a bat.

Somewhere in the mountains, coyotes were barking and howling, ignorant of the unnatural predator that had entered their midst. But not for long.

The creature drew breath into desiccated lungs and let forth a shrill cry the likes of which the Mojave Desert had never heard. Then it hopped once, twice, and took to the air, beating its wings in swooping, graceful arcs, as it soared above the landscape, looking for its next meal.

CHAPTER TWENTY-SIX

An hour after being shown to his room, Decker was back downstairs and on the hunt for a meal. His host, Robyn, had instructed him to come find her in the kitchen, but Decker didn't know where that was, so he wandered the first floor hoping to find it.

The first door he tried led into the bar, which looked just as an Old West saloon should. He could imagine old time cowboys sauntering in to quench their thirst. Except it wasn't a cowboy sitting at the bar nursing a bottle of bourbon right now. It was a grizzled old man with wiry white hair and sandpaper stubble covering his chin. He turned to greet Decker with an irritated tut.

"Who are you?" The old-timer asked.

"Name's John Decker. I'm looking for Robyn. She told me to meet her in the kitchen."

"Does this look like the kitchen to you?"

"No, sir, it doesn't."

The old man sighed. "Turn left, go past the stairs, and hang a right. You'll see a white door in front of you marked private. That's the kitchen."

"Thank you." Decker backed up. He was about to close the door when the old man spoke again.

"You one of them Feds?"

"I'm here at their request, but I don't actually work for the FBI."

"Who do you work for?" The old man's eyes narrowed. "NSA? CIA? Some other bunch of initials?"

"Definitely some other bunch of initials." Decker suppressed a smile. This must be Carlton Miller. His reputation preceded him, at least if you listened to Special Agents Fowler and Barnes. Not to mention Robyn herself.

"You one of the good guys?" Carlton asked. He picked up the bottle of bourbon and poured himself a large drink, then threw it back in one and smacked his lips with satisfaction.

"I can assure you I'm one of the good guys."

"Well, that settles it then. You aren't FBI."

Decker almost asked him what possible reason the old man could have for not liking the Bureau, but then he changed his mind. Chances were that Carlton Miller didn't like anyone who wore a badge. Decker had met his type before. He was most likely more than a little paranoid, distrustful of authority, and willing to believe any crazy conspiracy theory that came his way. In the end, Decker said nothing. He pulled the door closed and followed Carlton's directions to the kitchen.

When he entered, Robyn was sitting at a large antique table. Judging from the items spread upon it, the table served as both a place to eat and a place to prep food. Behind her was a six-burner range, a fryer, and a pair of commercial aluminum refrigerators. To her left was a sturdy metal door that he assumed led to a walk-in freezer. He shuddered when he looked at that. The last two walk-in freezers he'd encountered both ended up with bodies in them. Abraham Turner—a.k.a. Jack the Ripper—had kept one of his victims on ice in a London chip shop. Then, only a month ago, he'd carried a murder victim out of a sunken German submarine and stashed him in a similar freezer on a submerged research habitat. Decker wondered if he'd ever look at frozen food the same way again.

"Hey," Robyn said, glancing up from a magazine that was spread out before her on the table. "You found me."

"Not before I ran into the other occupant of your little town."

"Oh. You met Carlton." Robyn looked apologetic. "It was going to happen eventually."

"He's every bit as cheerful as you led me to believe."

"Isn't he, though?" Robyn pressed her lips together. "Take a seat. I'll rustle you up a quick supper. You like omelets?"

"Love them."

"Great, because we have a lot of eggs, a smattering of cheese, and not much else until I make a grocery run. I wasn't expecting visitors. I know this is more of a breakfast food, but…"

"It's fine. Really," Decker said. "Will the special agents, Barnes and Fowler, be joining us?"

"No. I already fed them. As soon as their plates were clean, they claimed they had paperwork to do and went back to their rooms."

"And Carlton?"

"He fends for himself. The type of things he likes to eat, I'm not cooking."

"That bad, huh?"

"Put it this way, he thinks it's easier to go find a jackrabbit in the desert than visit a grocery store. Claims it's *organic* without the price tag."

"He's a bit of an environmentalist, then?"

"Yeah, right. Cares so much about Mother Earth that he runs around polluting the desert." Robyn shook her head. "He has this old military Jeep. A relic from World War Two. It's a claptrap piece of junk that burns oil like crazy, but he drives it all over going on what he calls *Jackelope hunts.*"

"You're not exactly painting him in a better light," Decker said, bemused.

"Not trying to." Robyn returned to the table with two plates containing perfectly browned, fluffy omelets. She handed one to Decker and kept the other for herself. She placed salt-and-pepper on the table, then handed Decker a knife and fork.

He took them and cut a piece of omelet. He ate it, nodding with satisfaction, before glancing toward her. "I'm sure you've been asked this before, but I have to know. What drove you to come out here and live in the desert with Carlton?"

"Why not?" Robyn shrugged. "I always wanted to start a wedding venue. I ended up owning two thirds of the town and saw an opportunity. We are a stone's throw from the wedding capital of the USA, after all."

"I get that," Decker said. "But it must be lonely, living here all by yourself."

"Sometimes. That will change when the place is up and running." Robyn picked at her own food. "To tell the truth, I needed a change. I was in a relationship for the longest time, almost ten years. When it ended, I felt lost. Adrift. I wanted to put some distance between myself and Chicago."

"I see." Decker hoped he wasn't stirring up bad memories for her.

"Still, it's been a lot more work than I imagined. If I'd known then what I do now, I might have stayed put and rode it out."

"You've had issues?"

"And then some. The buildings were in worse shape than I thought. I had hoped to have the wedding chapel built by now, but as it is, I've sunk most of my cash into renovating the hotel. It needed so much more than I bargained for. We're months behind and way over budget." Robyn shook her head. "To tell you the truth, I'm a little worried. One more setback and that will be it. I don't have enough money to keep bankrolling this venture. I'm running on fumes, as the saying goes."

"I'm sorry to hear that."

"Thanks." Robyn forced a faint smile. "That's why the mine tours are so important. I need every dime I can get. Now even that looks like it might not happen."

"Maybe Carlton could help out."

"Not a chance. Whatever money he has, he isn't parting with. He's made that quite clear."

"Again, I'm sorry."

"Don't be. I got myself into this. Fools rush in, and all that." Robyn took a deep breath. "Goodness. I've only just met you and here I am unloading about my troubles. I should be the one apologizing."

"No need," Decker said. "I'm a good listener. Feel free to vent whenever you want."

"Thanks. You may regret that offer." Robyn looked down at her food.

Decker shrugged. "I doubt it."

Robyn looked at him and smiled, and he thought there was gratitude in her eyes, but she said nothing more, turning her attention to her food. Afterward the meal was done, she stood and cleared the plates away then turned back to Decker, all trace of sadness gone. "Fancy the two-bit tour?"

Decker shrugged. "Sure."

Robyn smiled. "Wonderful. Follow me."

CHAPTER TWENTY-SEVEN

Robyn led Decker from the kitchen and through the hotel lobby. She crossed to the saloon doors and opened them. "You've already seen the bar, but I'll show you again anyway, since I'm sure you didn't linger."

"I did not." Decker stepped across the threshold. Carlton was no longer there. All that remained was his empty glass on the bar. Even the bottle of bourbon had disappeared.

"This is the town's original saloon," Robyn said, following Decker inside. "Almost everything except the furniture is period, including the bar. We found over fifty bullet holes in this room during restoration. You can still see most of them if you look closely enough."

"Must've been a rough place," Decker said.

"It was. The prospectors were a rowdy bunch, and they were not exactly what you'd call law-abiding. This was the frontier, and the town didn't have a sheriff to keep the peace, so you can imagine the sort of shenanigans that went on. Local legend has it that six men got shot to death in this very room during the bar's original run. We even found an old Colt six-shooter hidden in the bar back, behind a removable panel. It probably belonged to some Old West bartender, who kept it handy to break up disputes."

"Interesting." Decker looked around. "Where is it now?"

"In our museum." Robyn beckoned for him to follow. "Don't get your hopes up, it's not exactly the Guggenheim. It's just an old storeroom we've converted to display the strange odds and ends found around here over the years."

"I'd love to see it."

"Good. It's our next stop," Robyn said, leading Decker toward a second door on the side wall of the saloon, and a narrow corridor beyond. "It is also our last stop. The hotel isn't large, and I figure you'd rather see the rest of the town in daylight."

"Sure," Decker replied, following Robyn into the corridor, which ran adjacent to the saloon bar. Apart from the door they had just stepped through, there were two others. One opposite, and another at the far end.

Robyn led him to the closer of the two. "This is the museum. The door at the end is my quarters. An old lean-to I converted."

They stepped inside.

Decker looked around, fascinated. Glass-fronted cabinets lined the walls. They contained a variety of artifacts, ranging from arrowheads, lumps of ore, and a variety of prospector's tools.

Robyn led him to a case on the far side of the room. "This is the Colt we found. It must've been a pretty expensive weapon back in the day. It has mother-of-pearl grips and an engraved barrel."

"That's a Colt Single Action Army revolver," Decker said, leaning close to study the weapon. "44-40 caliber. Four and three-quarter inch barrel. Looks like it's silver-plated. Probably manufactured in the late 1800s."

"Wow." Robyn sounded impressed. "You know your guns."

"I come from a law-enforcement family," Decker said. "It also helped that my father was a gun nut. He owned a couple of antique firearms. Nothing this interesting, though."

"Really?" Robyn nodded thoughtfully. "I should write this down so we can make an information card. To me it's just an old seized up revolver."

"I take it your dad didn't read Guns & Ammo to you before bed when you were young, then?"

"Not hardly." Robyn shook her head.

"You don't know how lucky you are."

Robyn stared at him, mute.

Decker wondered if she thought he was joking about the gun magazine. Unfortunately, he wasn't.

"What else have you got in here?" He asked, as much to change the subject as anything else. "Although I have to warn you, it's going to be hard to top that Colt."

"I might have something," Robyn said. She led him to a floor-standing glass display case in the middle of the room. "How about this?"

Decker peered inside the case and was shocked to see the skeletal remains of a person. Tattered clothing clung to the bones, including the remains of an old duster. "Now, that's pretty cool."

"Isn't it?" Robyn gazed down at the skeletal corpse. "We found him when we were blasting the mine entrance open. You can tell it's a male because of the pelvis."

"I realize that." Decker leaned in to study the bones in more detail. "I took a couple of pathology classes when I was a cop."

"Then you might be interested to know someone shot this unfortunate man in the back and dumped him over the side of the trail. We didn't find the bullet, that's long gone, but there's a tell-tale nick in the T3 thoracic vertebrae. You can also see a fractured rib where the bullet ricocheted inside the body."

"With the position of that wound, the bullet would've done a lot of damage, even if it missed the heart." Decker wondered who the man was in life, and what he'd done to earn himself a bullet in the back. "At the very least, his lung would have been toast."

"For sure," Robyn agreed. "He most likely died pretty quickly. The body was up near the mine entrance, and I find it unlikely anyone would bother to drag it up there back in those days. Like I said, there was no law enforcement to worry about. He was probably murdered pretty close to where the body was dumped."

"Makes sense. He would have bled out within ten minutes, maybe faster depending on what the bullet hit on the way through." Decker stared at the body. There was no flesh left, but he could still see tufts of straight black hair clinging to the skull. He wondered if the man was Native American. He ran his eyes over the length of the skeletal remains, overcome by a sudden feeling that they were not quite right, but he couldn't figure out why.

Then, while he was still pondering this, Robyn moved back toward the door. "I hope you don't mind, but I've got a few things to do before bed."

"No, not at all," Decker straightened up and followed her.

"You can stay and look around some more if you want," Robyn said as she stepped into the corridor. "It's no trouble."

"It's fine," said Decker. "I can always come back, and I hear my bed beckoning. I could use an early night."

"Okay, then." Robyn flicked the light off and pulled the door closed.

Decker glanced back, catching a last glimpse of the body in its glass tomb before his view was cut off. Then he followed Robyn back to the lobby, where he bade her good night, before climbing the stairs to his room.

CHAPTER TWENTY-EIGHT

When their fire burned down to glowing embers, Tiffany and Darwin retreated to the tent and settled in for the night. They zipped their sleeping bags together to create one large bed and crawled in beside each other. When Darwin turned off the lantern hanging from a hook on the tent pole, the darkness was absolute. Tiffany pressed against him, stared up into the swirling blackness, and listened to the breeze rustling through the sagebrush. The coyotes had stopped howling, at least for now, and that made her feel a little better. Yet Tiffany didn't think she would get a wink of sleep. She felt exposed and vulnerable, with nothing but a thin layer of fabric between herself and whatever predators might come prowling around their camp. Darwin sensed her discomfort and slipped an arm around her shoulder. He gently stroked the back of her neck, which sent shivers through her.

"There's no need to fret," he whispered, his lips inches from her ear.

"Easy for you to say," Tiffany replied. "You've done this before."

"And nothing has ever come sniffing around."

"That doesn't mean it won't," Tiffany said. "I heard those coyotes earlier."

"I thought you might feel this way," Darwin replied. He rolled over, dragging the sleeping bag, and her, along with him. He reached into his pack and withdrew a small bulky object.

At first, Tiffany didn't know what it was, but when he reached up and turned the lantern on again, she saw it was a small handgun.

"Where did you get that?" She asked, surprised. As far as she knew, he'd never owned a weapon, except for the baseball bat they kept in their closet.

"I borrowed it off Mitchel."

"That figures. He's like a walking armory," Tiffany replied. Mitchel was the first friend Darwin made after arriving in Nevada, but he was a little too obsessed with weapons for Tiffany's liking. "Is it loaded?"

"He said it was."

"You didn't check?"

"I figured he knew what he was talking about." Darwin returned the gun to his pack. "Besides, I don't intend to use it. I just thought it would help you sleep better."

"Do you even know *how* to use it?"

"How hard can it be?" Darwin reached up and turned the lantern off again. "You point it and press the trigger."

"*Pull* the trigger."

"Whatever."

"It was a nice gesture. Thank you." Tiffany rested her head on Darwin's shoulder and closed her eyes. Knowing the gun was there if the need arose, did actually make her feel safe. Which was why, after a few minutes, she fell into a deep sleep.

CHAPTER TWENTY-NINE

The high-pitched, undulating shriek jolted Tiffany from her slumber. She let out a startled cry and sat up, forgetting momentarily that she was cocooned in a sleeping bag with Darwin, and not laying in her own bed.

"What's going on?" Darwin asked, rubbing the sleep from his eyes, and pushing himself up on his elbows.

"I thought I heard something," Tiffany said, glancing nervously toward the tent flap. "It sounded really close."

"It was probably just a coyote." Darwin yawned and went to settle back into the sleeping bag. "Come back to bed."

"I swear, I heard something outside the tent. It wasn't a coyote. It sounded nothing like what we heard earlier." Tiffany reached up and clicked on the lantern, relieved to see that the tent flap was still closed and zipped shut.

"Whatever you heard, it's not making any noise now," Darwin said. "Coyote or not, it's probably miles away."

Tiffany strained her ears and listened, but now all she heard was the wind rustling the sides of the tent. Reluctantly, she slipped back down into the sleeping bag. "I know what I heard," she whispered.

"Are you sure you weren't just having a bad dream?" Darwin asked. "Maybe you only thought you heard something."

"It's possible, but..." Now that she thought about it, Tiffany wasn't certain what she'd heard. Maybe she had merely scared herself awake, although she couldn't remember having a nightmare. Then again, being stuck out here in the wilderness, it was no wonder she was jumpy. She wished, not for the first time, that Darwin had wanted to go to a hotel for his birthday trip, or maybe even take a cruise. She had never been on a ship before. That would be so much better than laying on the hard ground out in the Mojave Desert with coyotes prowling the hills. She turned to Darwin. "Maybe I did imagine it."

"There you go." Darwin opened an eye and looked at her. "You left the lantern on."

"Sorry." Tiffany pushed herself up again, careful not to jostle Darwin this time, and reached out to turn the light back off. As her finger found the switch, however, the inhuman shriek came again, long and warbling. And this time, it sounded closer.

"Holy crap," Darwin exclaimed. He scrambled to extricate himself from the sleeping bag, kicking up the fabric and pushing it aside. The tent was not tall enough for him to stand, so he crouched, bent over, wearing nothing but a pair of briefs. "Is that what you heard?"

"That's it, exactly." Tiffany noted. "I told you I wasn't dreaming."

"Okay. I believe you." Darwin was pulling his jeans on, trying to balance on one leg. He almost fell over, grabbing the tent pole at the last moment to save himself. "You're right. That doesn't sound like a coyote."

"Then what does it sound like?" Tiffany said. "Are there bears in this area?"

"I've heard stories of people spotting bears in the desert, but they shouldn't be this far south." Darwin managed to get both legs into his jeans and buckled them up. He pulled his shirt on. "But there's no way that was a bear. Sounded nothing like it."

"Mountain lion, then?"

"Possible. I have no idea what a mountain lion sounds like."

"I thought you were the big manly outdoorsman." Tiffany sat with her legs pulled up to her chest. She bit one of her fingernails nervously. "Isn't that why you wanted to go camping instead of going on a real vacation?"

"Just because I enjoy camping doesn't mean I'm an expert on every animal in the Mojave." Darwin kept his voice to a whisper. "For all I know, it was a damned jackrabbit."

"I'm pretty sure that was no rabbit." Tiffany glanced toward the pack with the gun in it. "Go outside and look."

"What?" Darwin shook his head. "There's no way I'm going out there."

"Fine," Tiffany said. She reached for the pack. "I'll go, then."

"What?" Darwin shook his head. "I don't think that's a good idea."

"Well, we sure as hell can't just sit here all night hoping whatever that was won't come sniffing around our tent."

Darwin put a hand on her shoulder. "Okay, I'll go look."

"Thank you." Tiffany felt a rush of relief. She wasn't sure she could actually have gone through with it.

Darwin pushed his hand inside the backpack and pulled out a flashlight, then dug back in for the gun. Armed now, he crawled toward the front of the tent. He pulled the zipper up to release the flap, clicked on the flashlight, and glanced back. "Stay here."

Tiffany nodded.

Darwin hesitated a moment, then he took a deep breath and pushed his way outside.

The tent flap fell closed behind him, cutting off Tiffany's view of the outside world. She rocked back and forth, hugging her knees, and waited for Darwin to return.

A minute passed. Then another.

She stared at the tent flap, feeling more nervous with each second now she was alone. She shouldn't have asked him to go outside. Whatever was she thinking?

Another two minutes ticked by.

Her distress was almost at breaking point. She leaned forward and reached out, pulling the flap open a couple of inches.

"Darwin," she whispered. "Where are you?"

Silence.

"Please, Darwin, answer me." Tiffany felt a lump form in her throat. She sucked back a sob. "I don't like this."

Still, there was no response.

Tiffany wriggled to free her legs from the sleeping bag and crawled to the flap. She pushed her head out and looked around. There was no sign of her boyfriend.

"Dammit," she cursed under her breath. The last thing she wanted to do was go outside, but she didn't want to stay in the tent either. Her mind was conjuring up all sorts of dreadful scenarios. Besides, if she found Darwin, they could hop in the Jeep and leave. She was sure he wouldn't want to stay here anymore, and she certainly didn't. To hell with the tent. They could come back for it later. With newfound resolve, Tiffany ignored the gut churning fear in her stomach and scrambled out into the chilly night air.

She stood up and glanced around. The Jeep stood off to her left, a dark outline against the deeper blackness beyond. The fire was nothing but smoldering ashes. A canopy of stars arched over the mountains like a million pinpricks in the heavens. But of Darwin, there was no sign.

A sudden panic gripped her. Why couldn't she see him? She edged further from the tent, wishing she too had a flashlight. Darkness folded around her like a blanket. She had the weird feeling of being totally isolated, as if she were the only person left on the face of the planet.

Then, out of the corner of her eye, she caught a flicker of movement. She swiveled as a panicked scream surged up, only to find Darwin's familiar form emerging from the darkness behind the tent.

"I looked everywhere, there's nothing." He walked toward her, flashlight bobbing.

"That's impossible. You heard that shriek."

"I don't know what to tell you." Darwin shrugged. "Maybe it was just a..." He let the words trail off, his eyes snapping skyward.

"What?"

"I don't know." Darwin looked in one direction, then the other. "I could have sworn something flew over us." Darwin craned his neck upward. "It was large, too. Bigger than a bird."

"Stop it, you're scaring me."

"I'm scaring myself."

"We should leave. Take the Jeep and get out of here." Tiffany didn't care if Darwin protested. She was driving back to Vegas with or without him. She was relieved when he nodded his agreement.

"Good idea." He turned back toward the tent, was about to duck inside, when the shriek came again.

A dark shape swooped from the sky, barely missing their heads, before climbing back into the darkness.

Darwin swung the gun upward into the night sky and pulled the trigger, but nothing happened.

The thrum of beating wings, much too loud, filled the air. It was coming back.

Darwin aimed loosely toward the sound and fired again.

Still nothing.

"Why won't this work," he said, frantically waving the gun up at the firmament.

"Is there a safety?" Tiffany asked.

"Shit." Darwin thumbed the push button safety behind the trigger guard, and this time the gun fired with a resounding crack.

Tiffany jumped and suppressed a squeal.

Darwin fired blindly into the sky, squeezing off two more shots in rapid succession.

"Did you get it?" Tiffany asked.

"I don't know." Darwin swiveled, eyes searching the heavens. "Maybe."

"We need to leave. Right now." Tiffany turned and took a step toward the tent. From behind her, Darwin let out a sharp grunt.

When she looked back, he was gone.

Fear, like an icy hand, twisted her gut.

"Darwin?" She screamed, hoping he would reappear.

And he did, but not from where she thought.

Her boyfriend's torn body dropped out of the cold dark sky and landed on the desert floor with a thud a few feet from her. It bounced and came to rest. Darwin's vacant dead eyes stared back at her. Blood seeped from a vicious gash across his belly and pooled beneath him.

Tiffany stifled a scream and backed away, horrified, while in the darkness above, came a beat of wings. Whatever killed Darwin was coming back. She could see it wheeling lower and lower in tight circles—a dark silhouette with red eyes blazing. And even though she was desperate to escape, wanted so much to flee for her life, Tiffany remained frozen, unable to tear her eyes away, as death barreled down toward her.

CHAPTER THIRTY

Decker was dreaming about Nancy when a distant crack roused him from sleep. It was gunfire. As a former homicide cop, he would recognize that sound anywhere. He lay there listening and soon heard two more sharp reports.

He rose and went to the window, pulling the curtain back and staring out into the night. Decker wondered who would discharge a weapon in the middle of the desert in the early hours of the morning.

Was someone in trouble?

If they were, he was powerless to help. The shots did not sound close. They could have come from anywhere, reverberating through the canyons and off whatever structures lay hereabouts. It would be impossible to pinpoint from which direction the gunshots had originated, especially since the sound could travel a mile or more. He stayed at the window for a while, listening, but heard no more gunfire.

He gazed out across the landscape, searching for any signs of movement, but saw nothing.

The cluster of tumbledown buildings that made up the ghost town of Haley stood out as stark black outlines against the surrounding landscape. There were no streetlights here, and when his gaze drifted upward, he marveled at the Milky Way arching overhead like some celestial river cutting through the deep emptiness of the cosmos. In that moment, he felt small. Insignificant. While somewhere out there, in the vast expanse of the Mojave Desert, another person, themselves minuscule in the grand scheme of the universe, had squeezed off three shots. Perhaps they were attempting to ward off some imminent danger, like a coyote or mountain lion, or maybe they were shooting at nothing in particular, just for the hell of it. Either way, they had stopped now.

Decker let the curtain fall back into place and returned to his bed. He slid under the covers and closed his eyes. Minutes later, he drifted away and rejoined Nancy in the dream that had been so abruptly interrupted.

CHAPTER THIRTY-ONE

Harlan Biggs slept through the night for the first time in weeks. He awoke refreshed and more optimistic than he had in a long time. He jumped up and went to the laptop in his office. When he checked his mail, there was a message from Sergeant Lawson. Attached to it was the LVMPD report filed by the two officers who had responded to the incident at the Ghost Canyon Mine. He read it with interest, then read it a second time, just to make sure he wasn't missing anything. Then he noticed the second attachment. An MPEG movie named BodyCam1. He clicked and waited for the file to load, his excitement mounting.

When it played, he maximized the window and leaned close to the screen. The footage was grainy and dark, clearly shot inside the mine. There was no sound. The picture jumped around all over the place. It was mostly just undefined shades of darkness, with an occasional flashlight beam highlighting rocky walls gouged by chisel marks. Once in a while it picked up another person as they stepped into the camera's path, but beyond this there was nothing of interest.

Harlan yawned. This was not as interesting as he'd first

imagined. He wondered why Lawson had bothered to send it. He fumbled for the mouse, intending to shut the video off, but then he froze, hardly able to believe what he was seeing. Now he knew why the sergeant had sent this to him. He clicked on the progress bar at the bottom and dragged it back a couple of minutes to watch the segment again, then did it a third time. His heart was beating fast against his rib cage. This video was better than any report. It was proof positive that his great-great-grandfather's journal was anything but the alcoholic rantings of a crazy old man.

Shaking, Harlan closed the video and made a copy which he stashed on his cloud account, just to be safe. Then he hurried to the bedroom and pulled on a pair of jeans and a denim shirt. He went to the closet and found a pair of hiking boots. Ignoring his Rolex watch, which he would never normally leave behind, Harlan raced from the penthouse and jumped in the elevator.

When he reached the lobby, he went in search of Wagner Mitchell. He found the GM in the casino overseeing the installation of the craps tables.

"You bring your truck today?" Harlan asked, rushing toward him.

"Sure." Wagner nodded. "Why?"

"I need to borrow it." Harlan held his hand out. "Give me the keys."

"What?" Wagner looked confused. "Why don't you take the Porsche?"

"Because I'm going out into the desert," Harlan said. "If I end up on a dirt road, it might bottom out. Besides, I don't want to get dust all over it."

"You don't mind getting my new truck dirty?"

"For Pete's sake, it's a truck. I'll give you twenty bucks to take it through the car wash if you're that worried. Hurry up. Keys," Harlan snapped his fingers, then he had a better idea. "You know what, on second thought, why don't you come with me. You can drive."

"Where?"

"An old ghost town called Haley." Harlan took off toward the parking garage.

"Haley?" Wagner hurried to catch up with him. "Isn't that where those folks got killed the other day while they were tromping around some abandoned mine? I saw it on the news."

"Yeah." Harlan was passing the buffet restaurant now. He glanced within, at the tables and chairs stacked against one wall, and the tarps laid out on the floor so that they could repaint the walls and ceiling. Once he was past the restaurant, he turned left and saw the exit leading to the parking garage directly ahead.

"Why do you want to go out there?" Wagner asked as they entered the garage and approached a red Ford F150 truck with gleaming chrome rims.

"Because it might be the only way I can pay Oscar Rossi back and save my hide."

"That doesn't make sense." Wagner unlocked the truck with the key fob remote and slid behind the wheel. "You sure you're feeling all right, Harlan?"

"I'm feeling fine. Just start the damned engine and get us out there. I'll tell you on the way."

"Take it easy, I was just asking." Wagner started the truck and steered through the parking garage to the exit. When he reached the road, he turned right toward East Flamingo Road. "You got an address for this place?"

"It's out on route Ninety-Five."

"Fine, put the address in the GPS." Wagner turned left on Flamingo, heading away from the Strip toward the interstate.

Harlan read the address from his phone and entered it into the navigation system, then sat back. "It will take about forty minutes to get there."

"Great, now maybe you can tell me why we're rushing out there in such a hurry."

"Because my great-great-grandfather, Travis Biggs, used to own a share of that mine. He went missing a few years after the mine dried up, but he'd already found a good amount of gold by then, which got passed down to his illegitimate son, sired with a town prostitute."

"I know all this, Harlan. Your grandfather built the casino using what remained of the modest wealth Travis Biggs accumulated as a prospector. I don't see what that has to do with paying off Rossi."

"It has everything to do with it," Harlan said. "It wasn't just the money that was passed down through the generations. Travis Biggs kept a journal. The Ghost Canyon Mine was an obsession. He claimed there was a huge seam of gold that no one else knew about."

"I still don't see how that helps us." Wagner steered the truck onto the interstate and joined the flow of traffic. "Even if there was gold in that mine, it's probably long gone."

"That's just it, Travis wrote in his journal that he had cursed the mine using the bones of a disgraced Paiute warrior, who's undead spirit protected the seam from other prospectors until he could extract the precious metals. When the mines stopped producing, the town's population left for richer pickings, like the Comstock Lode. Not Travis. He stayed behind, convinced he could still get gold out of the Ghost Canyon Mine. But he never did because he couldn't remove the curse."

"Harlan, listen to yourself. I know you're worried about this Oscar Rossi business, but you sound crazy. This is a fool's errand."

"I get it. It sounds nuts. I thought the journal was nothing more than a liquor induced fantasy. A tall tale written by a crazy old man. But it's not. The curse is real. Something supernatural killed those three people—"

"Harlan, come on—"

"And if the curse is real, then so is the gold." Harlan folded his arms and watched the desert landscape slip by.

"Even if it is, how are you going to get it?" Wagner asked. "You said it yourself, there's a curse on the mine."

"We don't have to get the gold out. All I need is enough gold in hand to convince Oscar Rossi that the seam is real. Then I can negotiate. He rips up the note on my casino, and I'll tell him where he can get enough gold to make us both rich. And the best of it is, he'll be the one who has to deal with any curse."

"And the fact that you don't own the mine?"

"I might not have the money to pay Oscar Rossi almost four hundred grand in interest payments, but I'm not completely broke. I'm sure I can pull enough cash together to make the current owners an offer. After what happened, I can't imagine they want to keep it."

"So that's what we're doing?" Wagner asked. "Buying that mine?"

"Not until I see the gold for myself. First things first, I want to look around up there and get the lay of the land. Check out the mine entrance. Then we'll come back when no one's around and actually go in, find the seam, and make sure the gold is really there. Maybe even snag a sample or two."

"And then?"

"Then we get ahold of that mine, cut a deal with Rossi, and save the casino."

CHAPTER THIRTY-TWO

The bright Nevada sunshine streamed in through Decker's window. It was a little after eight in the morning and he could hear hammering and sawing coming from further down the corridor. He rose and got dressed, then headed downstairs and made his way to the kitchen.

When he entered, Decker found the Feds, Barnes and Fowler, sitting at the table, eating bacon and eggs. A shaggy yellow-haired dog sprawled at their feet, looking up hopefully.

Robyn was fussing over the stove. She turned at Decker's arrival and smiled. "Sleep well?"

"I did, thank you." Decker took a seat. The dog dragged itself up and padded over to him, sniffing curiously.

"That's Tieg," Robyn said. "He's the official food taster."

"He's going to have to wait awhile to taste mine," Decker replied. "I'm famished."

"Good." Robyn turned with a plate of food and placed it in front of him. "Eat up."

"Thanks," Decker said. He glanced around the table. "Did anyone else hear gunshots last night?"

Fowler shook his head. "I slept like a log."

"Me too," Barnes said. "Although I did wake up around two, but I don't know why. What time did you hear the shots?"

"Around that time."

"It was probably yahoos out in the desert," Robyn said. "It's happened before. They drive up into the mountains to camp, party, and get shitfaced. I wouldn't worry yourself about it."

"Seems reasonable." Decker shrugged and turned his attention to the food. He ate quickly, digging into the hearty breakfast with gusto. When his hunger was sated, he glanced toward the two FBI agents. "I'm planning to look around this morning, maybe go up to the mine, just to get the lay of the land. Is that going to be a problem?"

"I don't see why it would be," Fowler said. "You're the specialist here. We've been told to assist you in any way possible."

"Are you planning to go inside?" Barnes asked.

"Not yet." Decker shook his head. "I'd like to get a better idea what we're dealing with before that happens."

"Makes sense." Barnes nodded.

"Do you have the medical examiner's report on the search team member that was killed, Sasha Martin?"

"Not yet in," Fowler replied. "It's only been forty-eight hours. I can call the Clark County ME's office and see where we stand if you like. Is there something in particular you're looking for?"

"Not sure," Decker replied. "But I would like to get their opinion on cause of death. If they think a human or an animal inflicted the wounds."

"I watched the body cam footage," Barnes chimed in. "That was no human, at least not a normal one."

"Didn't look much like an animal either," Fowler said. "Looked more like a walking skeleton."

"Which is precisely why I want a professional opinion. The ME hasn't seen that footage, therefore won't be swayed by presumption. Regardless of what the officer's camera filmed, we cannot jump to conclusions. Sometimes things aren't what they seem."

"Sometimes they are," Fowler said, grimly. "Pretty hard to mistake Sasha Martin's killer for a bobcat, at least if you've watched the footage. Regardless, I'll see what I can do. I can't imagine they'll have a full report typed up yet, but they should be able to tell us something."

"Perfect. I'd like to go there in person and speak with the medical examiner directly," Decker replied. "It might be helpful to see the body too."

"I'm sure I can arrange that."

"I'll leave it in your competent hands, then." Decker pushed his empty plate away and stood up.

Under the table, Tieg emitted a disgruntled snort when he realized there would be no table scraps forthcoming.

"I'm going to take that walk now," Decker said.

"You want some company?" Barnes asked.

"Sure." Decker turned to Special Agent Fowler. "How about you?"

"I don't think so," Fowler replied. "I'll stay here and call the ME."

Decker nodded. He glanced toward Robyn. "Thank you for the delicious meal."

"You're welcome," Robyn replied, smiling. "If you can figure out what's running around in that mine and take care of it, I'll make all the bacon and eggs you want for the rest of your life."

"It's a deal," Decker replied, grinning. He motioned to Barnes. "Ready to go?"

"Sure." Barnes pushed his chair back and stood up. "Just give me one minute to go upstairs. I want to get my gun. I don't feel like heading up there unarmed."

"A wise precaution." Decker started toward the kitchen door. "I'll meet you out front."

Decker made his way through the lobby. Behind him, he

heard Barnes climbing the stairs. He stepped out onto the veranda and leaned on the railing, taking in the ghost town during daylight for the first time. It was a town in name only. In reality, Haley was nothing more than a cluster of dilapidated buildings gathered next to a dusty road. The structures themselves were in various states of disrepair, and many of them looked like they would blow down at the first strong gust of wind. One building leaned at a precarious angle, part of the roof gone, windows nothing more than black oblongs devoid of glass. Thick support beams stood at forty-five degrees against the side wall, to prevent the building from collapsing completely. The skeletal frames of rusting cars and trucks sat baking in the sun. Some of them looked decades older than Decker. He wondered how much they would be worth, if restored. Then he decided they were too far gone to bother.

He glanced to his left, where a meandering trail followed the steeply rising land. Two A-frame barricades stood across the entrance, even though there was nobody to keep out except the ghost town's owners, Decker, and the FBI agents. Plus Tieg, of course, although Decker didn't think the dog cared one way or the other about the barricades.

He stepped down onto the dusty street. The sun was scorching on his head and shoulders. It was the exact opposite of the cold and rainy weather he'd left behind in Maine. Decker wondered if he should go back inside for a baseball cap. He didn't want to get sunburned. But then Special Agent Barnes appeared, his service weapon pushed into a holster worn over his polo shirt.

"Ready to explore?" Barnes asked, drawing level with Decker.

"Lead the way," Decker replied, deciding he couldn't be bothered to find a cap. "Show me that gold mine."

CHAPTER THIRTY-THREE

Harlan Biggs told his general manager, and the man currently driving the truck they were both riding in, to pull over onto the side of the road at the outskirts of the ghost town of Haley, Nevada.

While they were en route, he'd checked out the town's geography and discovered that the mine lay about half a mile distant, up a narrow trail that wound into the mountains. This tallied with the information gleaned earlier that morning from an old and fading map hand-drawn inside his great-great-grandfather's journal. It appeared that nothing much had changed over the intervening hundred and thirty years other than a steady decline in the condition of the town's buildings, and of course, it's population.

"Why are we stopping here?" Wagner asked as he maneuvered the truck off the road and onto the dusty shoulder.

"Look at that place," Harlan replied. "There's barely anyone around. We go driving in there, we'll draw all sorts of attention. I'd like to keep this little trip on the lowdown, at least for now."

"So how are we supposed to get to the mine?"

"Not this way, that's for sure." Harlan peered through the windshield at the A-frame barricades blocking off the trail. He also noted the unmarked Crown Victoria parked outside of the one building-the sign out front proclaimed it to be the Last Chance Saloon and Hotel-that didn't look like it was going to collapse at any moment. "That car must belong to the feds. My contact in the Vegas Police Department said there were a couple of FBI agents staying up here. Showed up and took charge within hours of the accident in the mine. Sent the local boys packing. I'd prefer to avoid a confrontation with the feds."

"I'm with you on that one," Wagner agreed. "Still doesn't help us reach that mine."

"Turn around." Harlan nodded back in the direction from which they had come. "There was a trail about a half mile back. Looks like it cuts around the back of the property, at least according to Google Earth. If we drive in that way, no one will see us."

"You want me to go off roading up that damned mountain?"

"It's not that far," Harlan replied. "A mile at most."

"It's not the distance that worries me, it's the damage to my tires. I didn't buy this truck so I could go driving all over the desert."

"Then why did you buy it?" Harlan asked. "Isn't that what a truck is for?"

"Whatever," Wagner replied, grumpily. He spun the wheel and steered the truck back in the other direction. The rear wheels kicked up gravel as he sped up away from the shoulder. "I get a flat, you're paying to replace the tire."

"We find that gold and get Oscar Rossi off our backs, I'll buy you a whole new truck."

"Your back, not mine," Wagner said. "I told you at the time not to do business with him."

"What choice did I have?" Harlan glanced down at the map on his phone, then back to the road. A moment later he slapped the dashboard with the palm of his hand. "There it is. The trail. Turn left here."

Wagner slowed and made the turn, then picked his way carefully up the trail. The truck had good suspension, but even so, they were jostled and bumped as the powerful vehicle clawed its way forward on the uneven surface. Soon they reached a flat, wide area crisscrossed with what looked like dirt bike tracks. An old fire pit was visible to their left, along with several crushed beer cans.

"Someone had fun up here," Wagner said, slowing the truck to a crawl.

"As long as they aren't here now." Harlan glanced toward the GM. "Why are you slowing down?"

"It looks pretty rough ahead," Wagner said, pointing toward the trail, which petered out to a narrow walking path strewn with boulders. "There's no way I'm taking the truck up that."

"Fine." Harlan didn't bother to hide his displeasure. "We'll hoof it from here. Probably best to keep the truck out of sight, anyway. The mine shouldn't be far now. Just over the next ridge."

"Great. Then maybe we can get back to civilization." Wagner pulled his door open and jumped out. He slammed it and rounded the front of the vehicle, a scowl on his face. "And FYI, you definitely owe me that car wash. The truck's filthy."

"Quit moaning." Harlan stepped past him and started up the trail on foot. "Your truck got a bit dirty, who cares? If we don't pull this off, I'll be part of the foundation for one of Rossi's building projects, and you'll be doing his dirty work for the rest of your life."

"I'm not complaining," Wagner said. "I just don't like the desert."

"And yet you live in Las Vegas." Harlan shook his head in bewilderment.

"Exactly. If I actually wanted to live in the desert surrounded by lizards and coyotes, I wouldn't have bought a condo on the eighth floor of a tower overlooking the Strip."

"Fair point."

They were approaching the end of the trail now, as it curved back down and ended at the entrance to the Ghost Canyon Mine. Harlan quickened his step, eager to see what awaited them.

"That looks like the mine entrance," Wagner said, pointing to a dark hole in the mountainside up ahead.

Harlan nodded and approached the entrance where a pair of security gates were standing ajar. "Not even padlocked. We can get inside."

"I didn't think you wanted to go in yet," Wagner said.

"I don't," Harlan replied. "But this might be our only chance. Once they lock it again we won't be able to get in."

"We'll still get in. I'll just use a pair of bolt cutters."

"And then the owners of this place will know someone was up here, genius." Harlan sighed. "They might decide to see what we wanted and find the gold, then we're screwed."

"Or they might not." Wagner glanced over his shoulder. "You saw those dirt bike trails. I'll bet teenagers come out here all the time to party. They'll probably just think it was random vandalism. Besides, they might leave it unlocked."

Harlan nodded. Wagner had a point, and he would have admitted as much, if it weren't for the unfamiliar voice that broke the silence behind them.

"Hey, you two. What are you doing up here?"

Harlan turned, surprised, and saw a pair of strangers striding toward them. The shorter man was armed with a Glock service pistol, which he was already pulling from its holster.

Harlan cursed under his breath. After taking the trouble to avoid going through town and making their presence obvious, they had been discovered anyway. Now the only question was how to handle it, especially since they had a gun pointed at them.

CHAPTER THIRTY-FOUR

Decker saw the two strangers as soon as they crested the trail. Special Agent Barnes had seen them too, standing near the entrance to the Ghost Canyon Mine, and was already pulling his gun, ready for trouble.

The pair of interlopers, on the other hand, didn't notice Decker and Barnes until the FBI agent shouted a challenge to them. They spun around, surprised, the look on their faces telling Decker that they hadn't expected anyone to discover them in such a remote location.

"Answer the question," Decker barked, employing the same authoritative voice that he'd used back in his days as a cop in New York. "This is private land. What are you doing?"

For a moment, neither man spoke. They just stared in mute shock as Decker and Barnes closed the distance between them. Then the smaller of the two men, who looked more like a weaselly accountant than a hearty outdoor type, appeared to pull himself together.

"Private land?" His face creased into a picture of innocence. "Are you sure about that? We thought this was a hiking trail."

"Well, it's not," Barnes said, keeping his gun leveled. "You have no business being here."

"Sorry, we didn't realize. We came across this here mine opening and thought we'd take a look. We were curious."

"You're out hiking, huh?" Decker asked.

"Sure." The man laughed nervously. "It's good exercise, don't you think?"

"We normally hike the Calico Basin Trail." The other man, who looked a lot more suited to the outdoors than his partner, spoke for the first time. "We decided to try something different today. I guess we messed up."

"You don't look very well prepared for a hike," Decker said, eying the men up. Neither wore a backpack nor carried water. They didn't even have hats, which was fine for a short stroll, but not for prolonged exposure in the wilderness. "Where's your gear?"

"We don't need much," the smaller man said. "We're pretty experienced at this."

"Is that so," Barnes said, narrowing his eyes. "You have so much experience that you don't need to hydrate?"

"Huh?" The man looked confused.

"It might be November, but it can still get up into the low eighties on a hot day. You'll lose a good deal of moisture on a long hike if you don't have any water on hand."

"Right. Thanks for the advice. We'll keep that in mind next time." The larger of the two men laughed nervously. He glanced toward the trail leading away from the mine. "I guess we'll be on our way now."

His partner nodded and took a step toward the trail. "Sorry to have troubled you. We wouldn't have hiked this way if we'd known it was private land."

"Not so fast." Decker raised a hand. "I don't suppose you'd mind telling us your names."

"What?" Now the man looked flustered. "Why?"

"Because I'm asking," Decker replied.

"And what gives you the authority to do that?" The man replied, growing bold all of a sudden.

"That would be the FBI." Barnes stepped forward. Holding the gun steady with one hand, he pulled out his credentials wallet with the other and held it up. "Special Agent Barnes. The man accompanying me is John Decker, on temporary assignment with the Bureau, and entrusted with the same authorization as myself." Barnes paused and drew a breath. "Now, if you wouldn't mind answering his question?"

"Very well," the man didn't look pleased. "My name's Bob Eastwood."

"And your friend?" Barnes asked, pointing to the larger man.

"My brother. Larry." A sheen of sweat glinted on the forehead of the man who called himself Bob Eastwood. "We're staying in Vegas. We drove here from Albuquerque yesterday."

"I thought you said you hiked around Vegas all the time," Decker said. "You even mentioned another trail."

"You did, indeed," Barnes added. "The Calico Basin Trail. Doesn't seem like a pair of brothers from Albuquerque would be too familiar with the hiking trails hereabouts. That's got to be what... a nine-hour drive?"

"What can I say, we like to gamble. We drive up at least once a month. Are we free to go now?"

"Go on, then." Barnes lowered his weapon but didn't holster it. "Get out of here. Make it quick before I change my mind and decide to dig deeper on the pair of you."

"Thank you, officer." The man calling himself Bob Eastwood wasted no time in scuttling back toward the trail with his brother in tow.

Decker watched them leave, climbing up through the canyon past the mine, until they crested a rise and dropped out of sight on the other side. He turned to Barnes. "You believe a word of what they said?"

"Not hardly. Albuquerque, my ass. They were lying. Body language was all wrong. I'll bet they didn't even give us their real names."

"That's what I thought." Decker stepped toward the trail. "I want to see where they're going."

"For sure. There's no way they hiked out here." Barnes followed Decker, and together they made their way up the trail, following the route taken by the two strangers.

They picked their way along the trail in silence, leaving the mine behind, doing their best not to alert their quarry of the pursuit. When they reached the high point of the trail, they saw the men below them, descending toward a red pickup truck.

Decker dropped to the ground so he wouldn't be visible if either man looked back. Barnes did the same, flattening himself against the rocky earth.

The men reached the truck. The shorter of the two glanced over his shoulder, as if he could sense Decker's gaze, then climbed into the passenger side. His companion jumped in the driver's side. Decker heard the engine start up. He reached into his pocket for his phone, bringing up the photo app and zooming in on the truck. As it peeled away, he took several pictures.

Soon the truck was gone, leaving behind only a cloud of dust that caught on the breeze and dissipated in twirling wisps.

Decker got to his feet and studied the photographs, finding one that showed the back of the vehicle, and the Nevada license plate it displayed. "Now we have proof. Everything they told us was bull."

"I thought as much." Barnes stared down at the photo on the phone's screen. "I would very much like to find out what their real names are."

"And what business they had up here at the mine," Decker said.

"I'll run the plate when we get back to town. That should

give us a name for one of those clowns, because I'm pretty sure it isn't Eastwood."

"And I'll bet you a hundred bucks they aren't brothers either," Decker added. "They don't even look alike."

Barnes nodded. He brushed the dust from his trousers and turned to head back toward the mine. "And when we find out who they are, we'll pay them a visit and ask those questions again."

"And this time, they had better tell the truth," Decker said.

"For damned sure." Barnes started walking back down the trail.

Decker turned and looked at the empty spot the truck had occupied before the two men climbed in and drove away. His cop's sixth sense was jangling. Whatever their game was, they were up to no good. Still pondering this, he stepped back onto the trail, and hurried to catch up with Special Agent Barnes.

CHAPTER THIRTY-FIVE

Harlan Biggs sat in the truck's passenger seat and stared out through the windshield, watching the dusty landscape slip by. When they reached the paved road again, and turned back toward Las Vegas, he let out a sigh of relief. "That was a close one."

"Close?" Wagner glanced sideways. "Are you kidding me? We almost ended up under arrest back there."

"No, we didn't. Not even close," Harlan snorted. "As far as they knew, we were just a couple of lost hikers."

"Yeah, until you went and told them we drove here from Albuquerque. What the hell was that?"

"I don't know. I got flustered and couldn't think straight. I figured if they thought we were from out of town, they wouldn't bother pressing the matter."

"Except that we'd already told them we hike around here all the time." Wagner let out a disgruntled huff. "And what was with those names?"

"What, you think I should have told them who we really are?"

"I never said that, but you could at least have come up with some better names. I mean, Bob and Larry Eastwood. Really?"

"What's wrong with those names?"

"Well, for a start, you told them we were brothers. We look nothing alike."

"For all they know, you're adopted."

"That's a hell of a back story. You're overthinking this," Wagner said. "One thing though, it puts an end to getting inside that mine."

"I don't see why."

"For a start, we're on the radar of two federal agents."

"No big deal. We've done nothing wrong."

"Yeah, except trespass on private land and then lie about who we are and what we were doing there. Sure, they might not be able to charge us with much of a crime just for that, but do you really want them looking into your business dealings?"

"Fair point. We'll just have to wait a few days before making the landowner an offer for the mine. Give those FBI guys time to clear out. In the meantime, I still want to confirm the gold is really there."

"And how are you going to do that? There's no way we can break into the mine now."

"Easy. We find another point of access. Sure, those FBI guys will keep a closer watch on that mine entrance now, but if we get in some other way, they won't even know we were there."

"Except we don't know if there even *is* another way in."

"These old mines always had more than one entrance."

"Even if you're right, how are we going to find it?"

"Shouldn't be too hard. There are hand-drawn maps of the mine system inside my great-great-grandfather's journal. That's how I know where to look for the gold once we get inside. I bet he marked other entrances on there, too."

"I don't know, Harlan, it's a long shot."

"Don't you worry about it. I'll take care of getting us inside. I have another job for you."

"What?" Wagner sounded suspicious.

"Find me a couple of men. Have them standing by later today."

"What do you need men for?"

"You think I'm going into that mine myself? Not hardly. I read the Vegas PD report on what happened in those tunnels, and there's no way I'm stepping foot inside. If there really is a curse, I don't want to come face-to-face with it."

"And you think sending a couple of unsuspecting men in there is a better idea?"

"Absolutely, I do. Pull some laborers off the casino floor renovation. If they come across anything, they should be able to take care of themselves, especially since they'll be armed with pickaxes to chip the gold samples out of the seam."

"And if there really is some sort of creature down there? What if it kills them?"

"Make sure that whoever you pick for the job won't be missed. Half the guys on the work crew don't have papers."

"You want me to find illegals?"

"Absolutely. It shouldn't be hard to figure out which ones arrived recently. Use them. Even if they go missing, their families will be too scared to report it." They were back in Vegas now, inching their way through traffic on East Flamingo. Harlan felt better now they'd put some distance between themselves and the federal agents. "And tell them to keep their mouths shut. I don't want any links to us if it all goes pear-shaped."

"I'll do what I can," Wagner replied. He maneuvered through the snarl of vehicles, pushing the accelerator to the floor, and speeding through a yellow light. Moments later, he arrived at the hotel's parking garage.

"Drop me off there," Harlan said, pointing to the hotel

entrance at the ground level. "If you need me, I'll be in the penthouse. When you find the men, tell them there's an extra day's pay in it if they get the job done and don't blab. That should make it easier to convince them."

"Right," Wagner replied. He came to a halt next to the hotel entrance and let his boss out, then continued on to the ramp leading to the second level, where he preferred to park the truck.

Harlan watched him go, then made his way inside to the bank of elevators. He felt a surge of optimism. If all went well, he would be in possession of enough gold ore to convince Oscar Rossi by the end of the day, and after that, he hoped, his money troubles would be over.

CHAPTER THIRTY-SIX

Decker followed Special Agent Barnes back down the trail until they arrived back at the mine entrance. Here he stopped, contemplating the set of sturdy metal gates installed to stop curious looky-loos like the pair they had just chased off from sneaking inside and getting themselves hurt or lost.

"It's been a couple of days since those two geologists went missing in the mine," Decker said. "If they were still alive and in a fit condition to do so, they probably would have found their way back out by now, don't you agree?"

"I'm thinking so." Barnes nodded in agreement. "Pretty sure they're dead, from the eyewitness account and available evidence."

"Glad we're on the same page." Decker strode toward the mine entrance and pulled the metal gates closed, then looped the dangling security chain around them and pulled it tight before slipping the padlock through the chain's links and snapping it closed. He turned back to Barnes. "No one's going to be mooching around in there now."

"And a good job too," Barnes said. "Or they might end up filleted like Sasha Martin."

Decker nodded and stepped past the FBI agent back onto the trail and started down toward town. He wanted to run that plate as soon as possible and see just who was loitering around the mine entrance. His sense they were up to no good had only intensified, and he always trusted his hunches.

Special Agent Barnes hurried to keep up. Halfway down they reached the battered remains of an old pickup truck that must've sat baking in the sun for decades, the harsh ultraviolet radiation doing as good a job of stripping the paint off as any sandblaster.

"Hold up a moment," Barnes gasped. "My leg's giving me trouble. I've got a cramp."

"Surely you're not that out of shape?" Decker said. "How old are you? You don't look a day over thirty."

"Thirty-six, if you must know." Barnes leaned against the truck. He glared at Decker. "And I'm just as fit as you, probably more so."

"Point taken. Didn't mean to rankle you."

"Don't worry about it," Barnes said. "I'm a bit sensitive, that's all. I've got pins in my leg from an injury I sustained in Afghanistan."

"You were in the military?"

"Green Beret. Got too close to an IED. Took four of us out, I was the only one that survived."

"I'm sorry to hear that," Decker said.

"Yeah. Me too. Pretty much ended my military career, so here I am."

"You joined the FBI."

Barnes nodded. "After I returned to the States. I wasn't quite ready to give up the excitement, and the Bureau makes it easy for ex-military to join."

"Especially if they're Special Forces, no doubt."

Barnes nodded again. "So, what's your deal? How did you end up chasing monsters for a living?"

"I'm surprised you don't already know." Decker walked to the edge of the trail and peered over. It fell away steeply toward the canyon floor, clogged by a tangle of thick bushes. He wondered if this was where they found the bones that now lay in a display case in the museum room at the Last Chance Hotel and Saloon. "People seem to make a habit of looking me up online whenever I go somewhere."

"I don't need to look you up online. I'm an FBI agent. I could just run a background check and find out everything I need to know from your driver's license number to what size shoes you wear."

"But you didn't."

"No." Barnes reached down and rubbed his calf. "When DC says they're sending a specialist like yourself, I find it's better not to pry. Too much curiosity can be detrimental to career advancement."

"Ah. Don't want to ruffle any feathers, huh?"

"Something like that." Barnes flexed his knee. "Cramps have gone off now. Let's go back to town and run that plate."

"Sure thing. I'm curious to see what we find."

"Me too." Barnes started back down the trail. "You still haven't told me how you ended up in your particular line of work."

"I spent years in law enforcement. First as a homicide cop and then a sheriff in Louisiana. That's where I ran across something I couldn't explain," Decker said. "A killer of supernatural origin. I took care of the situation but lost my job in the process. Then my current employer came calling. As the saying goes, they made me an offer I couldn't refuse."

"So now you hunt monsters like whatever is lurking inside that mine for a living."

"Given the choice, I'd rather have my old life back, investigating run-of-the-mill cases involving good old-fashioned human bad guys."

"Life don't work like that," Barnes said, with a hint of regret in his voice. "I'd prefer to be traveling the world with the Green Berets. I loved that job. But here I am, anyway."

"FBI agent sounds like a pretty good gig to me," Decker observed.

"Yeah. If you like paperwork. It's not exactly like you see on the TV shows."

"You could say that about anything." They were entering the town now. Decker led Barnes up the steps into the Last Chance.

Tieg bounded around the corner from the direction of the kitchen and ran up to them, wagging his tail furiously. Barnes kneeled and rubbed the top of the dog's head while the canine tried to lick him.

"I think he likes you," Decker said.

"He can spot a dog lover when he sees one," Barnes replied. "I used to have a mutt just like this when I was growing up."

"Don't flatter yourself," Robyn said, appearing behind the dog. She carried a tea towel in her hand. "He's not picky. He'll take the attention of anyone who will give it."

"Don't listen to her, boy," Barnes cooed at the animal. "I know you like me, and that's all that counts."

To reply, the dog let out a contented grunt.

"Did you find what you were looking for at the mine?" Robyn asked.

"And a whole lot more," Barnes said, climbing to his feet.

"We caught a couple of guys mooching around the entrance," Decker said. "Sent them on their way."

"You did?" Robyn looked alarmed. "I wonder what they wanted?"

"That's what we'd like to know, too." Decker took his phone out. "They claimed to be from Albuquerque. Told us they just came out here for the hiking trails."

"But we know that wasn't true because they had Nevada

plates on their truck." Barnes glanced at the phone. "Can you forward me the pics of that truck?"

"You have an email address I can send them to?"

Barnes gave Decker his Bureau address.

"Thanks." Decker tapped away at the screen. "All done. They'll be in your inbox."

"What about the mine?" Robyn asked. "Is it secure if they come back?"

"I closed the gates and put the chain back on," Decker replied. "They won't be getting in."

"Good. Honestly, we've never had a problem with trespassers before."

"Maybe it's all connected," Barnes said.

"Sounds reasonable." Decker nodded. "Feels like too much of a coincidence that we'd run across those two up there right now, after all that's happened, and I don't believe in coincidences."

"Neither do I." Barnes glanced toward Decker. "You going to be around for a while?"

"Yup."

"Great. I'm going to find out who owns that truck. I'll let you know as soon as I have the results." Barnes headed toward the stairs.

When he was gone, Robyn turned to Decker. "And what are you planning to do next?"

"Actually, I was hoping to have a chat with you," Decker replied. "I was wondering if you can tell me a little more about the town and its history."

"Sure," Robyn agreed. "Do you think there might be a connection to the attacks?"

"I have a hunch that whatever is in that mine, has been around a lot longer than the last few days." Decker glanced toward the saloon bar. "Why don't we talk in there, if it's not too much trouble."

"No trouble." Robyn moved toward the door. "It will be good practice, actually. When this place officially opens to the public, we're going to need a tour guide, and since we don't have much money, you can guess who that's going to be."

"You?"

"Yes indeed. So, you're actually helping me out too."

"I always like to be of help," Decker said, and followed Robyn into the saloon.

CHAPTER THIRTY-SEVEN

When he reached the penthouse suite atop the Prospectors Paradise Hotel, Harlan went straight to the desk in his office, upon which his ancestor's journal lay. He sat down, then reached out and touched it. The leather binding was coarse beneath his fingers. He couldn't help feeling a sense of awe. This little book had survived so much to end up with Harlan. His great-great-grandfather had started the journal when he left New York City to find his fortune out West. He made regular entries, detailing the hardships of a prospector's life in 1800s America. It was a fascinating historical document in its own right, but more than that, the unassuming leather-bound volume provided a roadmap through Harlan's current predicament. If the final entries in the journal were correct, and not merely the fevered rantings of an insane man, then a fortune in gold waited for Harlan inside the Ghost Canyon Mine.

The irony was not lost on him. While he struggled to make ends meet and keep the casino afloat, eventually resorting to a deal with the devil, this journal had sat upon his office shelf, just waiting to be taken seriously. And maybe Harlan would have given it a second glance, if it weren't for his preconceived notions hardened through childhood that it was nothing more than the frantic scribblings of a lunatic. After all, who in their right mind would think that monsters were real, or that a vast geological treasure lay undiscovered to this day beneath the mountains south of Las Vegas. His belief that the journal's contents were mostly nonsense had come from his old man, who had inherited the same sentiment from his own father. Harlan had never forgotten the stories contained within the journal, because they made such an impression on him as a kid. Which was why his thoughts turned to those journal entries when he saw the news report detailing the deaths in the mine.

Harlan opened the journal and thumbed through the pages until he came to the relevant section. The book had deteriorated over the years, with heavy foxing. The glue binding the spine had become brittle, and some pages had detached and were now loose. The writing was hard to read. Once black, it had turned a rusty brown thanks to the iron gall ink so prevalent at the time.

But Harlan wasn't interested in the pages of untidy, scrawled handwriting. What he wanted lay folded between the pages. A larger sheet of loose-leaf paper, itself showing signs of age. He removed it carefully and laid it out on the desk, careful not to damage the fragile document.

Unfolded, it was many times the size of the journal within which it had been stored. Harlan hunched over it. It was one of several maps of the Ghost Canyon Mine contained within the journal, and by far the most complete. Harlan suspected it was also the final one drawn by his ancestor, Travis Biggs, before the man went missing. It showed a labyrinth of tunnels that ran for miles. Some connected with each other, while others were dead ends. A cross-sectional view drawn beneath the main map showed the mine laid out on three distinct levels.

The map didn't explicitly indicate where the alleged untapped gold deposit was within the mine system—Travis

Biggs was not that stupid—but Harlan thought he'd figured it out already from the scribbled entries in the journal itself. What he was looking for right now was another entrance close enough to the gold to snag samples, while being far enough from Haley and those FBI agents to do so undetected. He already knew that the untapped lode, if his hunch was correct, was a good distance from the entrance they had visited earlier, so it stood to reason there would be another adit, or even a ventilation shaft. And when he worked his way back from the presumed location of the gold, he came across it. Just as he thought, there was a shaft running at a low incline from the surface on the other side of the canyon. It would be a bumpy ride to get there, even in Wagner's truck, but worth it. Now all he needed to do was make copies of the map—he didn't want to ruin the original—for the men Wagner Mitchell was hopefully rounding up right at this moment.

He felt a surge of optimism.

If all went well, his troubles would be over by day's end. He stood and went to the living room, poured himself a celebratory drink, which he polished off in one big gulp. He was about to pour a second, when there was a knock at the door.

Wagner Mitchell stood on the other side.

"All done, boss," he said, stepping into the penthouse. "I found a pair of suitable candidates."

"Expendable?" Harlan smiled. Everything was falling into place.

"Both here illegally. No family in the US. Came across the border last month in the back of a truck. I bet they're not even using their real names."

"Perfect." Harlan went back to the living room and poured himself another drink.

"You figure out how we're going to get in, yet?"

Harlan nodded. "There's a map on my desk. Take it down to the administration office and make copies."

"Right." Wagner turned to follow Harlan's orders.

"And be careful with it. It's really old. Fragile. I don't want it damaged."

"Sure thing." Wagner turned back to Harlan. "When do you want to go up to the mine?"

"As soon as possible. Make those copies first, and then we'll leave."

Wagner nodded.

"When you're done with the map, bring it straight back up here."

"Anything else?"

"Make sure the men have tools. Pickaxes would be best. Flashlights too."

"On it." Wagner moved to leave, but then stopped. "I hope you're right about all this, Harlan."

"Me too," Harlan replied. "Because I've kind of grown attached to my kneecaps, and I'd like to keep them."

CHAPTER THIRTY-EIGHT

Decker was stumped. Robyn's account of the town's history, fascinating as it was, did nothing to shed light upon what was killing people inside the mine. When she left after forty-five minutes to check on the construction crew, who had now moved on to the hotel's third floor, he stayed on in the saloon. He sat on a barstool and stared absentmindedly into the smoky antique mirrors lining the bar back. After a few minutes he caught a movement in the reflection and turned to see Carlton enter clutching a bottle of bourbon.

"What are you doing here?" The old man asked with a scowl. "Shouldn't you be running around looking for the monster?"

"Bit early in the day for the hard stuff, don't you think?" Decker shot back, eyeing the liquor bottle clutched in Carlton's gnarly fingers.

"You try spending a lifetime living alone out here in this godforsaken desert and then we'll talk about when it's suitable to start drinking." Carlton stomped across the bar and climbed onto a stool as far from Decker as possible.

"Your choice to live here, surely?" Decker watched the old

man twist the cap off the bottle, then reach over and grab a glass. "You could've gone somewhere else."

"Hardly. Someone had to stay here and look after this place, and it wasn't going to be either of my brothers. They were too busy with their fancy careers and families." Carlton poured himself a generous measure of whiskey. "They wouldn't sell the place either. Said it had sentimental value, even though neither of them ever bothered to come here."

"And does it?"

"Does it what?" Carlton asked.

"Have sentimental value?"

"Hardly. It's a big fat mistake, more like."

"Why do you say that?" Decker asked.

"Didn't Robyn just tell you the history of the place? I heard the two of you when I came over here. Thought I'd wait outside until you were done."

"She did."

"Then you know how the town came to be in our family."

Decker nodded. "Your grandfather came out here to work on the Hoover Dam back in the 1930s. He came across the place and fell in love with the town, so he bought the land."

"That's the romantic version. The reality was different. My grandfather did come to work on the Boulder Dam, as they called it at the time. But he didn't fall in love with this land. When the Federal Government erected Boulder City to house the workers, he realized this ghost town wasn't far away. By then, gambling was legalized. He figured he could capitalize by building a town full of casinos and loose women right here where you're sitting."

"But he didn't."

"Obviously. The Federal Government wasn't too keen on its workers gambling and carousing and did all they could to curtail it. It was during prohibition after all. My grandfather couldn't find any backers for his idea, and he didn't have the money to do it himself. He'd spent every dime buying this dusty scrap of scorched earth. Of course, it didn't help that the mob had moved in and were putting their money into Fremont Street."

"What happened after that?"

"What do you think happened?" Carlton sipped his drink and observed Decker with beady eyes. "My grandfather was a failure. Worse than that, he was broke. He ended up going back to Chicago, where he was born, and left the town to rot and ruin. Died without ever stepping foot in the place again."

"Then how did you end up here?" Decker asked.

"I grew up hearing stories about the town. When I was old enough, I came out to Vegas and got a job in one of the new hotels on the Strip. Figured I'd save my money and build a house out here. As you can see, I didn't. I ended up fixing one of the old shacks and I've been living here ever since. It'll be going on five decades next year."

"That's a long time," Decker said. "You must know a lot about the area."

"I know some." Carlton gulped the last of his whiskey and poured another. He didn't offer Decker a drink. "More than Robyn, that's for sure."

"Great," Decker said. He took his phone out and pulled up an image of the three mummified prospectors the geologist had found huddled deep in the mine. He stood and approached Carlton, holding the phone out so the old man could see it. "Did you know there were bodies in the mine?"

"How would I know that?" Carlton studied the image, scratching his fingers across the gray stubble lining his chin. "First I heard of it was when that geologist ran back here screaming blue murder."

"You'd never been inside the mine?"

"Never. The entrance was blasted back around the time the town was originally abandoned. Local legend claims they did it because they thought the mine was haunted, but the truth is, it was tapped out and dangerous."

"What about this?" Decker brought up another photo. An enlargement of the strange symbol scratched in the earth near the dead men. "You ever see this symbol before? Do you know what it means?"

"Nope. Can't say that I do." Carlton shook his head. "Looks kinda Native American to me."

"Is there anyone around these parts who *would* know what it means?"

"I thought you people did everything on the internet these days. Why don't you try that?"

"I did." Decker returned the phone to his pocket. "Came up with some similar symbols, but not this exact one, and without knowing what it's called I have no idea where to search."

"Shame."

"Well?"

"Well, what?" Carlton replied.

"Do you know of anyone I can talk to?"

Carlton shrugged. "Maybe. There's a Paiute reservation a drive away up near the top end of Red Rock Canyon. You could try there. Don't know how much help they'll be."

"Thanks." Decker heard a noise behind him. He glanced around to see Special Agent Barnes standing there.

"Hey. I got a name for that plate."

"Let me guess, not from Albuquerque."

"You must be psychic." Barnes licked his lips. "The registered owner of that pickup is one Wagner Mitchell. Single. Forty-four years old."

"You have an address?"

"Sure do. He owns a condo off the Strip. Figure it might be worth knocking on his door. You up for a field trip?"

"Hell, yeah. Lead the way." Decker turned back to Carlton. "And you, take it easy on that hooch."

"Any particular reason?"

"I can think of several," Decker said. "But the fact that it's not even two in the afternoon seems like a fine one."

CHAPTER THIRTY-NINE

For the second time that day, Harlan sat in the passenger seat of Wagner Mitchell's truck as they drove out of town and through Boulder City, toward Haley. This time, though, they were not alone. Behind them, in the truck's rear cab, were a pair of Mexican laborers pulled off their job installing new floors inside the casino.

The two workers, introduced to Harlan as Hector Ramirez and Emmanuel Garcia, sat in silence, occasionally exchanging glances, but otherwise making no attempt to talk. They spoke little English, and Harlan wasn't sure if they fully understood why he and Wagner were driving them out into the desert, or if they even cared. They knew enough to comprehend there was extra money in the unusual task they were being asked to perform, and that appeared to satisfy them. Had they realized the danger that awaited them, they would have reacted differently.

Wagner initially followed the same route as before, but then he took a different road into the canyon and bypassed the ghost town altogether. He followed his dash-mounted GPS, into which he had already fed the coordinates of the second entrance

Harlan had found on his ancestor's old map by matching it with topographical features and roads on its modern digital counterpart online. The coordinates would not be completely accurate, because there was no way to pinpoint the exact location of the mine entrance, but it would get them close enough.

"You sure you want to go through with this?" Wagner asked as they left the paved road behind and bounced up a rocky trail toward their destination. "If there really is some sort of creature in that mine, those men will be walking into a pretty dangerous situation."

"Quiet, you fool," Harlan said. "They can hear everything we're saying."

"And they can't understand a word of it." Wagner brought the truck to a halt.

"Why are you stopping?"

"To prove we can talk freely." Wagner twisted to look at the two Mexicans in the back seat. "Hey guys, how's it going?"

The two men grinned but said nothing.

"We're giving you extra pay for this job. You understand?"

The men grinned again, and this time they nodded.

"And then we're going to set you free in the desert and hunt you for sport. Understand?"

This elicited the same response as before.

"See?" Wagner said. "What did I tell you?"

"All right, you proved your point." Harlan was eager to get to the mine entrance. It was already mid-afternoon, and they only had a few hours of daylight left.

"Damn right, I did." Wagner started moving again, gripping the steering wheel tight to control the truck as the terrain deteriorated. A few minutes later, the GPS announced they had arrived at their destination.

Harlan unclipped his seatbelt and leaned forward, peering through the windshield at the desolate desert landscape. After a while he let out a frustrated grunt. "I see nothing that looks like a mine entrance. Are you sure this is the place?"

"I'm sure. I verified the landmarks on the hand-drawn map against Google Earth. Maybe your great-great-grandfather marked the entrance wrong."

"If he did, we're screwed."

"Or maybe it got covered up over the years." Wagner opened the truck door and jumped out. "Why don't we look around?"

"Good idea." Harlan exited the truck and shielded his eyes against the sun, scanning the rocky outcrops and steep slopes surrounding them.

Wagner was cutting across the patch of flat ground upon which they parked toward a narrow crevice clogged with sagebrush. He pulled the bushes aside and stepped through, then shouted for Harlan. "I think I found it."

Harlan rushed over to the spot where his general manager had disappeared. He edged his way past large boulders and pushed the sagebrush aside.

Wagner stood ten feet away in a cleft between the rocks, pointing at a square entrance in the rock face, locked by white planks nailed into thick support beams at the opening's edges. A faded sign attached to the planks read, DANGER-MINE SHAFT-KEEP OUT.

"Good job," Harlan said, barely able to keep the excitement from his voice. "We'll need to get those planks off. You brought a crowbar, right?"

"Sure did," Wagner replied. He climbed back out of the cleft toward his boss. "It's in the truck bed along with the pickaxes. I brought a sledgehammer too. It never hurts to be prepared."

"Perfect." Harlan stood aside to let Wagner pass and followed him back to the truck. He realized the Mexican laborers were still sitting inside, apparently waiting for someone to tell them what to do. "What's up with them?"

"Beats me." Wagner pounded on the quad cab's rear door and

motioned for the men to get out, then led them behind the truck and dropped the tailgate. He handed both men a pickaxe, backpack, and flashlight. Finally, he grabbed a heavy crowbar and started back toward the mine entrance with the laborers in tow.

The crowbar made quick work of the planks, which were rotten and probably decades old. They practically disintegrated when Wagner pried them off. The mine entrance beyond was a yawning black chasm. Harlan smelled fetid, stale air. He wondered if some animal had crawled in there to die.

"You got the map copies showing the location where you want them to go?" Wagner asked.

"Right here." Harlan clutched three sheets of paper in his hand, which he'd grabbed when they returned to the truck. He handed one to each of the laborers and kept the third for himself. He pointed to a mark on the map representing the entrance they were currently standing beside and then motioned to an X drawn in red ink over one of the tunnels. He traced his fingertip back from the entrance to the X, to show the Mexicans where to go.

They watched with narrowed eyes, then nodded their understanding.

Harlan glanced toward Wagner. "Do they know what they're looking for when they get there?"

"Sure." Wagner confirmed. "I had a work supervisor back at the casino translate my instructions into Spanish. I made it clear what we were looking for and how they were to extract it."

"You didn't mention gold, did you?"

"Do I look that dumb?" Wagner retorted. "They think we're looking for samples of quartz to use for a themed mine display in the hotel lobby."

"That's a pretty weak cover story." Harlan wasn't pleased. "We could get ahold of that stuff anywhere."

"I told them your ancestor worked this mine, and you wanted the real deal. Sentimental reasons."

"Still sounds pretty lame, if you ask me."

"Who cares?" Wagner replied. "They're here, aren't they?"

"I suppose." Harlan glanced toward the sky. The sun was already dipping low. "Can we hurry this up?"

Wagner huffed, obviously annoyed by Harlan's attitude, but said nothing. Instead, he motioned for the laborers to enter the mine.

They nodded, their faces displaying no discernible emotion, and switched on the flashlights. A moment later they stepped over the threshold, pickaxes in hand, and were soon swallowed up by darkness.

CHAPTER FORTY

Decker sat in the passenger seat of the government issued black Crown Victoria, driven by Special Agent Jackson Barnes. They followed route 95 toward the interstate. This would bring them through Henderson, into Las Vegas, and Wagner Mitchell's high-rise condo unit overlooking the Strip. At least, if the address on his vehicle registration was correct.

As they approached Boulder City, Decker spoke. "I'm surprised that Agent Fowler didn't want to come on our little jaunt."

"It was our lead. He figured the two of us could handle it," Barnes replied.

"Speaking of which, how *are* we going to handle it?" Decker asked. "We're still not sure how those two bozos fit into any of this, other than lying about their identities."

"Which is good enough reason for me to think they have something to hide. Innocent people don't panic and make up stories when confronted by the law." Barnes glanced in his rearview mirror, then pulled out around a slow-moving dump truck that was trundling along the road as if it had nowhere better to be. "Even if they have nothing to do with whatever killed those folks inside that mine, they were up to something, for sure."

"And it's not like we have any other leads," Decker said. "I've learned over the years that you can never tell where an investigation will take you. Even seemingly inconsequential details, or unrelated events, have a habit of proving useful."

"My thoughts exactly," Barnes agreed. "Since I have the FBI badge, I'll take the lead when we get there."

"If you like," Decker said. "A suggestion, though. Let's not mention anything about the deaths in the mine or the creature. I'd like to see if he trips over himself and lets something slip that he shouldn't know."

"They reported the deaths on TV, even though there was a media blackout. Probably some loose lipped sergeant in the LVMPD."

"They didn't report everything."

"And if he knows details that weren't released, we'll have cause to take him into custody and continue the conversation in an interrogation room."

"Let's not forget the other guy," Decker said. "We still need to find out who he is."

"I haven't forgotten that. That's one of the first things I'm going to ask. And he'd better tell me the truth this time."

"If we're lucky, they'll be together."

"When have you ever been that lucky?"

"Rarely," Decker agreed. "It would sure make this easier though, don't you think?"

"Then let's keep our fingers crossed that—" Barnes cell phone rang before he could finish. He glanced down toward it in the compartment between the seats and furrowed his brow. "It's Fowler."

"I wonder what he wants?" A sense of foreboding overcame Decker.

"Only one way to find out." Barnes snatched up the phone

and answered, putting it on speaker so that Decker could hear. "Hey. What's going on?"

"A hell of a lot," Fowler's voice said on the other end of the line. "Family out for a day trip made a gruesome discovery this afternoon. Two bodies at a campsite, pretty mutilated. They called in to Vegas PD, who gave me the heads up."

"Aw, shit." Barnes exchanged a quick look with Decker. "You think it's related to the incidents in the mine?"

"Can't be sure until I have more information, but it feels like a hell of a coincidence. Crime scene is less than a mile away as the crow flies. I borrowed Robyn Miller's car. I'm heading there now. I'll text you the coordinates. You can meet me there."

"Sure thing. We haven't even made it halfway to Vegas yet."

"Great. Then it won't take you long to get there." Fowler's phone signal was breaking up. "I'm entering the canyon. I'll send that text now in case I lose service."

"Roger that," Barnes replied, but Fowler had already hung up. He slowed the car, swung the wheel hard, and pulled a U-turn to head back in the other direction. "I guess our investigation just took a turn for the worse."

"Looks that way," Decker replied. He hoped the newly discovered bodies had nothing to do with the creature in the mine, but deep down he was sure they did.

CHAPTER FORTY-ONE

When Decker and Barnes arrived at the coordinates Special Agent Fowler had sent, they discovered a hive of activity. Police cruisers were parked blocking the trail leading into the site where the two bodies lay, light bars silently flashing. Beyond this stood a couple of unmarked cars and two white vans-one marked Crime Scene Investigations and the other, Coroner.

Barnes came to a stop behind the police cruisers and together he and Decker made their way toward the activity, stepping between the parked vehicles. A uniformed officer came toward them, raising a hand to wave them off until Barnes flashed his FBI credentials.

As they approached the scene, Decker saw a red Jeep Cherokee parked several feet from a small tent. Nearby were the remains of a fire pit. But it was the two bodies, both laying on their back, that drew his attention. They were young, mid-20s. A man and a woman, probably a couple. Even before he drew close, Decker could see the massive injuries to their torsos. The skin had been flayed back, abdomens ripped open. A medical examiner was kneeling next to the woman, examining the corpse, while a crime scene photographer was circling the other victim snapping photographs.

When they drew close, Special Agent Fowler turned to meet them, a stony expression upon his face. He looked at Decker. "Hope you're not squeamish."

"I was a homicide cop in New York. Not squeamish."

"Good. Because whatever tore these two up, did a fine job of it." Fowler stepped aside to let his partner and Decker move closer. "Glad I only had a light lunch, or it might make an encore appearance."

Decker doubted that. Fowler was a seasoned FBI agent unlikely to be phased by the sight of a corpse, no matter what its condition. He glanced toward the bodies. "What do we know so far?"

"Victims are Darwin Andoe and Tiffany Kent. Twenty-six and twenty-four, according to their driver's licenses. Obviously out here together. They were sharing one tent."

"How were they found?"

"Family on vacation from Pittsburgh. They wanted to see a real Western ghost town. They found a Yelp review of the unofficial tours that old man Carlton used to give and thought it would be a neat afternoon out. Hadn't even heard of the killings in the mine."

"So how did they end up here?"

"Took a wrong turn. Don't ask me how when every car has GPS."

"Huh. That was fortuitous. Might have been weeks before these bodies were found otherwise."

"Someone would have come across them, eventually. This area is a pretty popular camping spot. I came out here a few times myself back in the day, when it still felt like an adventure to sleep outdoors on the hard ground instead of in a soft bed."

"You don't strike me as the camping type," Decker said, looking at Fowler. "No offense."

"No offense taken. I'm older and wiser now. Camping just seems like an unnecessary hardship."

Decker's eyes drifted back to the pair of corpses. "We have a time of death?"

"Sometime between midnight and six, according to the coroner. We should be able to pin that down further once we get them back to the lab."

Decker scratched his chin. The girl was wearing flannel pajamas, or rather, what was left of them. The male was wearing jeans and a T-shirt, but no shoes or socks. A pistol lay nearby in the dirt. Decker's gaze strayed from the bodies toward the tent. The flap was open. A ruffled sleeping bag was visible within. "They were asleep before the attack. Their killer must've woken them."

"Why do you say that?" Fowler asked.

"Look at the sleeping bag inside the open tent. Plus, the man isn't wearing shoes or socks, which denotes he dressed in a hurry. The girl is still in her night attire, so she probably sent him out first to look around and then followed when she became worried about him. There's a gun too. If you check, I bet you'll find it's been fired, but it didn't do any good."

"You can't possibly know that."

"Sure, I can. Whatever roused them from their sleep was disturbing enough to warrant grabbing a gun before investigating. Under the circumstances, it's more than likely they would use that gun when faced with a deadly threat. Obviously, it was a waste of time because both victims are deceased." Decker studied the surrounding area. "There isn't any blood to indicate they injured their attacker, and no third body, so firing the gun achieved nothing."

"Makes sense." Fowler nodded.

"And we don't need to speculate on the time of death. It was around 2 AM."

"The gunshots you heard last night."

"Precisely. I bet we're not more than a mile from the ghost town. A mile and a half at most. The sound of gunshots can travel pretty far, especially in a landscape like this where they can echo off the rocks and canyon walls. There's also no noise pollution to mask the shots out here."

"That still leaves the question of who killed these people," Barnes said, speaking for the first time since they'd arrived at the site.

"Those wounds don't look like a human made them. These unfortunate people were violently ripped open. Remind you of anything?"

"The search and rescue team member. Sasha Martin."

"Precisely."

"You think it's the creature from the mine," Fowler said.

"Yes." Decker glanced at his watch, then looked at Fowler. "Did you speak to the ME's office about my request to view her body?"

"I did. They performed the autopsy but haven't released the remains yet. They're holding them until we give permission."

"Then that should be our next stop," Decker said. "I'd like to compare the wounds on these people to those of Sasha Martin. If they match, it will rule out a regular animal attack."

"What about the plate we ran?" Barnes asked. "Wagner Mitchell?"

"That will have to wait. This is more important." Decker turned away from the bodies. "I'd like to go right now, if you don't mind."

The two FBI agents exchanged glances, then Barnes turned toward his car. "Come on, then. I'll drive you. Afterward we can stop at In-N-Out and you can buy me a burger."

"Fair enough," Decker replied. He turned toward Fowler. "Want us to bring one back for you?"

"Nah." Fowler shook his head. "After spending the last hour looking at the remains of those campers, I'm not sure I'm in the mood for ground meat."

CHAPTER FORTY-TWO

The sun had dropped below the mountains and long shadows crept across the twilight landscape. Harlan Biggs looked around, peering nervously into the gathering darkness. It was two hours since the men went into the mine and there had been no sign of them since. Now Harlan sat on a boulder near the entrance, with Wagner on a similar rock on the opposite side. He wished they'd waited until the next morning to come out here, when there would be more hours of daylight available. But he hadn't thought it would take this long to get the samples of gold ore out of the mine.

"What are they doing in there?" He asked, rubbing his hands together. The temperature was dropping. The weather forecast said it would get down to fifty degrees overnight. He didn't want to be out here when it did. "I hope they didn't get lost."

"Me too," Wagner replied. "It's hard to find good labor."

"Did you bring a spare flashlight?"

"Yeah. Two of them. They're in the back of the truck. Why?"

"Because if those Mexicans don't come back soon, you'll have to go in and find them."

"Like hell I will." Wagner shook his head. "The whole point

of using laborers was to avoid dealing with whatever is lurking in there ourselves."

"Well, we need to do something. I don't want to stand out here all night."

"And you think I do?" Wagner let out a disgruntled huff. He stared into the sooty darkness beyond the mine entrance. "How much longer do you intend to wait before we give up on this?"

"I don't know," Harlan admitted. He was tempted to have Wagner drive him back to the hotel right now and retreat to his penthouse suite to regroup. But that would solve nothing, and the clock was still ticking. He had less than two weeks to renegotiate his deal with Oscar Rossi or end up as a piñata for the mobster's goons. He couldn't afford to waste time. "I sure wish we'd thought to give them two-way radios to keep in contact with us."

"What good would that have done?" Wagner asked. "We couldn't even get them to say anything in the truck, let alone over a radio."

"It would be better than nothing."

"And it's moot. We didn't give them radios, so it doesn't matter."

"Which brings us back to the question, what do we do now?"

"I guess we wait," Wagner said. "We don't have a choice."

"That doesn't work for me." Harlan stood and fought his way back through the sagebrush toward the truck. The desert fell away into gloom on all sides. The flashlights were sitting in a cardboard box in the truck's bed. He grabbed them and clicked one on. Playing the beam across the ground ahead of him, Harlan picked his way back to Wagner.

"Here," he said, offering his general manager the second flashlight. "I brought this back for you."

"I'm still not going inside that mine," Wagner said, accepting the offering.

"Have you forgotten I'm your boss?"

"And have *you* forgotten that I can quit whenever I want. I'm your general manager, not a prospector. None of this is in my job description."

"Would you rather work for Oscar Rossi?"

"No," Wagner answered. "But I don't want to go in there, either. Why don't we just go back to the hotel and worry about this tomorrow? There are plenty of other workers. I'll just round up a couple more."

"And what if they come across their friends in there?" Harlan asked. "What if they find them dead?"

"Who cares as long as they find what we want?" Wagner said. "It's not like they'll run to the cops or anything. Not given their status as illegals."

"Maybe." Harlan still felt it would be a shame to waste an entire day. They were already here. But if the men didn't come back, they would have no choice. He decided to compromise. "Why don't we both go into the mine, just a little way, and see if we can find them."

"How far are we talking?" Wagner asked, suspicious.

"I don't know, far enough to see down the tunnel."

"All right. But we're only going a little past the entrance, no further. I'm not running around in there."

"Deal." Harlan took a step toward the mine entrance and shined his flashlight inside. "You go first."

"Not likely, you'll stay out here."

"Fine. I'll go first, but make sure you follow behind." Harlan hesitated a moment, building his courage, then stepped past the support beams holding up the entrance. He moved slowly, sweeping the flashlight beam across the ground ahead of him. At his rear, he heard his general manager's footfalls.

"It sure is black in here," Wagner said. "How far inside the mine do you think the gold is?"

"Beats me," Harlan said. "Who knows if that map was to scale. It might be a mile deep, or five miles."

"Great. No wonder they haven't come back yet."

Harlan came to a halt and waited for Wagner to draw level. He pointed his flashlight down the empty tunnel. "This is a waste of time. Maybe you're right. Let's go back to the hotel. We'll find more workers and try again tomorrow."

"And if the Mexicans find their way out?"

"They can thumb a ride back to Vegas." Harlan was already heading back toward the entrance. "Or they can sit here and wait for us to come back. Either way, I don't care."

"Suits me." Wagner hurried to keep up with his boss.

They stepped back out into the cool desert air. Harlan pushed through the bushes clogging the path leading up to the mine on his way back to the truck. When he realized Wagner wasn't following, he turned back, perplexed. "You coming, or what?"

Wagner was back near the mine entrance, peering inside. "They might be coming. I hear something."

"About freaking time." Harlan took a step forward, eager to see what the two men had found inside the tunnels. "Tell them to hurry."

But Wagner didn't answer. He stood transfixed, gazing into the darkness beyond the mine entrance.

"Wagner?" Harlan drew closer. "You hear me?"

Still nothing.

Harlan was about to weave his way through the prickly bushes one more time on his way back to the general manager, when he noticed an emaciated figure in the tunnel, approaching through the darkness.

He faltered, stopped.

His heart raced.

A blast of chill air swept past him. And with it came a foul odor, like rotting flesh. But worst of all were the eyes. Two glowing red coals that held him, enthralled. While inside his head a soft voice whispered, and even though he didn't understand the language, he knew what it wanted.

Yet he couldn't run, despite the terror that tightened his chest and made his eyes grow wide. He willed himself to move but could not make his legs obey. And when the creature came into view, a demon conjured from the depths of hell with a rakish frame and translucent skin stretched so tight it looked like it would tear, he still didn't run. Because even though Harlan Biggs knew that he would die if he stayed there, even though he saw the horrific things it was doing at that moment to his friend, Wagner Mitchell, a part of Harlan embraced the voice inside his head that promised everything would be alright. That if he just let it happen, a swift release from this world was imminent, and all his problems would go away. After a little pain, of course...

CHAPTER FORTY-THREE

The Clark County Coroner's Office was a squat one-story tan colored building occupying an entire block west of the interstate in downtown Las Vegas not far from the outlet mall and Fremont Street, where legal gambling first sprung up in the city back in 1931.

It was getting dark, and Decker could see a glow settling over the city to the east, where the downtown casinos and hotels were firing up millions of twinkling lights and neon signs to draw tourists into their glittering dens of excess. Towering above it all was The Strat Hotel, taller than every other building.

Special Agent Barnes pulled into the parking lot and stopped beside a row of white SUVs bearing the Coroner's Office emblem. They made their way to the public entrance at the front of the building. The office was already closed for the day, but Barnes made a call on his cell phone, and soon a man wearing black scrubs unlocked the doors and let them inside before disappearing back into the building. Moments later a second man arrived, this time wearing a white lab coat.

"Jackson, it's been a while," the man said, referring to Barnes by his first name.

"The I-15 Strangler case," Barnes replied. He nodded toward Decker. "This is my colleague, John Decker. He's a specialist on loan from another agency."

"Pleased to meet you, Agent Decker." The man said. "I'm Doctor Sam Callow."

"Pleased to meet you too," Decker said. "And it's not Agent Decker. Mister will do. Or better yet, just call me John."

"My apologies," Callow replied. "You're here about the Sasha Martin case, is that correct?"

"Yes," Decker said. "We'd love to get your opinion and also see the body."

"Sure." Callow motioned for them to follow him toward the door marked staff only. He produced a key card and swiped it through a reader, then opened the door and held it for them. As they made their way to the pathology lab, he spoke over his shoulder. "I have to say, this was not your run-of-the-mill autopsy."

"What do you mean?" Decker asked.

"We get a lot of suspicious deaths come through. People who've met violent ends. Gunshots, stabbings, suicides. We've had the occasional animal attack too, but we rarely see these kinds of wounds inflicted on a body."

"Really?"

"It was like an animal attack times ten. If I didn't know better, I'd say an entire pack of animals set upon this poor woman. The damage to her abdomen was extreme. There were signs that the killer was attempting to eat her internal organs. There are bites taken out of her liver," Callow led them to a door marked Pathology Room Two. He opened it and they entered. "She's in here. I had the remains transferred from the cooler after the viewing request came through."

"Thank you," Barnes said. He glanced toward a metal dissection table where a body lay under a white cloth. "Is that her?"

"Yes." Callow crossed to the table. "I have to warn you, it's not a pretty sight."

"We'll be fine," Decker said. He motioned for Callow to remove the sheet.

"We've just come from a crime scene containing two victims that we suspect were killed by the same creature that attacked Sasha," Special Agent Barnes said. "Your colleague, Doctor Lyle, was there."

"Oh, right. Out near Ghost Canyon?"

"Yes."

"I was there when the call came in. Thankfully, I wasn't the ME on duty, or it would've been me driving out there, and I'd like to go home on time tonight."

"We won't keep you long, then," Decker said.

"I appreciate that." Callow gripped the edges of the sheet and folded it back to expose the upper half of Sasha Martin's body.

Her skin was pallid and tinged blue. A Y-shaped incision, now sewn up, ran from her neck down between her breasts and followed the line of her rib cage. But it was the mess of torn flesh beneath her chest that drew Decker's attention.

"Remind you of anything?" He asked, looking sideways at Barnes.

"Yeah. Looks very much like the wounds on the two bodies we just left."

"I think it's safe to assume the same culprit killed all three."

"I concur." Barnes nodded his agreement. "Still doesn't get us anywhere closer to identifying who or what is responsible, except that it was in the Ghost Canyon Mine at the same time as Sasha."

"It's unlikely a human did this," Callow said. "It has all the hallmarks of an animal attack, but it's too..." He paused a moment, searching for the right word. "Frenetic. I've seen bites from coyotes. Black bear attacks. I even attended the autopsy of a woman mauled by a mountain lion several years ago when I was working in California. This is nothing like those. The weirdest thing is the lack of defensive wounds. Normally there would be bites and scratches to the forearms and hands from the victim's attempts to fend off the attack. We see none of that here. Frankly, it's perplexing. Honestly, I have no idea what kind of wild animal could have done this."

"That's because it wasn't a wild animal," Decker said. "It was something much more dangerous. A supernatural creature."

"A what now?" Callow looked at Decker as if he'd misheard. "Did you say supernatural?"

"He did," Special Agent Barnes confirmed. "And that information is to go no further than the three of us."

"Don't worry about that," Callow replied. "I have no intention of mentioning the supernatural to anyone or putting it in my report. Frankly, if that's your working theory, I think the pair of you are nuts."

"Wouldn't be the first time someone came to that conclusion," Decker said ruefully. "Will you send me a copy of the report when you have it?"

"Sure. It's going to be a few days, though. We're pretty backed up right now."

Decker nodded. He turned to Barnes. "I think we've seen enough to confirm that we're dealing with one assailant."

"Agreed." Barnes let his gaze drift to the dissection table as Dr. Callow replaced the sheet, hiding Sasha from view. "Which means it's not in the mine anymore."

"Maybe," Decker replied thoughtfully. "But Sasha's attack occurred in the mine where it's dark. The campers were killed in the middle of the night, also under the cloak of darkness. My hunch is that the creature does not like daylight. And don't forget the mine entrance was left unlocked last night."

"You think it came out, attacked those poor people, and then returned to the mine before dawn?"

"That's exactly what I think. If I'm right, it's been stuck in those tunnels since pioneer days. It would return to the place it knows."

"At least we can rest easy tonight then," Barnes said. "You padlocked the mine entrance after we ran those two guys off."

"I did," Decker said. "I wasn't sure if it was the right thing to do at the time, but now the decision appears to have been prudent."

Callow cleared his throat to let Decker and Barnes know he was still there. "Gentlemen? If it's all the same with you, I'd like to get this body back to the cooler and finish up my day."

"Absolutely." Decker shook the man's hand. "You've been very helpful."

"Anytime," Callow said. "If you'd like to follow me, I'll show you both out."

CHAPTER FORTY-FOUR

After they left the coroner's office, Decker and Barnes made their way over to the Strip and stopped at the condominium tower address the license plate check had turned up. They parked inside the first level garage but when they arrived at the entrance found it locked, with a key code required for entry. It only took Special Agent Barnes a few minutes to get them in. He placed a call to the Las Vegas PD, who had an emergency access code in their computer database. This was standard procedure with restricted access buildings. Decker had used many such codes to gain entry to similar apartment and condo blocks when he was with the NYPD.

They crossed the lobby and took the elevator to the eighth floor, but when they arrived at Wagner Mitchell's door, there was no reply. They waited a few minutes and tried again, to no avail. Wagner Mitchell was not home.

"What now?" Barnes asked. "You want to hang around a while and see if he shows up?"

"Nah. He might not be home for hours," Decker replied.

"Or he might not come back tonight at all," Barnes observed.

"He could've gone home with a date, or even be out of town entirely for all we know."

"It's unlikely he's out of town. We only ran into him this morning." Decker looked back along the corridor. "I can't see the point in staying here, though."

"Me either." Barnes started back toward the elevator. "I'm getting hungry, and you owe me that burger."

"I was hoping you'd forgotten about that."

"Not likely," Barnes pushed the elevator call button. The car must've still been there because the doors slid open immediately. He stepped inside and waited for Decker. "I never forget a free burger."

By the time they arrived back in Haley, it was almost nine o'clock. Special Agent Fowler had returned from the crime scene in the desert and was now sitting at a table in the saloon, making idle conversation with Robyn. Tieg lay at their feet, his head between his paws. When they entered the bar, his tail wagged.

Barnes petted him and told the senior agent about their visit to the coroner's office. Fowler, in turn, filled them in from his end.

When they were done, Robyn stood up. "If the pair of you are hungry, I still have some food left over from dinner in the kitchen. It's not fancy. Just chicken salad, you're welcome to it."

"That's mighty nice of you," Barnes said. "But we stopped and ate on the way back."

Robyn nodded. "Are we going to be safe tonight? Agent Fowler said two more people died. It sounds dreadful."

"I wouldn't worry yourself," Decker said. "The mine is secure. Whatever is inside, can't escape now."

"That makes me feel a better," Robyn said. "I still don't like the thought of that creature living in my mine. Have you figured out how to stop it yet?"

"No," Decker admitted. He still wasn't sure what the creature was, let alone if it could be vanquished. "My primary concern right now is making sure no one else gets hurt."

"Of course."

"As soon as we have a solution, you'll be the first to know." Decker glanced around. "Where's Carlton?"

"Beats me," Robyn replied. "He keeps to himself unless he's in here drinking. He's probably in that falling down cabin of his."

"I'm not sure him being there is a good idea," Decker said. "I'm pretty confident that we're safe here in town, but I would feel better if everyone were in one location given the circumstances. I know the two of you don't get on very well, but it might be for the best if he stayed in the hotel until we resolve this situation."

"He won't do that. I've already tried. When Special Agent Fowler first told me what was going on, I told Carlton he could stay here. He declined, in no uncertain terms."

"He wasn't friendly about it either," Fowler said. "It's a good job he lives alone out in the middle of nowhere, because he wouldn't last ten minutes if he had to interact with folk on a regular basis. He's not what you'd call personable."

"That's the understatement of the year," Robyn agreed. "Although I think in this case, his dislike of me is the driving force as much as anything else."

"You tried, and that's all that counts," Decker said. "If he refuses to accept your hospitality, we can't force him."

"Still, I'd hate for anything to happen to the old coot." Robyn managed a weak smile. "He might be a rude and angry jerk, but he's still family."

"You're more forgiving than I would be," Fowler said. "There's no excuse for behavior like that."

"Maybe not." Robyn shrugged. "But that's Carlton, and he's a bit long in the tooth to learn new tricks."

"I meant what I said as a compliment to you, more than a recrimination of him," Fowler replied. "Actually, on second thought, I think it was both things at the same time."

"I know." Robyn's smile widened.

"And on that note, I think I'll bid you all goodnight." Fowler pushed his seat back and stood up. "Dead bodies create an inordinate amount of paperwork, and I should probably retire to my room and start in on it."

"Me too," Barnes said. He turned to Decker. "If you don't need me for anything else, I'll see you in the morning. I'd still like to chase down Wagner Mitchell and talk to him if you're up for it."

"Sure," Decker replied. "We'll go first thing after breakfast."

Barnes nodded and followed his partner out of the saloon toward the stairs.

Robyn watched them go, then turned to Decker. "I'm going to hit the hay too. I've had no time to myself since this all kicked off, and there's a period romance that I'm dying to finish reading. Gotta find out if the scullery maid gets her prince."

"If they are anything like the books Nancy reads, I have a feeling she will."

"Nancy?"

"My better half."

"Ah." Robyn nodded then turned toward her quarters.

Decker watched her go and headed toward the stairs. It was a little before ten o'clock, which would be almost midnight central time. It was late, but Nancy would still be awake to take his call, and he was looking forward to hearing her voice.

CHAPTER FORTY-FIVE

The screech jolted Decker awake, his eyes snapping open. He lay still and listened, waiting for the eerie sound to repeat itself, but there was only silence. He wondered if he'd dreamed the strangely plaintive cry, but he didn't think so.

It was still dark. The clock on his nightstand read 3 AM. The pillow under his head was wet, the sheets sticky. The room was too warm. He must've forgotten to set the temperature on the AC unit when he went to bed. He sat up and turned on the lamp next to the bed. Climbing out, he crossed to the air conditioning control panel near the bedroom door and adjusted the temperature down by five degrees. Soon there was a low hum as the unit kicked on.

Decker was about to climb back into bed when the sound came again, a plaintive high-pitched cry that rose in intensity before dying away.

He hadn't dreamed it after all. Was it a coyote? He didn't think so. He'd heard plenty of coyote calls and this had a different timbre.

Decker turned off the bedside lamp and went to the window. He pulled the curtain back enough to see outside. He was the only person sleeping on this side of the building. Robyn's quarters were at the rear behind the saloon bar, and the two FBI agents occupied rooms on the other side of the hall. Their windows faced the other direction. Only his own room looked down upon the ghost town's dusty main street, which was lit only by a single exterior lamp affixed to a pole near what had once been the town's assay office. He could still make out the faint lettering identifying it as such across the wooden building's weathered frontage.

He let his gaze wander over the landscape, from the road at the far end of town that led to Boulder City and Vegas, to the dirt trail winding up to the gold mine.

He saw nothing untoward.

Yet something had disturbed his slumber, and the cry sounded closer the second time.

He lingered at the window, unable to find the source of the odd caterwaul. Then, after a few minutes, he noticed a disturbance that hadn't been there before. It wasn't much. Just a shifting of blackness upon blackness. But it was enough to draw his attention. There was something there, after all, lurking in the shadows beyond the thin pool of light cast by the lone streetlamp.

Decker made a note of the location and let the curtain fall back into place. He went to the nightstand and opened the drawer, retrieving a black Sig Sauer M17 handgun provided to him by CUSP prior to his departure from Maine. It was the same model used by the Armed Forces, and his own employer issued it for the same reason. It was rugged, with good weight and tighter dispersion than many of its predecessors. The extended magazine contained twenty-one hollow point rounds. More than enough for most situations.

Decker closed the drawer and slipped from his room into the corridor beyond. The hotel was quiet. The odd warbling cries had not disturbed anyone else. He debated waking one or both of the FBI agents, but then changed his mind. He wasn't even sure what was out there. Most likely, it was some wild animal that strayed down from the mountains. It would probably be gone by the time he got outside.

Leaving the Feds to their slumber, Decker descended the stairs and crossed through the lobby to the hotel's main doors. As he reached out to pull the latch back, there was a noise to his rear. He turned and saw Tieg, Robyn's dog, standing several feet distant watching him. After a moment, the animal turned and padded back toward the small office behind the stairs, where the mutt slept at night.

Decker turned his attention back to the street. He opened the door a crack and stepped outside onto the veranda. Here he paused, looking to his left and right. He kept the gun to his side, ready to use it should the need arise. After affirming there were no immediate threats around the veranda, Decker turned his attention to the area where he'd seen movement from the hotel window.

Whatever had been moving through the darkness was not there now. Decker descended the steps. He was halfway to the spot where he had seen the shape slinking along, when he stopped, overcome by a sudden sense that he was no longer alone.

He held his breath, feeling exposed and vulnerable. A crazy thought popped into his head. That he'd been lured out here. That whatever he'd seen from the window above possessed enough intelligence to trick him into leaving the safety of the hotel. His immediate instinct was to retreat, even though he couldn't identify an actual threat. Was he just reacting to the quiet and spooky surroundings? He didn't think so. Decker had an innate ability to sense danger. It was what made him a good cop back in New York. It was how he'd survived more than one encounter with the supernatural over the past several months. Now his inner alarm was blaring as loud as it ever had.

Decker decided to trust his gut and go back inside. Until he caught a movement from the corner of his eye. He turned toward the leaning shell of a building with a broken and rotten boardwalk. And there, standing in the doorway, was a figure.

Decker drew a sharp breath. His heart pounded against his ribs. Blood rushed in his ears.

The figure stepped out of the gloom. It lurched toward him. An impossibly animated skeleton held together by dry, coriaceous skin mottled brown with age. And the sound when it walked... Like old bones grinding together.

Decker had seen enough.

He raised the gun and started backwards toward the hotel. His finger flexed on the trigger. But then he lost the will to fire. Worse, he couldn't tear his gaze from the creature's hypnotic eyes. Two burning pits of luminescent red fury that held him immobile as inexorably as if he were a fly caught in a spider's web. Then he understood why the other victims hadn't fled from this abomination. Because they couldn't. And as the skeletal demon bore down upon him, Decker understood something else too. He might very well be living the last moments of his life.

CHAPTER FORTY-SIX

Decker watched the creature advance toward him, unable to do anything about it. On some level he knew he should defend himself, or at least retreat, but the voice inside his head sent a different message. It overwhelmed his sense of self-preservation. Melted it away. It spoke softly and soothed his fears, even though he didn't understand the strange language. It told him not to worry, that everything would be over soon, and all he needed to do was keep watching those red burning eyes. And that's exactly what Decker did, even as another part of his mind struggled to break free of the creature's mesmeric gaze.

Then, from Decker's right, more movement. A blur of light-colored fur that sped forward and leaped at his chest. The impact sent him tumbling to the ground, breaking the spell. As Decker's senses returned, he found himself looking up into a pair of large brown eyes above a furry snout and lolling tongue. Tieg. The dog, apparently unaffected by the creature's aura, had rushed to push Decker out of harm's way.

Realizing the danger had not yet passed, Tieg jumped from Decker's chest and turned back toward the approaching menace, lips curled back, teeth barred. The dog let out a guttural, low growl, and stepped forward, ready to attack.

Decker had lost his grip on the gun when he fell. He scrambled to his knees and hunted for it, frantic, before spying the weapon several feet away laying on the dusty ground. He lunged forward, scooping it up. He rolled sideways and raised the gun in a fluid movement, bringing the creature into his sights. He was careful not to look at those eyes again, though. If he did that, it would all be over.

Tieg was tensed to pounce. The dog's hackles were up, fur bristling. The canine was about to attack. An effort that could only end one way.

Decker wasted no time.

Careful to fire above the defensive canine, he squeezed off three shots in rapid succession, each of which slammed into the creature's chest, driving it backwards. He stood no chance of killing it. He knew this already because a gun hadn't saved the two campers, whose remains he'd witnessed earlier that day. But it bought him time, and that was good enough.

Decker jumped to his feet and called to the dog, praying the animal would listen. For a moment Tieg ignored him, tensed to attack, then it turned and lopped over to Decker, casting a wary glance back toward the creature. He nudged the dog toward the hotel and ran alongside, taking the steps up to the veranda two at a time. He practically fell through the open doorway then turned and slammed it shut.

He leaned against the door, breathing heavily.

Robyn was standing in the lobby, eyes wide with fright. Moments later, the two FBI agents raced down the stairs, guns drawn.

"What's going on?" Barnes asked, going to the window, and peeking out. "I heard shots."

"The creature. It's outside," Decker said. He rubbed his forehead where the start of a headache pulsed. He almost felt hungover, even though he hadn't been drinking. Was it a side effect of the creature's mesmerism? "Everyone be careful. Don't look it in the eye. It has a hypnotic gaze. That's how it immobilizes victims."

"There's nothing there." Barnes shook his head, bewildered. "The street is empty."

"Are you sure?" Decker went to the other window. He pushed the curtain back with the barrel of his gun, keeping his eyes low to avoid being ensnared by the creature's gaze yet again.

Special Agent Fowler came up behind him and peered over Decker's shoulder. "I don't see anything either."

"I'm telling you. It was there. Damned thing almost got me." Decker stepped from the window, lowering his gun. He glanced toward Tieg, who was now pressed against Robyn's leg, the dog's aggression having given way to fear. "The dog saved my life. If he hadn't pushed me out of the way, I'd be a goner."

"Good boy," Robyn said, kneeling next to the dog and patting his head. She looked up at Decker. "How could that creature be here? I thought it was in the mine?"

"Me too." Decker was baffled. "It escaped last night and killed those poor campers, but we locked the gates and secured the mine entrance this morning. It should have been trapped."

"Well, it wasn't," Fowler grumbled. "Everyone should stay inside until dawn. If Decker's theory is correct, it's sensitive to daylight and we'll be safe then."

"What about Carlton?" Robyn looked worried. "He's all alone in the shack at the other end of town. I might not like him much, but I'd feel guilty if something happened."

"I hadn't thought of that," Fowler replied. "Someone will have to go check on him."

"Right," Barnes said. "And bring him back here for the night, if he'll come."

"Good luck with that." Robyn stood up and pushed her

hands into her pockets. "I've already had that conversation and he refused."

"The situation has changed. He'd be a fool to stay on his own tonight."

"He is a fool," Robyn replied. "And a stubborn one, at that."

"We have to try," Decker said. "Warn him of the danger, at least."

"I'll go," Barnes said, although he looked none too pleased.

"I'll accompany you," said Decker. "It will be easier with two of us. We can watch each other's backs."

Barnes nodded. "That makes me feel better. You ready to do this?"

"No time like the present." Decker checked his gun. He still had eighteen rounds. That should be enough for whatever trouble they encountered. "If we come under attack, whatever happens, do not look into the creature's eyes. Understood?"

"Gotcha."

Decker glanced back at Agent Fowler. "Lock the door behind us and don't go outside for any reason."

Fowler nodded.

"And look after Robyn. Make sure she stays safe," Decker added.

"You two keep your eyes peeled out there," Fowler said. "Take nothing for granted."

"Always." Decker exchanged a look with Barnes, then he pulled the door open and stepped back out into the night with the FBI agent right behind.

CHAPTER FORTY-SEVEN

Decker and Barnes made their way down the street toward the ramshackle cabin inhabited by Carlton Miller. They moved carefully, senses on high alert. Decker scanned the landscape ahead of them while Barnes brought up the rear and covered his six.

Decker felt uneasy. Wherever the creature had gone, it couldn't be far. He wondered if it was watching them right now, biding its time, waiting for the pair to be far enough from the hotel to render them vulnerable. It was intelligent. Of that, he was sure. The voice that whispered in his head, lulling him into a deadly trance, was all the proof he needed. But he couldn't dwell on the ramifications of that right now. There was a job to do, and he needed to stay sharp.

Carlton's shack was even more shabby up close than he expected. The entire building was leaning. A pane was missing from the only frontward facing window, and two more were cracked. There was barely any paint left on the battered and warped siding. The steps up to the front door sagged, and Decker wondered if his foot would go right through them. Next to them was a sign screwed onto the railing. It read, YOU KNOCK, I SHOOT.

"Charming," Barnes whispered as they reached the building, turning his attention from the open road behind them to the old man's shack. "Shall we flip a coin to see who's going to knock?"

"I'll do it," Decker said. "I've already escaped death once tonight, I'm on a winning streak."

"Or your luck's about to run out," Barnes observed flippantly.

"Yeah. Just watch my back." Decker approached a dented World War Two Jeep parked up in front of the cabin. It looked like a derelict, but according to Robyn it was Carlton's pride and joy. Skirting the aging vehicle, he climbed the steps and used the butt of his gun to rap three times on the cabin door.

When there was no answer, he tried again.

This time there was movement inside the cabin, and then a reedy voice spoke. "Who is it? Who's out there? What do you want?"

"Carlton. Open the door," Decker said, relieved the old man wasn't following through on the warning sign nailed to his railing.

"Go away."

"He sounds just fine to me," Barnes said. "Tell him not to go outside and let's get back to the hotel. Standing out here in the street like this, knowing what's out there, is giving me the willies."

"Carlton. Open up. We need to talk." Decker tried the door handle and found it locked. "It's important."

For a moment nothing happened, then he heard a lock disengaging. The door creaked open to reveal the old man dressed in a pair of boxer briefs and a stained white T-shirt. "Talk then. Make it quick. You woke me up."

"We came to check on you. Make sure you're safe." Decker could see past Carlton into the shack. It was a mess. From his vantage point, he could see a rickety wooden table piled with dirty plates. A sweaty odor wafted out as the humid air inside the cabin escaped, causing Decker to wrinkle his nose.

"What? Why wouldn't I be?" Carlton shook his head. "You got me out of bed for this?"

"You didn't hear my gunshots?"

"Can't say that I did." The old man poked his finger toward his left ear. "I'm deaf on one side. Can't hear for shit. If I'm lying on my good ear, the sky could fall, and I wouldn't notice."

"Sorry to have bothered you," Decker said. "A word of advice, though. After we leave, lock up and don't go outside until morning. It's not safe."

"No worries there. I'm going right back to bed." Carlton scrunched his face up and let out a grunt of annoyance. "Which is where I'd still be if it weren't for you."

"Point taken." Decker decided it wasn't worth getting into a spat with the old man. "We'll be on our way back to the hotel now."

"Um. Maybe not." Barnes backed up toward the cabin steps. He craned his neck upward into the night sky. "It's coming back, and I swear, it sounds like the damned thing's right above us."

"That's impossible." Decker swung around, bringing his gun to bear, ready to fire. Above them, in the darkness, he could hear a beat of wings. He looked upward, searching the blackness. And then he saw it, soaring across the tops of the buildings and spiraling downward.

"Holy hell." Carlton's eyes flew wide with fear. "It's a monster."

"It always is," Decker said dryly, as the creature touched down in the middle of the street twenty feet distant. He glanced between the two men. "Remember, whatever you do, don't look into its eyes. That's how it gets you."

"Yeah." Barnes scrambled up the steps. "What now?"

As if to answer his question, the creature threw its head back and let out a shrill screech. It lowered its arms, folding leathery, batlike wings to its sides. Then it started toward them in a shambling, creaking gait.

"Inside. Now," Decker shouted, grabbing Barnes by his shirt collar and yanking him backwards toward the door. "If we stay out here we're doomed."

"Now wait a minute, you can't just barge into my home." Carlton tried to close the door.

"Not so fast." Decker stuck a foot in the jamb and tugged it open again, then bustled the shocked FBI agent inside, before following him and slamming the door. There was a large bolt attached to the frame. He drew it across.

"I don't trust that to hold," Barnes said, pulling himself together. "We need to put something in front of that door. Barricade it."

"How about this?" Decker crossed to an old chest of drawers standing against the cabin's sidewall.

"Perfect." Barnes joined him and together they dragged the heavy piece of furniture across the floor and pushed it up against the door. "That should hold it."

"Hey." Carlton was standing, hands on hips, a look of indignation on his face. "You're wrecking the place."

"I hardly think so," Decker replied. "Five decades of neglect appear to have beat me to it."

"You don't need to be mean after I let you in here." Carlton was sucking on his lower lip. "I probably saved your lives."

"You didn't save our lives," Decker said. "You tried to slam the door and leave us to fend for ourselves against that creature out there."

"I panicked, that's all." Carlton waved a dismissive hand and hobbled across to the bed in the corner of the one-room shack, where he flopped down.

"Whatever you say." Decker went to the window. The creature was still there, standing in the street, observing the shack. But it made no move to approach. Then, with another warbling screech, it unfurled a pair of hideous wings and took to the sky where it disappeared from view.

"It's gone again," Barnes said from his position at Decker's rear, peering over his shoulder. "Thank the heavens for that."

"For now." Decker searched the sky but could not see the creature anymore. "But I'm not sure I want to step out there again anytime soon. How many hours until dawn?"

Barnes checked his watch. "Three, give or take."

"Then I guess we hunker down here until then." Decker glanced toward Carlton, who sat perched on the edge of the bed glaring at them. "Looks like you've gotten yourself a couple of roommates."

CHAPTER FORTY-EIGHT

Decker and Barnes spent the rest of the night huddled inside Carlton Miller's cabin. Neither man felt comfortable sitting on the stained sofa facing the sooty stone fireplace, so Barnes took the only other place to sit, a solitary dining room chair next to the table. He pushed the piles of dirty plates away with a grimace and shot Carlton a disapproving look, but kept his mouth shut. Another confrontation with the crotchety old man would only make their forced stay in his cabin that much more uncomfortable.

Decker decided the floor was his best option and sat with his back to the chest of drawers they had used to barricade the door. Neither man slept. Decker was worried about Agent Fowler, Robyn, and Tieg. He trusted them not to venture outside, but they would worry, none-the-less. Regardless, a return to the hotel before daybreak was too risky, and neither he nor Barnes had brought their cell phones. With no other option, he settled down to wait out the hours.

When dawn broke, they left and made their way back toward the hotel. They had barely covered half the distance when the hotel doors flew open and Robyn hurried down the steps. She rushed toward them, a big grin on her face. Tieg, elated, ran ahead of her. Special Agent Fowler followed behind at his own pace, obviously relieved to see the pair, but unwilling to express it with such exuberance.

"Oh my God, I'm so happy to see the pair of you." She flung her arms around Decker, then did the same to Barnes. "We couldn't tell what was happening. I thought that hideous creature might've gotten you."

"Not a chance," Decker said, faking a nonchalance he didn't totally buy into. "We were fine."

"Except we had to spend the rest of the night locked inside with Carlton in that mangy old cabin," Barnes said, a tinge of disgust in his voice. "That guy needs a maid more than anyone I've ever met."

"He doesn't get many visitors," Robyn replied.

"And I can see why." Barnes frowned. "The signs he has peppered around warning people off are bad enough, but man, does it reek in there. I used to play football back in high school, and it smelled worse than my old locker room. I was holding my breath for the first fifteen minutes we were there."

"The place could certainly use an air freshener or ten," Decker agreed. "But that's not what I'm worried about. I miscalculated."

"How so?" Fowler asked.

"I thought that padlocking the mine entrance would keep the creature contained. I was wrong. It escaped anyhow. I only hope it didn't kill anyone else."

"Might be an idea to check the mine," Barnes said. "If that thing busted through the gates, we need to know."

"Agreed." Decker nodded. "Probably sooner rather than later."

"How about now?" Fowler suggested. "I'll come with you."

"Suits me," Decker replied.

Robyn shook her head. "Not until all of you have eaten

something." Her gaze shifted between Barnes and Decker. "You must be famished."

"This is more important." Decker was, in fact, hungry, but he didn't want to waste another moment. If there was a problem with the mine entrance, they would need to figure out how to solve it before darkness fell again and the creature emerged once more.

"All right," Robyn said. "But I'm going to rustle up some breakfast, anyway. Don't be too long. When you return, I expect you to eat."

"Yes ma'am," Barnes said with a chuckle. "You're worse than my mother."

"Dang right I am." Robyn pursed her lips. "Now scoot. And don't be long."

"We'll do our best," Decker replied. Then he turned toward the trail with the two FBI agents at his side.

CHAPTER FORTY-NINE

They made their way up the trail as the sun rose higher in the sky. Far above them, a prairie falcon rode the thermals in lazy wide circles looking for prey, hoping to snag a jackrabbit, or possibly even an unlucky collared lizard or desert iguana. After his encounter with the creature the night before, Decker could easily sympathize with whatever poor desert dweller fell victim to the prowling raptor.

After a ten-minute hike, they reached the flat plateau in front of the mine. Beyond this the trail wound higher, creosote bushes and sagebrush pushing in on all sides. It was up this path that Decker and Barnes had followed the pair of interlopers the previous day.

Decker came to a halt and looked around. Nothing looked out of place, and when he approached the mine's entrance, he discovered the gates were still padlocked.

"All secure," he said, tugging on the chains just to make sure. "The creature didn't get out this way."

"That's a relief, at least." Barnes wiped a bead of sweat from his brow.

"On the contrary, it's worse." Decker scanned his

surroundings, paying close attention to the sandy earth under their feet. If the creature had been here recently, it would have left faint but distinguishable tracks. He could easily see their own boot prints, and those of the two men they encountered the previous day. He even noticed the impression of older footprints, probably left by the geologists and search and rescue team earlier. "It means the creature is escaping the mine from another location."

"Or it left the mine after the first killings and hasn't returned," Fowler said.

"It's possible." Decker rubbed his chin. "But I still think my original assessment is correct. The creature has been trapped in the mine since pioneer days. That's the only scenario that makes sense given the original incident and the fact that the mine entrance was blocked until recently. Those geologists were the first people to venture that deep into the mine since Robyn reopened it. The three corpses they found appeared to be hiding from something. They were afraid. There was a symbol drawn into the earth nearby, which denotes a superstitious angle. The geologists found bones too, suggesting violent deaths occurred in the tunnels prior to their own fatal encounter. This is ground zero, I'd stake my reputation on it. The creature probably has an attachment to this place. I'll further speculate that it doesn't do well in daylight given the circumstances of each attack. I'm sure it returns here before dawn."

"And let's not forget that it can fly." Barnes looked unhappy. "As if a demonic mummified skeleton with hypnotic eyes wasn't enough."

"It flies too?" Now it was Fowler's turn to look distressed. "How is that even possible?"

"How is a walking homicidal skeleton possible?" Decker countered. "Sometimes it's better to worry less about the how, and a little more about the why. In this case, what purpose does the entity serve and who summoned it?"

"You think that abomination was put here deliberately?"

"I think it's a strong possibility. How many other gold mines do you know that have their own resident murderous corpse?"

Fowler shrugged. "You're the expert, I guess."

"This is all very well," Barnes said. "But it doesn't get us anywhere. Regardless of its origin, we know there's a creature that shouldn't exist running around killing people, because we've seen it with our own eyes. Heck, it almost killed us. We know it can fly, which means it can cover longer distances than would be possible on foot, especially over this terrain."

"We also know it didn't leave the mine through this entrance," Fowler added. "And if we work from Decker's assumption that the creature uses the mine tunnels as its home base, that only leaves one conclusion."

"It's getting in and out through a second location," Decker said. "One that must have also been opened recently, because the killings only started when the geologists entered the mine."

"Robyn never mentioned blasting a second entrance, or even knowing one exists," Fowler said.

"There would be no need for her to open another way into the mine," Decker replied. "She only wants to run tours through the closest tunnels to the surface. She won't be going deep, for liability reasons, as much as anything else. We can check with her when we return, but I don't expect her to be any help in this matter."

"That tears it, then." Barnes peered past the locked gate into the dark tunnel beyond. "We could wander around this desert for six months and not find another entrance."

"Which is why we aren't going to conduct our search on foot." Decker glanced skyward and watched the still circling hawk for a moment. "We need a higher vantage point. We need to be in the air."

"A helicopter?" Fowler's demeanor brightened at this idea.

"Precisely. It will enable us to cover a lot of ground in a short amount of time. I don't suppose you'd have one on hand?"

"Sure. It's tucked away in my desk back at the field office." The sarcasm in Fowler's voice was hard to miss. "I was kind of hoping your organization might arrange one. They appear to have their fingers in every pie."

"I'm sure I could arrange it," Decker agreed. "But we don't have time to throw it up the chain of command and see what shakes loose. Besides, I'd rather keep my organization's involvement in this under the radar."

"What about LVMPD?" Barnes asked. "They have helicopters."

"And you think they'll just lend one to us? After all, they contacted us for help with this and we sent everyone home, including their SWAT team." Fowler didn't look convinced. "Against normal operating protocol, I might add. The FBI doesn't take over, we assist."

"They'll lend us one if we give them a good enough excuse."

"Like?"

"We'll tell them we have a missing person, possibly abducted. We can say they'll get credit for the recovery. They're always looking for good press."

"And if they prevaricate, we'll remind them of the bad press if they don't work with us and provide a helicopter."

"My thoughts exactly," Barnes said.

"Then what are we waiting for?" Fowler asked. "Let's get back to town and make it happen."

"And get some breakfast," Barnes added.

"Naturally. Robyn makes a mean pancake." Fowler looked at Decker. "You ready to go flying?"

"The quicker the better," Decker replied. He hoped their plan worked, because if they failed, more innocent people would end up dead once the sun went down.

CHAPTER FIFTY

Two hours after returning to town, Decker stood on the veranda of the Last Chance Hotel and Saloon and watched an Airbus H145 helicopter painted in the black and white livery of the Las Vegas Police Department fly into view over the scraggy peaks of the mountainous terrain.

As it circled and came in for a landing, the two FBI agents exited the hotel, along with Robyn. Further away, standing in the doorway of his shack, Decker could see Carlton shielding his eyes against the sun to watch the large helicopter touch down.

"Told you our cover story would work," Barnes said with a grin.

"Never doubted you," Decker replied as the aircraft came to rest on a patch of barren land at the far end of town. He stepped between the two agents, descended the veranda steps, and started toward the waiting copter. "Let's get this taken care of."

"You don't need to tell me twice," Fowler said, falling in behind.

Leaving Robyn to watch, the three men made their way toward the helicopter. As they neared, Decker ducked instinctively to avoid the spinning rotor blades, and approached the aircraft side door, which now stood open. A man in an orange jumpsuit and crash helmet appeared in the door to greet them.

"You must be the FBI team," the man said, raising his voice over the helicopter's twin engines.

Decker nodded.

"Great. Climb aboard." He stepped aside and waited until all three were in the cabin before sliding the door closed. The noise level dropped by half.

"Welcome aboard," a fresh voice said.

Decker turned to see a pilot sitting up front in a glass cockpit that surrounded him like a bubble. "Glad to be here."

"I'm Officer Michael Glendale. You can call me Mike," the pilot replied. "My colleague is Officer Robbie Parsons."

"Hey." The man who'd met them at the helicopter's door raised a hand.

"Dispatch says you're looking for a missing person with a possible abduction element," Glendale said. "You know which way they might be heading?"

"Not for sure. The Ghost Canyon Mine is close by. We think they might take shelter in an old entrance or ventilation tunnel," Decker replied, sticking to the story details he and the two FBI agents had concocted while they were waiting for the helicopter. "We've already secured the main entry into the mine, but we need to search for other ways in."

"We'll give it a good try," Glendale replied. "But I have to warn you, these old mine shafts and entrances can be pretty well hidden. A lot of them date back over a hundred years and are in some mighty rugged terrain."

"Understood," Decker replied. "Let's do our best, anyway."

"Okey-doke. First things first, we need to get you guys strapped in." Officer Parsons motioned toward a row of seats along the side wall of the helicopter. Upon each one sat a bright green crash helmet and headset with built-in speakers and a microphone for easy communication over the engine noise once the copter was in the air. Decker was about to move toward the seats, when Parsons spoke again. "Since you guys have a better idea what we're looking for than us, one of you should sit up front in the cockpit. I'll take a seat back here with the others."

"That sounds like a job for you," Barnes said to Decker.

"Makes sense," Decker said. He squeezed past Parsons and slipped into the cockpit seat next to the pilot. There was a helmet here too, sitting on the floor next to him.

"Put that on," Glendale instructed.

Decker nodded. He picked up the helmet and put it on, along with the accompanying headset, then clipped himself in using the harness style seatbelt. The two FBI agents and Officer Parsons followed suit in the helicopter's rear cabin. Moments later the engine noise rose in pitch, the aircraft lifted from the ground, and they were airborne.

CHAPTER FIFTY-ONE

They flew low over the uneven landscape. The pilot expertly adjusted to the rise and fall of the rocky landscape beneath them. The glass bubble surrounding the helicopter's cockpit provided an excellent field-of-view, allowing Decker to see far and wide. This was clearly why the Las Vegas Police Department had selected the Airbus H145, which was designed specifically for operations such as the one they were now conducting. It was an amazing machine, barely a year old according to its pilot, who peppered them with abstract facts as he flew. Unlike the other helicopters operated by the LVMPD, which were used as eyes in the sky during police pursuits and for surveillance, this one was kitted out for search and rescue and medical transport flights. It had a large rear cabin area, able to support up to nine passengers, not including a two-man crew, and boasted clamshell doors at the back for easy loading and unloading. A rescue hoist was fitted near the side sliding door, although they wouldn't need that capability on this excursion.

"Let me know if you want to circle back and look at anything," Glendale said after fifteen minutes had passed.

"Will do," Decker replied, never taking his eyes off the barren desert slipping away beneath them.

After a while, when they had traveled to the edge of their useful search area, the helicopter banked and turned back upon itself. They were using a creeping line search pattern, flying back and forth across the landscape, and moving outward with each successive pass. They had started above the known entrance to the Ghost Canyon Mine and flew due east following the ridgeline of the mountain and proceeded from there. It was tough going. The arid desert terrain, while vast and open, was full of peaks and valleys that cast deep shadows and could easily hide an entrance. Not only that, any remaining ventilation shafts or adits would be over a century old and overgrown with vegetation such as creosote bushes and sagebrush, which were abundant in the area.

After an hour, Decker started to lose hope.

The Mohave looked even bigger from above than it did from the ground. It was like looking for one grain of sand on the beach. Twice he thought they had something, and instructed the helicopter to backtrack, only to discover that it was nothing more than a tantalizingly shaped outcrop with dark shadows beneath.

Then, just as he was about to suggest they return to their original starting point and take a second pass over the search area, he spotted a glint of light from the base of a wide canyon ahead of them.

"There." Decker tapped the pilot on the shoulder and pointed. "Can we get lower?"

"These canyons are treacherous, but I'll see what I can do," Glendale said. He pushed on the stick and tilted the helicopter's nose down into the canyon.

A dirt trail snaked across the canyon floor, weaving away until it was lost behind a rise of land. Further away, toward the horizon, Decker could see a thin line of asphalt standing out against the ochre red background of the desert. This was the road leading to Haley. In the other direction would be Boulder City and Las Vegas. Then, as they approached the area where Decker had noticed the sun glinting, he saw something that he wasn't expecting.

A red pickup truck.

It was parked at the edge of the trail, near an outcrop of rocks that created a natural cleft in the landscape. Sagebrush and creosote bushes choked the crevice. But it was what lay between the truck and the rocks that caused Decker to draw a sharp breath. Sprawled on the ground in a dark patch that could only be blood, arms spread wide, lay a corpse.

CHAPTER FIFTY-TWO

The helicopter had barely touched down before Decker was unclipping his seatbelt and making for the door. He jumped out, followed by the two FBI agents, and raced the short distance to the truck, and the body beyond.

It was a man, laying on his back with glassy dead eyes staring up into the bright blue desert sky. His torso was flayed open, exposed innards already crawling with flies.

Decker recognized him at once.

So did Special Agent Barnes. "This is one of the two guys we caught up at the mine entrance yesterday."

"And that's the truck they were driving," Decker said, jerking a thumb back toward the red pickup sitting some fifteen feet away.

"Then where's his friend?" Barnes asked.

Decker circled the body, careful not to disturb anything a forensic team might want to examine later. "Good question. Maybe he came up here alone."

"Or maybe he didn't. Either way, judging by those wounds, he ran into the same creature that tried to kill us last night. Body's been here a while, but not too long. I'd say less than twenty-four hours, although the ME will be able to give us a better estimate. Question is, what was he doing here?"

"We need to search the area." Decker stepped away from the body. "See if he was alone. I would also like to know what he found so interesting about this particular spot."

"I'll take the truck," Fowler said, pulling a pair of blue nitrile gloves from his pocket and putting them on.

"Here." Barnes offered a pair of gloves to Decker.

"Thanks." He took them and looked past the FBI agent at the two Las Vegas PD officers. "One of you should call this in, get a team up here. Secure the scene."

"I'll handle that," Glendale said, turning back toward the helicopter.

"Officer Parsons, you can help search. If this guy's friend is around here, we need to know."

"Sure thing," Parsons replied.

"We'll fan out from the body. Each person in a different direction. If you find anything, call out. And expect the unexpected. This isn't a regular crime scene. Ready?"

"Ready." Barnes nodded.

They set off in different directions. Fowler headed toward the truck. Parsons followed his colleague back toward the helicopter. Moving past it, he started to search up the trail. Barnes made his way toward the rocky outcrop. Decker headed down the trail in the other direction. He could see the tire marks left by the truck, but no footprints, which meant it was unlikely the truck's occupants had ventured this way. It turned out he was right. He was only a few minutes into the search when Barnes let out a loud holler.

"Over here. I've found another one."

Decker turned and hurried back toward the scene, and at first, he couldn't tell where Barnes was. But then he saw the FBI agent's head and shoulders above a tangle of bushes. He was in the cleft formed by the rocky outcrop, standing near a jagged escarpment.

The Vegas police officers were heading back. Agent Fowler was already pushing his way through the bushes, cursing as branches caught on his bare arms and scratched him.

Decker quickened his pace, reaching the narrow crevice at a jog and following the FBI agent along the narrow path between the rocks. He pushed the bushes aside and emerged into a wider area surrounded by large boulders. At one end was a gaping hole in the earth, the interior nothing but an inky black void. Broken and rotten timbers lay scattered about. A crowbar sat discarded in the dirt near the entrance. Nearby, a few feet from the dark mine entrance, lay a second body.

"I guess we know what these two jokers were doing up here," Barnes said, glancing toward the hole in the rocks. "After we chased them away from the mine, they came looking for another way in."

Decker looked down at the ruined body, desecrated in the same manner as Sasha Martin and the two campers. "And in the process, they released something they weren't expecting."

"Looks that way." Barnes kneeled beside the body. With his nitrile gloves on, he patted the man down. "Under normal circumstances, I'd wait for forensics to process the scene before searching a victim, but time is ticking."

"Forensics aren't going to be much good to us anyway," Decker said. He moved close to Barnes and kneeled next to him. "We've already met our killer, and it's not one of the usual suspects."

"I agree." Barnes had found something in the dead man's back pocket. A wallet. He opened it and studied the driver's license contained within, then glanced between Decker and Fowler. "Gentlemen, I'd like you to meet Wagner Mitchell, owner of that truck parked yonder, and the man we've been trying to find since yesterday."

"Looks like he's beyond giving an interview at this point," Fowler observed.

"Which is a shame, because I'd really like to know what business he had in that mine." Decker glanced back toward the other body. "I'd also love to know who his friend is."

"Let's find out," Fowler said. He turned and pushed his way back through the bushes toward the second corpse. He bent down—careful not to step in the pool of congealed blood—and rummaged through the man's clothing until he came up with a second wallet. He flipped it open, then closed it again as Decker and Barnes approached. He rubbed his chin thoughtfully. "I know this guy."

"What?" Decker glanced down at the corpse. "Who is he?"

"Name's Harlan Biggs. Owns a casino off the Strip. A real dive, although he's been renovating it. He's a smalltime hustler who thinks he's a big shot."

"Harlan Biggs. Why do I know that name?" Barnes asked.

"Probably because we've had a file open on his family and their associates for decades. His father used to launder money for a local mobster named Oscar Rossi. The Bureau tried to turn his old man years ago, even tried to have his gaming license revoked to force his hand, but he'd never squeal. That was before my time, of course. Harlan isn't like that. Never had the stomach for it, although there's talk that he got himself mixed up with Rossi all over again. Probably how he came up with the dough for the casino renovation."

"Guess he won't be paying the loan back now," Barnes said.

"Not unless Rossi has some contacts on the other side." Fowler dropped the wallet into an evidence bag handed to him by the Vegas cop, Glendale, and sealed it. "I think it's time we find out what these two jokers were up to before they got themselves killed."

"Best place to start would be their home premises."

"It's like you read my mind." Fowler nodded. "You think Judge Rodrigues is in a good mood today?"

"Probably not," Barnes replied. "But he'll still give us search warrants, I'll bet. He wants nothing more than to clear the organized crime out of Vegas once and for all."

"My thoughts exactly." Fowler turned to the helicopter pilot. "You call this in?"

Glendale nodded. "CSU are on the way."

"Perfect. We'll let PD clean up." Fowler started back toward the helicopter. "Take us back to town, quick as you can."

"Wait," Decker said. He turned and made his way back toward the cleft in the rocks. He pushed his way past the bushes and approached the mine entrance, stepping around Wagner Mitchell's body.

"What are you doing?" Barnes said, following behind. "There's no time to waste."

"I have a hunch," Decker said. He pulled his phone out and found the photo the geologists took deep within the mine. The three mummified bodies huddled against a rock wall. He zoomed in on the strange symbol drawn in the earth in front of them. Stepping a few feet inside the mine entrance, Decker kneeled down and used his finger to draw the same symbol in the dusty soil.

"I assume there's a reason you're doodling on the ground." Barnes looked perplexed.

Decker straightened up. "There is. Those three corpses the geologists found weren't mutilated." He held the phone up and showed Barnes the picture. "Look at their stomachs. Intact. Not a scratch."

"So?"

"That symbol. It looks Native American. If I'm right, it's for protection. That's the only thing that makes sense. Why else would the creature leave them alone?"

"Maybe their deaths were nothing to do with the creature," Barnes said. "There might be no connection."

"Possible. But I don't think so. It was stalking them, I'm sure of it." Decker slipped the phone back into his pocket. "There's no other reason they would sit there and not walk out. They were hoping the creature would go away, but it didn't, so instead they had no choice but to wait and starve to death."

"What a horrible way to die. Stuck in the darkness knowing you can never leave." Barnes shuddered.

"If my hunch is correct, their deaths were not in vain." Decker looked down at the symbol he'd drawn on the tunnel floor. "This will contain the creature. It won't be able to pass beyond it."

"Only if your hunch is correct. And that's a big if."

"Yes." Decker started back toward the helicopter. "You'd better hope I'm right. We don't have time to reseal the mine entrance before dark."

"And if you're wrong?"

"Then the creature will return again tonight," Decker said as they reached the helicopter and climbed in. "And we'll have to be ready for it."

CHAPTER FIFTY-THREE

By two o'clock that afternoon, Decker was standing outside the Prospectors Paradise Hotel and Casino, with Special Agent Barnes at his side clutching the newly minted search warrant issued by Judge Rodrigues and collected from the Las Vegas Municipal Courthouse only a half hour before. Three miles away, at the Sunset Towers condo building overlooking the Las Vegas Strip, Special Agent Fowler was getting ready to search Wagner Mitchell's home with a junior agent in tow.

The hotel casino was closed for renovations, with scaffolding covering the front façade, and construction materials piled high in the parking lot. The lobby doors, though, were not locked, and Decker could see workers wearing hard hats moving about within.

"Looks like business as normal here," Decker commented. "They obviously haven't missed their boss yet."

"I bet work will come to a screeching halt when they find out Harlan Biggs is dead. There won't be anyone to pay the construction company."

"Not our problem," Barnes replied. He took his credentials

out and headed toward the main doors. They hadn't gotten more than a few feet across the hotel lobby when a booming voice shouted in their direction.

"Hey, you two. What are you doing in here? Can't you see the casino's closed? This is a construction site."

Decker turned to see a stocky man wearing a fluorescent jacket and yellow hard hat stomping toward them. He carried a walkie-talkie in one hand, and a clipboard in the other.

"We're not here to gamble," Decker said as the man drew close to them.

Barnes held up his credentials. "FBI. We have a warrant to search the hotel and the owner's personal accommodation."

"You want Harlan Biggs, then," the worker said. "He ain't here. Haven't seen him all day."

"We're aware of that." Barnes slipped the credentials wallet back into his pocket. "You are?"

"Matt Campbell. Site supervisor. I work for Calder Construction. We're handling oversight of the renovation, including the hotel rooms."

"Pleasure to meet you, Matt," Barnes said. He glanced toward the casino, where a dozen or more workers were busy laying floors. "These are all your employees?"

"Some. Depends what job they're doing. A majority are subcontractors. Electricians, carpenters, day laborers, and the like. They come and go. It's hard to keep track."

"I see." Barnes nodded. "When was the last time you saw Harlan Biggs?"

"Yesterday. Early afternoon. That goes for his general manager too."

"Wagner Mitchell."

"Yeah. He was running around the construction zone, getting in the way. No clue what he was doing. Then the pair of them disappeared. Haven't seen 'em since."

And you won't see them again, thought Decker, but he said

nothing. Instead, he glanced toward the elevators. "Where can we find Harlan Biggs' personal accommodation?"

"Top floor." Campbell snorted. "He's got a couple of guest rooms up there that he knocked into one and likes to call the penthouse suite. Thinks he's the king of the castle."

"Is it only the penthouse on the top floor?" Barnes asked.

"Nah. There are other guestrooms up there, but he ain't renovating them. Doesn't want people staying on the same floor as him. Claims he's going to rip them out and put a VIP bar and restaurant up there instead. You can't miss his penthouse suite. He's actually got it written on the door."

"You know where we can find a key for that unit?" Barnes asked.

"You could try Penny Blake, the office manager. She'd probably have one."

"And where would we find her?"

"Go through that door over there," Campbell said, pointing across the lobby away from the casino to a door marked STAFF ONLY. "That's the administrative offices. She'll be the first door on the left."

"Thank you," Barnes said. "Are you going to be here for a while?"

"Until at least six," Campbell replied.

"Perfect. If we have any further questions, we'll come find you."

"Sure." Campbell shrugged and turned, making his way back into the gutted casino.

Barnes and Decker headed in the other direction and soon found Penny Blake's office.

Barnes knocked.

"Come in," a voice said from within.

Barnes opened the door and stepped inside with Decker right behind.

Penny Blake was a rail thin woman in her early fifties who

wore too much makeup and obviously bleached her hair. If it surprised her to receive a visit from the FBI, she didn't show it.

Barnes handed her the search warrant and explained the situation. This time he didn't hold back the news of Harlan and Wagner's deaths.

Penny looked shocked. The color drained from her face. "Oh my, that's terrible." She sniffed and pulled a tissue from a box on the desk, then dabbed her eyes. "I wondered why I hadn't seen them today. I never imagined they were dead."

"I'm sorry to be the bearer of tragic news," Barnes replied. "We found them in the desert, near an old mine entrance. You wouldn't happen to know what they were doing there, would you?"

"An old mine?" Penny shook her head. "I can't imagine. Harlan wasn't exactly the outdoors type."

Barnes nodded.

Penny glanced down at the search warrant. "I suppose you want access to the penthouse?"

"That would be helpful."

Penny stood and crossed to a safe set into the wall behind her. She dialed a combination and opened it. Decker saw rows of keys hanging on hooks inside. When she turned around again, there was a plastic card in her hand.

"Here," she said, offering them the key card. "Harlan always keeps a spare in the safe."

"Thank you." Barnes accepted it. "We'll let you know when we're done up there. I don't know how long it will be."

"Okay. I'll be here for a few more hours, at least." Penny gave them a sad smile. "Although who knows if I'll be here tomorrow. Guess I need to look for another job."

Barnes looked uncomfortable. "If you're not around when we're done, I'll slip the key under the door."

Penny nodded and pulled another tissue from the box with a

loud sniff. A tear ran down her cheek. She was still crying when they left the office, closing the door behind them, and turned back toward the lobby.

CHAPTER FIFTY-FOUR

The penthouse belonging to the recently deceased Harlan Biggs, on the top floor of the Prospectors Paradise Hotel and Casino, was a world away from what most people would consider swanky living. A set of keys that bore a Porsche logo sat on a side table next to the door, and the living room contained a wet bar fit for an alcoholic, but other than that, the place was tired and old. The furniture, though high-quality, bore the scars of faded opulence. The walls were covered with framed photographs, many of them black and white and obviously harkening back to the glory days of the brat pack. Some were signed. Most were not. Decker recognized such luminaries as Wayne Newton, Sammy Davis Junior, Elvis Presley, and Bob Newhart. He wondered if these performers had any connection to the hotel, or if they were just stage dressing for Harlan Biggs' ego. Not that it mattered anymore. The man who lived in a faded penthouse suite atop a struggling hotel and casino would never be back.

"What's that god-awful stench?" Barnes asked, wrinkling his nose.

"Smells like garbage," Decker said, crossing the living room and approaching the bar. "It's worse, closer to the window."

"Some penthouse. Smells more like a flophouse." Barnes spent a moment studying the collection of photographs, then turned away, his eyes roving around the room. "Doesn't look like there's much of interest in here."

"Agreed. Although I'm not exactly sure what we're even looking for."

"We'll know when we see it, I guess." Barnes pointed toward a door near the bar, beyond which an unmade bed was visible, sheets ruffled. "I'm going to check in there."

"Sure. I'll take the kitchen," Decker said. He crossed back through the living room to the entrance hall and was about to turn right into the small kitchen, when he saw another door to his left. He poked his head inside and discovered an office with dark wood shelves lining the walls. A desk occupied the center of the room, over which hung a brass ceiling fan.

Decker stepped inside, curious. If Harlan Biggs had left any clues regarding his activities out in the desert, and why he was so interested in the Ghost Canyon Mine, this felt like the logical place for them.

When he saw a leather-bound volume, much older than the rest of the books in the room, his hunch was rewarded. It lay on the desk next to an empty whiskey glass. Decker felt a tingle of anticipation. It was conspicuous enough to be what they were looking for.

Decker approached the desk and sat down. Putting on a pair of nitrile gloves, he opened the book, careful not to damage it, and studied the first page. There was an inscription in spidery cursive.

A TRUE AND ACCURATE ACCOUNT
OF THE EXPLOITS OF TRAVIS WILLIAM BIGGS,
PROSPECTOR AND PIONEER.

BEGUN IN THE YEAR OF OUR LORD, 1868.

Decker turned the page, his excitement growing. Travis Biggs was obviously an ancestor of the recently departed Harlan Biggs. That the casino owner was reading this book, clearly a journal kept by his ancestor, at the same time he was skulking around the Ghost Canyon Mine could not be a coincidence. Especially since the man who penned the journal, Travis Biggs, identified himself as a prospector.

Decker leafed through the pages. The first half of the journal described the author's departure from the East Coast and his grueling cross-country journey. He endured one hardship after another, including a food shortage, an outbreak of cholera among the larger group he was traveling with, and a Comanche attack which left one man dead and three more with arrow wounds. But it was an entry toward the middle that caught Decker's attention. A passage that recounted Travis Biggs arrival in the bustling frontier town of Haley, Nevada, malnourished and suffering from dehydration. He scanned the page, and then the next one. By the time he'd reached the last pages, his hunch turned into a certainty. This was what they were looking for, and it explained so much more than why Harlan Biggs was sniffing around the mine. It also told Decker what the creature was, and why it was there. He read the relevant passages again, digesting every word, and then he closed the journal and stood. The pieces were falling into place. The long dead prospector, Travis Biggs, had provided him with most of the answers, but he needed more information in order to defeat the creature, which he now knew certain Native American tribes referred to as the Baykok. And he needed the information quickly, because once darkness fell the creature would want to kill again, and he wasn't completely sure the symbol he'd drawn in the earth at the second mine entrance would actually hold the creature at bay.

"Hey." Barnes appeared in the office doorway. "Fowler just texted. Wagner Mitchell's place is clean. He's going to borrow a pool car and head back to Haley."

"I figured it would be, considering."

"You find something?"

"I found everything," Decker said, holding up the journal in a gloved hand. "You fancy making an unscheduled stop?"

"Sure," Barnes said, shrugging. "Where are we going?"

"Downtown," Decker replied. "Out past Fremont Street."

"That's in the opposite direction to Haley." Barnes looked confused. "Why would you want to drive out there?"

"Because that's where the Paiute Tribe live." Decker stepped past Barnes toward the penthouse door. When he reached it, he turned to look back over his shoulder. "Don't stand around. Hurry. We don't have much time."

CHAPTER FIFTY-FIVE

The Las Vegas Paiute tribe's downtown reservation sat on North Main, two-and-a-half miles away from Fremont Street, the area that most tourists associated with downtown. The small reservation, deeded to the tribe at the start of the twentieth century by a sympathetic landowner, was only a fraction of the lands now controlled by the Paiute. Further away, at the north end of Red Rocks Canyon, was another four thousand acres returned by the Federal Government, which the Paiute operated as a golf resort. But it was the administration building on the downtown reservation that interested Decker.

"I still don't see why we need to go here," Barnes said as they drove toward their destination.

"Because the answer to our problem may lie there," Decker said. He patted the journal, which he'd brought from Harlan's office. "This tells us how the creature was created, and its purpose. Harlan's ancestor was a greedy man, and when he found a rich vein of gold in the Ghost Canyon Mine, he didn't want to share it. Most of the other mines in the area were already tapped out by then, and the prospectors who called Haley home were already departing for better opportunities. He knew if word spread of a fresh discovery, he'd never contain the flood of new prospectors."

"Okay. I still don't see what that has to do with the murderous creature prowling about."

"There was a man of Native American ancestry living in town. Travis Biggs, the author of the journal, refers to him as a half-breed. He was part Ojibwe, and part Western descent. Consequently, he was an outcast. But he knew things. When he arrived in Nevada from the Great Lakes region, he brought the knowledge of his ancestors with him. This included an entity known as the Baykok, a terrifying creature with glowing red eyes, a hypnotic gaze, and the ability to fly." Decker waited a moment for this to sink in before continuing. "Does that sound familiar?"

"Chillingly so," Barnes replied. "You think Travis Biggs summoned this entity?"

"I do, with the help of the part Ojibwe outcast. A man referred to in the journal only as Karuk."

"But how?"

"The Baykok is created from the scattered bones of a disgraced warrior. In this case, they used the remains of a man interred outside the traditional burial grounds. A Paiute named Shilah. Travis doesn't say what caused Shilah's fall from grace and subsequent burial so far from the rest of the tribe. I suspect he didn't know, since the grave was already ancient when they visited it. Suffice to say, they desecrated the remains and stole some of the bones, which they scattered in the mine."

"There must've been more to it than that." Barnes didn't look convinced. "Just taking a few bones from a grave and putting them somewhere else doesn't create a monster."

"I assume there was an incantation or some other magic at work. Regardless of how Karuk accomplished it, we've already met the result, and it almost killed us."

"True. Although it's a lot to get my head around," Barnes

said. "And it still doesn't explain why we need to visit the reservation."

"Because Travis Biggs failed, which is why the creature is still with us. After Karuk placed the bones in the mine and summoned the tortured soul of the disgraced warrior, he got a bullet in the back for his troubles. It was a brazen admission of murder written by the very man who committed the act. But this was the Old West, and Haley had no law enforcement."

"That solves another mystery," Barnes said. "The skeleton Robyn has in her museum. She found it up near the mine and it dates back to that era."

"Precisely. The skeleton displays damage consistent with being shot, which matches the confession in this journal."

"We can safely assume the skeleton is Karuk, then."

"It's a reasonable hypothesis."

"That still doesn't explain why the creature is still around. Travis Biggs must've had an exit strategy, or he wouldn't have killed the only person with the knowledge to summon the Baykok."

"Because he made a mistake," Decker replied. "After murdering Karuk, he stayed out of the way and let the creature do its work, killing the other miners. Presumably, word spread that the mine was haunted."

"Which is why the area was consequently named Ghost Canyon."

"Exactly. Other prospectors would have been loath to step foot inside the mine, especially since Travis was now the only one who knew about the gold still contained there."

"Right." Barnes nodded.

"Except that he could never reach the gold. He went back into the mine and gathered up the scattered bones, just like Karuk said to do. He returned them to their original burial spot, which should have appeased the angry spirit, and caused it to depart. But when he tried to reach the gold, the Baykok was still there. Knowing not to look directly at it, he was able to escape, but only barely. This is where the journal ends. The last pages are blank."

"Something must've happened to Travis Biggs."

"Clearly. While we will never know the circumstances of his demise, it's reasonable to assume that he kept trying to reach the gold and eventually fell prey to the creature. My guess is that his bones are somewhere in those tunnels to this day."

"The man he murdered, Karuk, must've done something to ensure his own safety."

"That's what I'm thinking," Decker said. "He knew Travis Biggs might try to double-cross him. He just didn't expect it to happen so soon. He made sure Travis could not get rid of the creature alone. The most obvious way to do that would be to keep one of the bones and hide it. Then, even if Travis reinterred the remains, the skeleton would not be complete, and thus Shilah's energy would not dissipate."

"Makes sense," Barnes agreed. "It also explains why Harlan Biggs was so interested in the mine. Gold. He was heavily in debt to a mobster and might lose his casino, or worse."

"He must've seen news reports about the deaths inside the mine and realized his ancestor's journal was true," Decker said.

"It's all falling into place," Barnes said. "You still haven't said why we're visiting the Paiute. We know what the creature is and how it came into existence. We know how to defeat it."

"But there are still two things we don't know," Decker replied.

"What happened to the bone Karuk held back in anticipation of Travis Biggs deciding he was a liability," Barnes said.

Decker nodded. "And where Shilah's grave is located."

"You think someone in the modern Paiute Tribe has those answers?"

"I believe they can point us to Shilah's grave," Decker said as Barnes pulled up in front of their destination, the Paiute Tribe's administrative center. "And as for the bone Karuk kept back, I may already have solved that mystery. But we won't know until our return to Haley."

"Then what are we waiting for?" Barnes asked, turning the engine off and jumping from the vehicle. "Let's take care of this and get back there quick as we can."

CHAPTER FIFTY-SIX

Decker and Special Agent Barnes approached the Las Vegas Paiute Tribe's administrative building but were disappointed to find the lobby doors locked.

"Doesn't look like anyone's home," Barnes said.

"It would appear that way." Decker peered through the glass, noting that the lights were off. "There are no opening hours posted."

"We might need to come back tomorrow. Get here earlier in the day."

"I'd rather not wait that long," Decker said. "We'll have to find another way. This is too urgent."

"Short of walking around knocking on random doors, hoping someone hereabouts knows something, I don't know what else we can do."

"If that's what it takes," Decker said, "that is what we should do. I'd rather not risk the Baykok escaping again tonight and killing anyone else."

"I hear that." Barnes rubbed his chin thoughtfully. "I'm just not sure it will get us very far."

Decker was about to reply, when he heard a door slam

around the side of the building. Moments later, a slender woman of no more than thirty years of age, with long dark hair, and an olive complexion, appeared in the parking lot. She carried a bag over her shoulder, a bunch of keys in one hand, and a can of soda in the other.

She looked surprised to see Decker and Barnes at the building's front doors. "Can I help you, gentlemen?" She asked, changing course, and walking toward them.

"Maybe," Decker replied. He lifted a hand and shielded his eyes from the sun, which was now low on the horizon. "Do you work here?"

"Right now, I'm the only one that works here. At least, full time." The woman drew level with them. "Is there something in particular you're looking for?"

"Yes, there is," Decker replied. "My name's John Decker, and my colleague here is Special Agent Jackson Barnes. We're looking for information regarding the tribe's history, and in particular, the final resting place of a warrior known as Shilah."

"I'm Sandra Levi. I'm the administrator here. Actually, I'm the entire staff."

"Really?" Decker looked surprised.

"There are less than sixty Las Vegas Paiutes left. Most of us work in one of our smoke shops, or at the golf resort out on Route Ninety-Five."

"I see," Decker said. "Can you tell us anything about Shilah? It's important."

"I'm sorry," Sandra said, shaking her head slowly. "I've never heard that name. How long ago did he live?"

"We don't have an exact date, but he would've died before the 1870s. Possibly even a century or more before that."

"That far back." Sandra looked thoughtful. "Our history, especially centuries ago, was mostly oral. There is someone that might help you, although I can't guarantee he will have the information you need. His name is Bobby Yellowhorse. He's been collecting the history of the tribe for as long as I can remember. If anyone knows of Shilah, it would be him."

"Fantastic," Decker said. "Is he close by?"

"Yes." Sandra nodded. "He only lives a block from here on Sackett Street."

"Great, would you mind giving me the address?"

"I think I should call him first and make sure he's willing to see you," Sandra said. She finished the rest of her soda and deposited the empty can into a trash receptacle, then took out her cell phone. "Just give me a second, and I'll see what I can do."

"Sure." Decker waited while the young woman placed the call. She conversed with Bobby Yellowhorse for less than a minute and then hung up. "He says he'll see you. Actually, he sounds rather excited. He likes to talk about our history." She removed a business card from her bag along with a pen and scribbled on the back, then offered it to Decker. "This is where he lives. My phone number is on there too, if you need anything else."

"Thank you," Decker said, accepting the card.

"I hope you find what you're looking for."

"Me too," Decker replied. "Because lives may depend upon it."

CHAPTER FIFTY-SEVEN

Bobby Yellowhorse lived in a small cinderblock house painted yellow with sky-blue trim. A barn stood to one side of the main structure, in front of which was an old Camaro that looked like it hadn't moved since Bill Clinton was in the White House. Another vehicle, a dusty Ford Mustang at least a decade newer, stood on the driveway.

Barnes pulled his Crown Victoria behind the Mustang and came to a stop, and together he and Decker approached the house. The front door opened before they even reached it.

The man they had come to see was so old Decker couldn't begin to guess his true age. His dark tanned face was wrinkled like a roadmap. His hair, thinning but still down to his shoulders, was pure silver. As they drew close, he turned and hobbled back into the house, using an intricately carved cane to support his weight. As he went, he motioned for them to follow him inside.

He moved to an armchair that took up a corner of the room opposite a tube television with rabbit ears on top and sat down with a relieved grunt. "Pardon me for not standing on ceremony," he said, leaning the cane against the side of his chair.

"But my legs aren't what they used to be, and if I'm on my feet for more than a few minutes, the arthritis pain is unbearable."

"Not a problem," Decker said, closing the door behind him and moving further into the room with Barnes at his side.

"Sandra tells me you have questions about a Paiute warrior," said Bobby, getting right down to business. "Can you give me some details?"

Decker told him about Shilah, and their belief that the warrior's spirit had transformed into a Baykok and was prowling still, looking for new victims.

"A Baykok? That's northern folklore. Ojibwe." Bobby said. If he found Decker's claim far-fetched, he made no show of it, save for a raised eyebrow. "What proof do you have of this?"

Decker had brought the journal in with him. He approached the old man, kneeled next to the chair, and opened it, then explained about Travis Biggs and Karuk. He spoke fast, realizing time was slipping away. It was already almost five in the evening. It would be dark soon.

When he was done, the old man sat with his hands placed in his lap, deep in thought. Then he motioned to a dresser on the far side of the room. "Go look in there. You'll find a binder marked pre-1850. Bring it to me."

Decker complied.

Bobby took the folder with a grunt. "This binder, along with the others in that dresser, represent the information I have gathered about our people. Much of it was handed down to me by my parents and grandparents, or other elders of the tribe, many of whom have now passed on. It's far from complete, but I've done the best I can."

"Can you tell us what we need to know," Barnes asked.

"Maybe." Bobby opened the binder and leafed through the pages for many minutes, occasionally making small tuts of frustration. Eventually, he looked up, his eyes sparkling. "There was a member of the tribe called Shilah, a long time ago. He was indeed a warrior who was interred outside of the traditional burial grounds, although what crime he committed to be treated so, has been lost to time. There are no other entries for that name matching the information you've given me, so he must be the ancestor you seek."

"Fantastic," Decker said. "Do you know where he's buried?"

Bobby nodded. "According to my records, his last resting place is at the far end of Ghost Canyon, on an elevated plateau overlooking the Colorado River, near Eagle Wash."

"I know that area," said Barnes. "It's only a couple of miles from Haley. It would've been easy enough for Travis Biggs and Karuk to walk there from the town."

"Can you show us the exact location on a map?" Decker asked.

"I think so." Bobby nodded.

"I have a map in my glove box," Barnes said.

"You do?" Decker glanced toward him, surprised.

"Sure. GPS is great, but an old school paper map comes in useful when you want to mark locations down, especially if they are off the beaten track." He turned toward the door. "I'll get it."

Decker watched the FBI agent step outside, then turned back to Bobby and took out his phone. There was one other thing he wanted to ask. "Would you mind if I show you something, while we're waiting?"

Bobby shrugged.

"Perfect." Decker brought up the photograph of the dead miners huddled in the passageway that became their tomb. He enlarged the section showing the symbol scratched into the earth—two inward facing arrows within a roughly drawn circle—and held the screen toward Bobby. "Do you recognize this?"

"Let me get a closer look." Bobby leaned forward, squinting at the screen. He pursed his lips. "That's a protection symbol. The arrows represent a defense against harm. The unbroken circle signifies safety. Together they act as a powerful shield against those of malevolent intent."

"Will it restrain the Baykok?"

Again, the old man shrugged. "I do not know. I've never met a Baykok. In theory, the spirit should not be able to pass beyond the protection symbol and harm those on the other side of it. At least, that's what the dead prospectors pictured in this photograph clearly believed. One of them must have possessed at least a smattering of Native American knowledge. According to legend, the Baykok rips its victims open to reach their internal organs, which it then devours, after leaving stones as replacements. Those men might have died sheltering there, but they show no signs of being attacked, so their assumption regarding the symbol was probably correct."

"Good enough for me," Decker said. The legend of the Baykok was accurate on some counts, but wrong on others. It did indeed rip its victims open, but it didn't leave stones in place of their internal organs. At least if the bodies he'd examined were any indication. He didn't mention this to Bobby, though. He slipped the phone back into his pocket as Barnes returned, map in hand.

"Here we are." Barnes spread the map on the coffee table and offered Bobby a pen. "You think you can mark Shilah's location on this?"

"I believe so." The old man leaned forward in his chair, studying the well-worn map with a furrowed brow. He reached out with a shaky hand and marked a spot southeast of Haley and the Ghost Canyon Mine. "This is where you will find the warrior, Shilah."

"Thank you." Decker picked the map up and folded it, feeling a renewed hope. With this knowledge they could defeat the creature, at least if Travis Biggs had correctly interpreted Karuk's instructions about returning the warrior's summoned spirit back to the realm of the dead. Yet a lingering doubt remained at the back of Decker's mind since Biggs himself had not managed to lift the curse.

"You ready to get back to Haley?" Barnes asked.

"Yes. The sooner the better," Decker replied. He turned to the old man. "No need to get up. We'll show ourselves out. You've been most helpful."

"My pleasure. If you need more information, please do come back." Bobby looked up with watery eyes. "I assume that you're going to visit Shilah's grave."

"We are." Decker nodded.

"I have just one request then," Bobby said. "Tread lightly and treat the site with reverence. Shilah might not rest in our traditional burial grounds, but his grave is still a spiritual place."

"You have my word," Decker said. Then he turned, clutching the map, and started toward the door.

CHAPTER FIFTY-EIGHT

Decker and Barnes left the Paiute colony behind and drove back toward Haley. It was rush hour now and getting dark, the November sun already out of sight behind the distant mountains. The traffic on the interstate was bumper-to-bumper. Decker fidgeted in his seat, frustrated by the slow going. After fifteen minutes, during which they only moved half a mile, Barnes reached the limit of his patience. He switched on the car's strobes and steered into the emergency lane. Soon they were around the worst of the downtown traffic. He turned the strobes back off and they continued to their destination, arriving back in Haley a little before 6 PM. The sun had set now. The rugged desert landscape was bathed only in the reflected light of the moon. Decker wasted no time in jumping from the vehicle and heading inside, where he encountered Robyn and Special Agent Fowler standing in the hotel lobby, deep in conversation.

When he entered, Fowler turned. "You're back. Good. I hope you have some clue how to proceed, because the raid on Wagner Mitchell's house was a complete bust and I'm out of ideas."

"He does," Special Agent Barnes replied, following behind Decker.

"The skeleton in your museum," Decker said, looking at Robyn. "Where did you find it?"

"Up near the mine entrance, along the trail," Robyn answered. "I already told you that."

"No. I mean, where *exactly* did you find it? You said the body was dumped over the side of the trail. How far from the mine?"

"Not far. Maybe a few hundred feet. The body was at the bottom of an overgrown ditch. We were cutting back the creosote bushes to run a power line up there from town. That's when we found him."

Decker turned to Barnes. "It has to be Karuk. The skeleton's location and method of death fit."

"Who's Karuk?" Fowler asked.

"He was an associate of Travis Biggs, a prospector back in the late 1800s. The two of them are responsible for the creature in the mine."

"Travis Biggs?" Fowler shook his head. "Who's he?"

"An ancestor of Harlan Biggs, one of the two men we found at the second mine entrance. Travis wrote a journal detailing everything he'd done and the reason. Harlan still possessed the old journal—it was probably a family heirloom—which is what prompted him to seek out the mine," Decker said, quickly explaining about the previously undiscovered gold the prospector had found, and his plan to use Karuk's knowledge of Native American belief to keep it for himself. "The disgraced Paiute warrior, Shilah, is the key to all of this. His restless spirit became the Baykok. That's what has been killing people."

"This is getting weirder by the minute," Fowler grumbled. "I've never even heard of a Baykok."

"Neither had I until today." Decker was already crossing the lobby toward the corridor leading to the museum room. "Right now, I must see that skeleton."

"What does the skeleton have to do with all this?" Robyn asked, as the other three tagged along behind.

"Everything. It's the key to defeating the creature." Decker waited for Robyn to unlock the door and then stepped inside, hurrying across to the glass display case in the center of the room. "Something's been bothering me ever since I first looked at the skeleton, but I couldn't figure out what. It was only after I read the journal that I realized."

"Are you going to share?" Fowler asked.

"Just as soon as I confirm my suspicion." Decker turned to Robyn. "Do you have the key to this cabinet? Can we open it?"

Robyn hesitated a moment, then nodded. "It's in the office. I'll get it."

"Hurry," Decker said. "It's already dark out and we have a lot to do."

"Wait here." Robyn hurried from the room. Less than a minute later she returned with a bunch of keys. She pawed through them until she found the correct key and unlocked the case. She lifted the entire glass side panel out and set it down, leaning it against the stand. She looked sideways at Decker. "Done. It's all yours."

"Thank you." Decker bent over and reached inside the case, nudging the remains of the tattered duster gently aside to avoid damaging it. He pointed to the area below the skeleton's pelvis. "See here? There are more bones than there should be."

"Oh my God," Robyn whispered. "You're right. There's an extra leg bone up by the left femur. I've seen it before, but I just assumed it was misplaced from somewhere else in the body. I never gave it any thought. Now it seems so obvious. It can't be from the same skeleton. How did it get there? And where did it come from?"

"Ladies and gentlemen, I'd like you to meet Shilah," Decker said. "Or at least, his fibula."

"That's why the creature didn't leave after Travis Biggs

returned Shilah's bones to the grave," Barnes said. "That's the reason it's still here."

"Exactly." Decker smiled. "Travis couldn't return all the bones, although he didn't know it at the time. Karuk didn't trust the shifty prospector. He kept the bone hidden in his duster as insurance. Probably figured he'd hide it when they got back to town so that Travis would still need him."

"But that's not how it worked out. Biggs figured he had no more use for Karuk, since he already knew how to lift the curse on the mine," Barnes said. "He wanted the gold for himself and couldn't see any point in waiting around to dispose of the only other person who knew of its existence."

"But he wasn't aware of the bone Karuk had kept back. When he shot him and pushed his corpse off the trail, he also lost the ability to send Shilah's spirit, and the supernatural creature he'd become, back to its resting place and make the mine safe again."

"So, if we return that bone to Shilah's grave, the creature will go away?" Barnes asked.

"That's the theory," Decker said. He turned to Robyn. "Was the skeleton articulated when you moved it?"

"Partly, yes." Robyn motioned to the upper body. "The torso was still complete. The scraps of clothing still adhering to the corpse kept it together. We were able to move it with little trouble. The arms and legs, not so much. As you can see, we're missing small bones in the feet. Scavengers probably carried them off. Some of the leg and arm bones got scattered too. We had to search for them in the surrounding area. That's why I thought the third fibula was just a bone we hadn't placed correctly when we reassembled the skeleton. It's not like I'm an expert on this stuff. I wasn't expecting there to be one bone from a second body."

"That presents a problem," Barnes said. "All three fibulae look similar. If the leg bones became scattered and were only put back in place after being moved to this display case, how do we know which belong to Karuk, and which one must be returned to Shilah's grave?"

"We don't," Decker said. "Maybe a trained medical professional could tell us, but as it stands, any of the three could belong to Shilah. And if we return the wrong one, the creature will remain and most likely kill again."

CHAPTER FIFTY-NINE

Hector Ramirez and Emmanuel Garcia were more scared than at any other time in their lives. The two Mexicans sat huddled in the darkness, with only the beam from their flashlights to illuminate the tunnel in which they had remained hidden for much of the past twenty-four hours. They had entered the mine the previous afternoon and followed the map provided by the owner of the casino where they had spent the last three weeks working as low-paid day laborers. What began as an easy, if unusual chore—retrieving some lumps of quartz from a location deep inside the mine—had quickly turned into a nightmare they had not yet escaped. As they followed the tunnels deeper underground, nearing their destination, Hector had noticed an object on the ground ahead of them, laying half buried in the sandy ground.

A skull.

It gleamed white in the twin beams from their flashlights, hollow eye sockets staring down the tunnel in a deathly gaze that would never end. Scattered nearby were more bones and threads of clothing, including a pair of rotten suspenders, dating the remains back to pioneer days. The two Mexicans continued on, disturbed by their grisly discovery, but more afraid of the two men that waited at the mine entrance than they were of a man who had passed on more than a hundred years since.

But when they arrived at the indicated spot, a dead-end tunnel far from the gold mine's entrance where twinkling rivers of quartz crystal weaved along the rocky walls, they came across something much worse. Three mummified corpses huddled together as if they had just sat down to wait for their own demise. Scratched into the earth in front of them was a strange symbol neither man recognized.

It didn't take long to decide it wasn't worth sticking around. The tunnels contained an ancient evil and these three corpses proved it. Besides, they could actually feel it oozing from the very rocks around them and permeating the atmosphere, thick and cloying. They didn't care now if the two white men waiting above wanted some stupid chunks of quartz, or more accurately, what was contained within the crystalline rocks. Hector and Emmanuel were not stupid. There was gold here. Lots of it. But not enough to lose their lives over and end up like the three unfortunate souls huddled at the back of the tunnel. Especially since they were not the ones who would benefit from the wealth of precious metals surrounding them.

The Mexicans turned to head back, clutching their pickaxes tighter, because now they believed they were not alone in the darkness.

And they were right.

Something was moving toward them, out of sight beyond a bend in the tunnel. They could hear its footfalls, and the strange shuffling, popping sounds that grew louder with each moment.

The two men froze, caught in a dreadful realization that they were trapped. If they continued upon their route back to the surface, they would run into whatever was coming their way, and they were sure it was nothing good. But if they retreated, there was nowhere to go except a dead-end, and judging by the corpses huddled there, it hadn't worked out too well for the last people to make that decision.

Yet they had no choice. Whatever was prowling the tunnels was surely not friendly, and they didn't wish to encounter it, so they did the only thing possible. They fled back into the tunnel as far as they could go. And there they waited, scared and alone, with only the three mummified corpses for company. And when the beast came into view, red eyes glowing like the fires of hell, they cowered and whimpered and prayed for deliverance from the evil drawing closer with each step.

At least until they heard the voice whispering inside their heads, telling them that everything would be okay. It would all be over soon. All they had to do was remain still and let the creature have its way.

But then something strange happened. The skin-draped skeleton slinking toward them came to a halt a few feet from the symbol drawn on the ground. It stood there, glaring at them, the fire in its eyes fading, and taking with it the whispered voice. Then, with a shriek of frustration, the creature turned back the way it came, leaving the pair of terrified Mexicans alone.

They hadn't seen it since.

Unwilling to move, fearful the nightmarish creature was waiting in the darkness beyond their flashlights, they settled onto the ground. After a while they turned one flashlight off to conserve battery power. And there they waited as day turned to night and back into day again. Now, as it approached nightfall for a second day, hunger gnawing their stomachs, they realized they must either move or starve to death just like their deceased companions.

After a brief discussion, they decided to try for the surface. They moved reluctantly, stepping past the protection symbol, and inching their way down the tunnel, using both flashlights even though one was visibly dimming, the batteries almost drained. They kept the beams aimed low and moved in silence lest they alert the creature to their presence.

For a while all went well. They followed the map back through the twisting maze of tunnels, and soon their spirits lifted upon the realization that they might actually make it out alive. Then, from somewhere deeper within the mine, they heard it. An inhuman shriek that echoed through the shafts and tunnels, bouncing off the narrow stone walls.

They quickened their pace, eager to escape, but it was not enough. The creature was coming. They could hear it growing closer, moving with surprising speed.

When Emmanuelle tripped, his foot catching a jagged rock and sending him sprawling, Hector turned back to help him up. But he'd fallen hard, his leg twisting at an unnatural angle as he landed. His scream of pain was only slightly less unnerving than the screech of anticipation from the darkness in the tunnel behind them. Hector summed up the situation, mumbled a brief apology in Spanish, then turned and fled despite his friend's desperate pleas for help. As he approached the mine entrance, another scream reached his ears, shrill and full of terror. At least, until it was suddenly cut off.

Hector stumbled forward, out of the mine and into the cool desert night. The full moon hung low in the sky, bathing the landscape in a silvery glow. He turned and looked back the way he'd come, expecting to see the creature giving chase, but the mine's entrance was nothing but a yawning, dark hole in the earth. And there, at the entrance, he noticed another symbol just like the one that had protected them the previous evening. Or at least, the remains of it. In his haste to escape, Hector had stood upon the crudely drawn symbol, scuffing it up and leaving it only half visible. He cursed his own stupidity. Someone had tried to keep the creature contained, until he'd come along and ruined it. Worse, he couldn't even redraw it, because he didn't remember exactly what the symbol was meant to look like.

Hector realized there was only one option. He must leave this place as quickly as possible. He turned and ran, clawing his way through the bushes clogging the rocky crevice. As he expected, there was no sign of his employers or the truck. Yet something was different. The entire area was ringed with yellow crime scene tape that flapped in the breeze. But there was no time to investigate this new development. Hector pushed his way past the tape and fled down the canyon trail as fast as his legs would carry him. A minute later the creature found the mine's entrance, and unhindered by the destroyed symbol, emerged and spread its wings, then took to the sky with a triumphant wail.

CHAPTER SIXTY

Decker stood in the Last Chance Hotel and Saloon's museum room, his gaze resting upon the skeleton of the man they believed was Karuk, shot in the back by his partner almost fourteen decades earlier. In particular, he studied the three leg bones, aware time was growing short. Realizing there was no definitive way to identify which belonged with the skeleton, and which one had been removed from the grave of Shilah, the disgraced Paiute warrior, he decided. "We take all three."

"Will that work?" Barnes asked.

"I don't know if any of this will work," Decker said. "I'm only going on the information Travis Biggs wrote in his journal. For all I know, Karuk lied to Travis about how to return Shilah's spirit to the other side and dissipate the energy that created the Baykok."

"We don't have any choice," Fowler said. "Crazy as this all sounds."

"I agree." Robyn nodded. "According to what you just told us, Shilah's remains need to be made whole again for the creature to go away. It shouldn't matter whether there are some extra bones included that aren't his."

"My thoughts exactly." Decker reached into the cabinet and removed the brittle bones. "I need something to wrap these and keep them protected."

"A bag would be good too," Barnes said.

"Coming right up." Robyn stepped out of the room and quickly returned with a backpack and a towel, which she spread across the top of the display case. "Here, use this."

Decker placed the bones on the towel and wrapped them carefully, then placed the precious cargo into the bag and zipped it up. "I'm going up to the grave."

"I'm coming with you," Barnes said.

"Me too," Fowler announced. "I'm having trouble getting my head around all this, but I'm not going to miss it."

"And me," Robyn added. "It's my mine. I have the most to lose."

"I think you should all stay here and let me do this on my own," Decker replied, glancing around the group. "It might not be safe."

"All the more reason for us to come then." Robyn met Decker's gaze. "The Baykok might not want to slip quietly into the night. You might need a distraction."

"Is this how you all feel?" Decker asked.

As one, they nodded.

"Fine. We don't have time to argue about it." Decker started for the door. He crossed the hotel lobby with the rest of the group in tow. As he reached the front door, he heard a patter of feet. When he looked back, Tieg was standing watching them.

The dog let out a single bark.

"No," Robyn said, crossing to the animal and patting its head. "You can't come with us. Go back to your bed and lay down."

The dog looked up at her for a moment, then turned and sauntered back toward the office, glancing over his shoulder once before turning the corner and disappearing.

Robyn rejoined the group. "Well, what are we waiting for? Let's vanquish a monster."

CHAPTER SIXTY-ONE

They passed through town under the cover of darkness and made their way to the trail leading up to the Ghost Canyon Mine with flashlights in hand. But they would not follow it all the way. At the midpoint, another less traveled path meandered up through the canyon and ended, finally, at a plateau overlooking the Colorado River. It was there the warrior, Shilah, was buried. And it was there the Baykok would be defeated. At least, if it all went to plan.

Decker took the lead, with the backpack containing the last of Shilah's remains slung over one shoulder. As they walked near Carlton's shack he saw a light burning, but there was no sign of the old man himself. Decker eyed the old WWII Jeep sitting to the side of the cabin, wondering if it would be able to make it up the trail, then decided against it. The thing would probably roll over and kill them all on one of the steep inclines, not to mention how narrow the trail became.

They continued on out of town, climbing until they reached the split. Here they turned left, away from the mine. As they went, Robyn spoke up, breaking the silence that had consumed them since leaving the saloon.

"Do you think this will really take care of the situation?" She asked. "I mean, it seems so easy, just putting an old bone back into the ground."

"Maybe there's some sort of incantation we need to recite," Barnes speculated. "Some ancient words that will open the portal between our world and wherever that creature came from."

"If there is, I don't know them." Decker had wondered the same thing, but the journal didn't mention any specific ritual. "We can only hope Travis Biggs didn't omit any information."

"Or that his buddy, Karuk, didn't withhold some vital tidbit in the same way that he concealed one of Shilah's bones."

"Yes. But we can only go on the available data, and I choose to believe we will be successful." Decker adjusted the pack on his shoulder and stepped over a boulder jutting from the earth. He played his flashlight beam over the ground ahead, aware of the danger posed by a careless misstep. The mountain pathway was treacherous in the darkness. If one were to slip and fall over the edge, it would be a long way down. Worse, the ground was uneven and scattered with loose rocks and gravel. But he didn't want to wait for daylight. If the creature escaped the mine, innocent lives would be lost, and he would be to blame.

"How far do we have to walk?" Robyn asked. "I don't like it out here."

"It shouldn't be much further," Decker replied. "We've covered a good distance already. Maybe another half-mile."

"Which will feel more like two miles on this terrain," Barnes said.

"If you're uncomfortable, I'm sure someone will take you back," Decker said to Robyn. "You don't need to accompany us."

"I'm coming, and that's all there is to it," Robyn replied with a determined look upon her face. "You're not getting rid of me that easily."

"Not trying to get rid of you. I'm glad you're here. You probably know the landscape better than any of us."

"Damn right. Plus, I want to see that bone put back in the ground. That creature, the Baykok or whatever you called it, is living inside my mine. I intend to evict it."

"That's the attitude." Barnes chuckled. "Don't give up. Fight back."

"I've never given up and I'm not starting now." "Speaking of which, don't you think this is too easy, us just wandering up here and planting a bone to solve all our problems?" Fowler said, glancing around nervously. "In my experience, nothing's ever this simple."

"Honestly, it's about time something was easy," Decker replied. "I'm due one."

"Not sure it works like that," Fowler said. "I think we should—"

The screech that echoed down the canyon cut him off mid-sentence.

Decker stopped and glanced skyward, searching the heavens for any sign of the creature. "I guess that answers your question. Happy now?" he said to Fowler.

"Not in the least." Fowler reached for his gun. "This is one instance where I would truly love to be wrong."

"It could've been anything," Robyn said hopefully. "Coyote or even an owl."

"That wasn't a coyote or an owl," Barnes replied, drawing his own service weapon. "And I think we all know it."

"I like my interpretation better," Robyn said, her voice cracking as she tried to swallow the fear that threatened to overwhelm her.

"I hoped the protection symbol I drew at the mine entrance would hold the creature back," Decker said. "It appears I was wrong."

"Unless it found another way out," Barnes said.

"It doesn't matter." Fowler turned and looked up the trail toward the gravesite. "Creature or not, we must get that bone up there."

"Which is why we need to keep moving," Decker said. He gathered the group together and nudged them forward. "Just keep walking, fast as you can, and be alert. Remember, it can fly."

"How could I forget," Barnes said, hurrying along beside Decker. "The image of that thing dropping out of the darkness and coming toward us is burned into my memory forever."

"Maybe it doesn't know we're here," Robyn said. "If we're lucky, it will leave us alone."

"I wouldn't bank on it." Fowler was bringing up the rear, craning his neck to watch their rear. "Like I said, nothing ever goes easy."

As if to prove him right, another screech ripped the air, this one closer.

Fowler stopped. He motioned for the others to keep going and pointed his gun upward. "You guys make a run for it. I'll see if I can distract the damned thing."

"Don't be a fool." Decker turned back. He took a step toward Fowler, hoping to dissuade him from his foolhardy plan.

He never got a chance.

Before Decker could reach the defiant FBI agent, a black shape dropped from the sky. Wings beating the air. Red eyes blazing. Then all hell broke loose on the ground.

CHAPTER SIXTY-TWO

Robyn screamed. Bullets started flying as the two FBI agents opened fire upon the angry creature. Decker leaped forward and took Robyn's arm, steering her further up the trail and out of harm's way. By the time he turned back, the Baykok was blocking the path behind them. Then Decker realized something else. Agent Fowler had stopped firing his gun and now stood transfixed with the weapon held in front of him like some kind of deadly offering.

Barnes was backing up, aware that his bullets were useless against the supernatural entity. He reached out and caught hold of Fowler's collar, tried to pull him backwards, but the senior agent merely shrugged off his partner's grip and walked forward, toward the Baykok.

"Elton," Barnes shouted, using Special Agent Fowler's first name. "Don't look at it. Keep your eyes down."

But if Fowler heard the frantic plea, he ignored it. And all the while, the creature stood waiting for its victim.

"It's no use," Decker said, drawing level with Barnes. "He's already under its influence. Take Robyn and get her to safety. I'll do what I can here."

"No." Barnes shook his head. "You take Robyn and get to that grave. You have Shilah's bone in your backpack. You need to bury it again. That's the best way to help. I'll get Fowler, and if I can't, I'll follow along after."

Decker knew the FBI agent was right, even though he didn't want to admit it. He hated leaving a man behind, let alone two. But there was no choice. He met the agent's gaze, briefly, and then sprinted back to Robyn, who was standing in mute horror, her eyes wide.

"We can't just leave them here," Robyn said, her voice strained. "We have to help."

"The best way we can do that is to get Shilah's bone back in the ground." Decker took her elbow and attempted to steer her further up the trail. "The faster we do that, the quicker we can banish that thing back to hell."

"All right." Robyn nodded and started back up the trail, away from the stricken FBI agents. "Let's do it, then."

Decker breathed a sigh of relief. He cast a quick glance backwards to see Special Agent Fowler standing before the creature, waiting for his death. Several steps behind, Barnes was standing with his gun leveled. Decker couldn't tell if he was aiming at the creature, or at his partner, ready to put him out of his misery if the need arose. Decker didn't wait around to find out. He hurried after Robyn, moving faster than he would've liked across the uneven surface. But he'd barely gone twenty feet when an angry shriek blasted through the night, accompanied by a whoosh of air above his head.

Decker ducked instinctively and twisted sideways just as razor-sharp claws reached for the bag on his shoulder. The Baykok had abandoned its pursuit of the FBI agents and was now focusing its attention on him.

"It knows you have the bone," Barnes shouted from his rear. "It's trying to stop you reaching that grave."

"I see that," Decker replied, dropping to the ground, and

rolling to the side of the trail as the creature made a second pass. It swooped overhead and then disappeared back into the dark sky.

"Throw me the bag." Robyn was gesturing wildly. "Quickly. I can run faster than you."

"Not going to happen." Decker scrambled up and looked around wildly, wondering from which direction the Baykok would attack next. "You won't stand a chance. It will rip you to pieces."

"Not if it can't catch me," Robyn countered. "It's the only way."

"A fair point." Decker considered his options. The only way to defeat the creature was to make sure it didn't get ahold of the bag. If that happened, they would never put it to rest. It would roam through the ages, murdering with impunity. He didn't have long to decide. He could hear the Baykok returning, the flap of its wings growing louder as it swooped down toward him. He dropped the pack from his shoulder and hefted it, ready to throw to Robyn. But just as he raised his arm, he felt a force like a freight train smashing to his back, sending him sprawling forward.

Decker hit the ground hard. The bag jolted from his grip. His flashlight smacked against a rock and went out with a tinkle of glass. He discarded it, rolled over and sat up, scrambling backwards toward the bag, even as the Baykok landed on the trail with a thud and started toward him.

Decker reached out, averting his eyes from the creature's hypnotic stare.

His hand curled around the bag's strap.

"Look out." Robyn screamed a frantic warning, too late.

The Baykok sprang forward with a shrill hiss, deadly talons extended.

Decker raised an arm in a feeble defense. He steeled himself for what was about to happen. A thought of Nancy flitted through his mind, and he felt a momentary pang of despair at the realization that he might never see her again. Then he heard a mighty roar, and his world exploded in blinding white light.

CHAPTER SIXTY-THREE

Decker shielded his eyes and squinted against the sudden onslaught of blazing light. The roar grew louder, and with it came a shower of gravel and dirt that rained down upon him. Decker twisted his head to avoid the worst of it, expecting to see the Baykok still dropping toward him with murderous intent. Instead, he saw a blur of tires, the twin beams from a pair of round headlights, and a hulking green shape that growled past at a clip.

Carlton's World War II era Jeep.

And behind the wheel, his face crunched with concentration, the man himself. He was tugging at the steering wheel, sending the vehicle into a sideways skid that caught the Baykok in mid-air, crashing into it and driving the howling creature toward the edge of the trail.

Decker scrambled backwards to avoid the churning tires. He scooped up the bag containing Shilah's remains and jumped to his feet in time to see the Jeep, with the creature still pinned to the hood, reach the edge of the trail, and take a nosedive into the canyon below.

"No." Robyn rushed forward, a frantic scream on her lips. She shined her flashlight toward the precipice. "Carlton."

"He's gone," Fowler said, now released from his fugue state and running to stop her getting too close to the edge. "We don't have time for this. We'll come back for the old man. Right now, we need to reach that grave."

"He's right," Barnes agreed. "Carlton bought us the time we need, but the creature probably isn't dead. It will be back."

"We're not far away," Decker said, brushing himself off and glancing around for his flashlight. He was disappointed to find the lens smashed. Even if it wasn't, the barrel was crushed where Carlton's tire had rolled over it. He stepped past the broken light and went to Robyn, then took her arm. "You have to come with us. We can't leave you here. It's not safe."

"We have to help him." Robyn was desperate. "He sacrificed himself for us."

"He did," Decker said. "And it will all be for nothing if we don't put Shilah's remains back in the ground where they belong."

"I guess you're right," Robyn said. She sniffed and wiped a tear from her cheek. "But we'll come back as soon as we've taken care of this?"

"You have my word." Decker met her gaze. "Carlton saved my life, and we'll do what we can for him. But first we do this."

"Okay." Robyn turned and followed the three men as they hurried up the trail.

Decker glanced backwards, nervous. He was sure the Baykok was still out there, and it would now be in an even worse mood than before.

They reached a wide, flat area at the end of the trail, dotted with scraggy sagebrush. On one side the land rose steeply, scattered with boulders. On the other it dropped off into darkness. Decker could hear water running. The Colorado River, a long way below them.

Toward the back of the flat area, partly concealed by creosote bushes and the remains of a dead Joshua tree, Decker spotted a rough pile of rocks, almost imperceptible against the backdrop of mountainous terrain beyond.

"That must be the grave," he said, pointing. "There's nothing else here that fits the bill."

"Then what are we waiting for?" Fowler started toward the rocks. He pushed the bushes to one side and heaved the Joshua tree's twisted carcass off the mound.

"Let me in," Decker said, stepping forward. "Help me with the rocks. And give me some light. I can't see what I'm doing."

"Sure thing," Barnes said, joining Decker.

Robyn trained her flashlight on the grave as the three men dropped to their knees and began pulling rocks aside. "Hurry," she said, glancing skyward. "I think it's coming back."

And sure enough, Decker heard the steady drumbeat of wings high above, soon accompanied by the creature's now familiar screech. He twisted around and looked up to see a dark shape flit in front of the moon. As suspected, Carlton's Jeep had not kept the creature away for long. He turned back to the rock pile and continued with renewed urgency.

The beat of wings grew louder.

Robyn's hand was shaking, the flashlight jumping. "If you're going to finish this, now's the time."

"Almost there," Decker said. He heaved another large rock sideways and underneath, pale and white in the flashlight's beam, he saw bones.

"Get the remains out of the bag," Barnes said, breathless. "Quickly."

Decker twisted sideways and dragged the bag toward him. He unzipped it and reached in. His hand curled around the bones within. But as he pulled them out, a set of powerful talons dug into his back and lifted him skyward, leaving the bag and his surprised companions on the ground.

Decker felt the earth drop away beneath him.

Robyn screamed, her eyes wide with fright.

Special Agent Barnes lunged forward and grabbed one of Decker's legs. Fowler followed his partner's example and wrapped his arms around Decker's other leg. Together they pulled against the Baykok's might as it fought to carry him away.

Decker grunted in pain as sharp claws sliced into his back. Worse, the FBI agents were losing their battle. He was being dragged higher and there was nothing he could do about it. Then he realized that even though the bag was gone, he still clutched the three leg bones. The grave was directly below him, where the rest of the Paiute warrior's remains now lay exposed. There was only one thing Decker could do now. Mouthing a silent prayer Decker gauged the distance and dropped the bones toward the opened grave.

They clattered to the ground, all three hitting near the same spot close to Shilah's unearthed rib cage. One bounced away and was lost in the bushes. Another slipped off onto the rock pile. The third one lay balanced atop the warrior's skeletal remains.

If Decker was expecting an instant reaction, he was wrong. Nothing happened. The bone that remained in the grave was not Shilah's.

With a victorious screech, the Baykok flapped its leathery wings and pulled him higher despite the two FBI agent's best efforts. Decker could feel the creature's taloned feet digging into his flesh as it tried to tear him from their grasp.

But Robyn wasn't ready to give up. She grabbed one of the discarded bones and lunged into the bushes to retrieve the other. She emerged a moment later with bloody scratches on her arms and face but clutching both bones. With a defiant scream, she pushed them into the grave.

This time the reaction was instant.

A light flickered within Shilah's rib cage. A curl of wispy gray smoke twisted upward, expanding to take on a vaguely human shape. A chest formed, and a face, and atop the smoky figure's head, the translucent outline of a feathered headdress. And there were arms too. They twisted outward and reached toward the Baykok, even as a pair of amorphous hands spun themselves into existence.

At this, realizing its own peril, the creature relaxed its grip upon Decker. He fell back to the ground and stumbled to remain on his feet.

When he looked up, tendrils of curling gray smoke were extending from the misty figure's hands and weaving around the Baykok's clawed feet, ensnaring it. They snaked up its body and dragged the struggling creature relentlessly toward the grave. The Baykok hissed and wailed, beating its wings in a frenzied attempt to escape, even as it grew ever closer to the Paiute warrior's remains. It clawed at the rocks surrounding the grave. But it was no use. The fiery red mesmeric glow that burned within the Baykok's hollow eye sockets was already fading, its struggles becoming feeble as it sank back into the earth. Then, as Decker watched, Shilah's smoky, amorphous spirit reached a vaguely defined hand over the Baykok's head and pushed the creature down, before they both faded from view and were gone.

CHAPTER SIXTY-FOUR

"Is it over?" Robyn asked, staring wide-eyed at the spot where the Baykok and smoke spirit had disappeared moments before. "Did we defeat it?"

"I believe we did," Decker replied. He reached around and explored his back where the creature had clawed him. His shirt was shredded. Touching the wounds elicited stabs of fresh pain. He withdrew his hand, now bloody.

"I don't understand what just happened," Fowler said. "If that creature was created from Shilah's remains, then what rose out the grave?"

"The warrior's true spirit?" Decker speculated. "In the Native American legends, the Baykok is the restless soul of a disgraced man. An undead creature, it wanders the earth unable to enter the afterlife. But no person is completely bad. The Baykok was evil, for sure, but there must've been goodness in Shilah too. I think that's what rose out of the grave."

"Shilah's soul was fractured. Split between light and darkness," Barnes said. "Is that what you're trying to say?"

"It's the best explanation I've got. Either way, Shilah is whole again. He's at rest."

286 | ANTHONY M. STRONG

"It all sounds crazy to me," Fowler grumbled. "All I want to do is get out of here."

"We should put the rocks back in place first," Decker said, approaching the grave and kneeling. One by one he piled boulders back over Shilah's remains.

The others joined in, and the task was soon completed. Decker stood up and said a silent prayer to whatever Gods the old warrior had believed in. That done, he turned back toward the trail in time to see a figure limping along toward them.

"Carlton," Robyn screamed, elated. "You're alive."

"Of course I'm alive, you foolish girl. You think I don't know how to drive a Jeep?" Carlton said, closing the gap between them.

"That's exactly what we think," Barnes replied, grinning. "You did go headlong into a ravine, after all."

Carlton came to a halt. Decker noticed a gash on his forehead. He was favoring his left leg too. "We should get you checked out," he said.

"I'm fine." Carlton waved a dismissive hand.

"You saved my life," Decker said. "If you hadn't come along, I would've been a goner."

"Don't mention it."

"The trail is so narrow," Barnes said. "How did you even get a Jeep up it?"

"Why wouldn't I be able to, boy?" Being a hero had not dampened Carlton's grouchy demeanor. "Damn thing's built for off roading. Not in good shape now though." He glared at Decker. "You owe me a Jeep."

"I'll see what I can do." Decker couldn't help but grin.

"Why were you even there?" Fowler asked.

"I saw you bunch of fools heading out of town and figured you'd get yourselves in trouble. And I was right." Carlton folded his arms. "If I hadn't done something, that creature would've killed the lot of you. I'm not Robyn's number one fan, but I like her a whole lot better than a bloodthirsty monster."

"Thanks," Robyn said, bemused. "I think."

"That's probably as close to a compliment as you'll ever get from him," Decker said. "I'd take it if I were you."

"And with the creature gone, you'll be able to extract the gold from that mine," Barnes said. "You probably aren't going to run tours down there anymore, given what's happened, but if Harlan Biggs' hunch was correct, there should be more than enough precious metals in there to open ten wedding venues if you want."

"One will be enough," Robyn replied. "But we can worry about that later. Right now, I'd really like to get out of here. Angry skeleton creature or not, this place gives me the creeps."

"You won't get any argument from me," Decker said as they started back down the trail, with Barnes assisting Carlton even though the old man was doing his best to shrug the FBI agent off. He was bruised and battered, but alive, and that was a good day in Decker's book. Tomorrow he would check the mine and make sure the creature was really gone for good. But right now, all he wanted was a fresh shirt, his wounds patched, and a hot shower.

EPILOGUE

THREE DAYS LATER

Decker was in his room, packing up to depart the Last Chance Hotel and Saloon and head to the airport. He'd spent the last few days making sure the Baykok really was vanquished, tidying up loose ends, and writing a lengthy report to his superiors back in Maine regarding the activities at the ghost town. The two Special Agents, Barnes and Fowler, had left the hotel forty-eight hours before and resumed their regular duties at the Las Vegas field office. But not before all three, along with Robyn, had entered the mine and navigated their way to the tunnel discovered by the geologists, where three mummified corpses sat in silent darkness. They also found the deep vein of gold that Harlan Biggs and his general manager, Wagner Mitchell, had lost their lives over. This was confirmed by one of their employees, a Mexican laborer found wandering, hungry and dehydrated, in the desert. He told a tragic tale of the pair's greed and how it had resulted in the death of his friend, whose corpse had subsequently been located and removed from the second mine entrance to be returned to his family. Now all that remained for Decker was to say his goodbyes and leave.

He was almost finished packing when there was a light knock at the hotel room door. When he answered, Robyn was on the other side with Tieg. She was smiling.

"How are you getting along?" she asked.

"Almost done," Decker replied. "Another half hour and I'll be out of your hair for good."

"You don't have to run off so soon."

"Actually, I do," he said, touched by her sadness at his departure. "My employer is sending a jet. It will be here within the hour."

"That's a shame. Tieg will miss you."

Decker looked down at the dog, who returned his gaze with trusting brown eyes. "Well, I'll miss him too. He saved my life, after all."

"Maybe you could come visit him once in a while."

"I'd like that."

"Or you could stay a few days longer and hang out with him," Robyn countered.

"Nice as that sounds, I really can't."

"What would it take to change your mind?"

"I'm not sure you can change my mind," Decker said with a smile. "Unless you want to call my boss, Adam Hunt, and demand he give me a few days off."

"Maybe I don't need to," Robyn said, enigmatically.

"And why is that?" Decker asked.

"Because your fiancé already has," a new voice said.

"Nancy?" Decker asked, confused, and delighted.

"Do you have another fiancée I don't know about?" Nancy said, appearing from the corridor.

"What are you doing here?" Decker's smile widened into a grin.

"Adam said you cleared things up here quicker than he

expected, so he didn't need you back for a few more days." Nancy stepped into the room. "He thought you would have more fun in Las Vegas than sitting at home, so he flew me out here."

Robyn coughed gently. "I'm going to leave the two of you alone. I'll be downstairs if you need anything." With that, she turned and left.

"I must say, the ride out here was plush."

"Ride?"

"The private jet. Is that what you're doing when you're not with me, riding around in swanky jets sipping champagne?"

"No one's ever offered me any champagne." Decker rubbed his chin.

"Huh." Nancy furrowed her brow. "Hunt must like me more than you."

"I hardly think so," Decker joked. "Seriously, how did you pull that off?"

"Because it's a special occasion." Nancy crossed the room and sat on the bed. "Speaking of which, I booked us a suite for a couple of nights at the Bellagio. I thought you might like to enjoy Vegas instead of chasing monsters all over it."

"Sounds like fun," Decker said. "What did you mean when you said it was a special occasion?"

"Well, I was going to wait until we got to the hotel room to mention this, but what the hell." Nancy shrugged. "I've been thinking. Our lease is almost up on the house in Mississippi, and I'd love to be closer to Taylor while she's at college."

"You want to move to Boston?"

"Not exactly. I know how hard it is on you, going back and forth between Mississippi and Maine, so I figured we should just move there. That way I can be close to Taylor, and you can be close to work."

"What are you going to do in Maine while I'm working?"

"What do I do now while you're working?"

"Good point."

"Maine might actually be good for me," Nancy said. "A new start. I could open another restaurant. Get back to doing what I love."

"You want to open a diner?" Decker joined her on the bed.

"Not a diner. I was thinking a bakery and coffee shop. Might be fun." Nancy took a deep breath. "So, what do you think?"

"I think if it's what you want to do, then let's move to Maine." Decker put his arm around her. "I don't see how that counts as a special occasion though."

"It doesn't." Nancy met Decker's gaze. "That's the other thing I want to talk to you about. You're always off running around the world putting yourself in danger, and I worry that one day you won't come back. I can't stop you doing the job you love, but I can make sure I'm your wife."

"I thought we already agreed you were going to be my wife. We're engaged after all."

"I know. But I don't want to be engaged. I think we should get married. As soon as possible."

Decker remained silent for a moment, letting this sink in, then he said, "I think that's a great idea."

"You do?" Nancy replied, excited.

"Sure." Decker nodded. "And we're in the right place. We could find a preacher and get married under the Las Vegas sign."

"I didn't mean that quickly." Nancy shook her head. "You're impossible."

"What? You said you wanted to get married as soon as possible."

"But I still want a real wedding. A dress. Our family and friends there. Sometimes I wonder about you."

"Understood. No shotgun wedding under the Las Vegas sign. Got it. You will have to give me a few weeks to come up with an alternate venue, though."

"How about we work on it together."

"I'd like that," Decker said.

"Me too." Nancy laid back on the bed and kicked her shoes off. "Lay down and join me."

"What about the Bellagio?"

"We don't check in until tomorrow." Nancy grabbed Decker's arm and pulled him down, kissing him. "We're staying here tonight. Robyn insisted."

"She's in on this too?"

"Yup." Nancy kissed him again. "Will you just shut up and relax? I want to cuddle with my future husband."

"It doesn't look like I have much choice," Decker said, slipping his arms around her.

"No, you don't." Nancy said resting her head on his shoulder. "And for once, Adam Hunt isn't going to call and ruin everything."

"You sure about that?"

"Pretty sure," Nancy replied. "Because I told him what would happen if he did."

ACKNOWLEDGMENTS

The author would like to thank his wife, Sonya, for her tireless efforts to make his books better. Also, many thanks to Barbara Gorman, James Facey, and the entire advanced reader team for their time and dedication, and willingness to be the first eyes on my work. I would also like to wish Darwin Andoe a happy birthday, and a big thank you for allowing me to put him face-to-face with the Baykok.

Printed in Great Britain
by Amazon